# "I took your virginity.

"As a gentleman, I must ask you to be my wife," Will stated quietly.

"No. Go away," Rachel replied nervously.

"Your father thinks we're truly married. He doesn't think licenses and ordained preachers are necessary. We said the words, and I bedded you—"

"He knows?"

Will saw her white nightdress. Her legs dangled over the edge of the bed. "He asked me directly. I couldn't lie."

"Dear Lord in heaven! He'll parade us to Reverend Ludlow in front of his rifle—!"

"No. He's enlisting your friends to persuade you. He'll figure ways to get us alone together."

"I don't care what he does!" Rachel cried.

"Would you marry me if you felt a grand passion?"

"I don't know what grand passion is. Do you love me?" she asked.

"No. I respect you. You're a fine woman. But you want grand passion—"

"Not anymore! I've had enough passion to last a lifetime…!"

Dear Reader,

If your mother didn't tell *you* about Harlequin Historical, this Mother's Day might be a good time to let *her* in on the secret. The gift of romance can enhance anyone's life, and our May books promise to be a spectacular introduction. With two 5★ reviews from *Affaire de Coeur* already under her belt, up-and-coming author Rae Muir returns with *Twice a Bride,* the second book of her unforgettable WEDDING TRAIL series about four friends who find love on the road to California. In this authentic tale, a trail scout's daughter marries a rugged hunter to fulfill her father's dying wish—only her father doesn't die....

We are delighted to bring you *Lion's Lady,* the fourth title in Suzanne Barclay's highly acclaimed SUTHERLAND SERIES. Here, a newly widowed noblewoman contrives to secure her son's inheritance and is shockingly reunited with the valiant warrior who is her child's natural father. Ana Seymour has penned her ninth historical title, *Jeb Hunter's Bride,* the story of a feisty adventuress whose journey west heals the haunted soul of a handsome wagon train leader.

And if you haven't yet discovered Lyn Stone, don't miss *The Wilder Wedding.* In this wonderful Victorian, a sheltered heiress who believes she is dying and wants one last adventure proposes to a worldly—and utterly irresistible—private investigator whom she has just met.

Whatever your tastes in reading, you'll be sure to find a romantic journey back to the past between the covers of Harlequin Historical. Happy Mother's Day!

Sincerely,

Tracy Farrell
Senior Editor

Please address questions and book requests to:
Silhouette Reader Service
U.S.: 3010 Walden Ave., P.O. Box 1325, Buffalo, NY 14269
Canadian: P.O. Box 609, Fort Erie, Ont. L2A 5X3

# RAE MUIR
## THE WEDDING TRAIL

# TWICE A BRIDE

## *Harlequin Books*

TORONTO • NEW YORK • LONDON
AMSTERDAM • PARIS • SYDNEY • HAMBURG
STOCKHOLM • ATHENS • TOKYO • MILAN
MADRID • WARSAW • BUDAPEST • AUCKLAND

ISBN 0-373-29014-4

TWICE A BRIDE

Copyright © 1998 by Bishop Creek Literary Trust

**Books by Rae Muir**

Harlequin Historicals

*The Pearl Stallion* #308
*The Trail to Temptation* #345
*All But the Queen of Hearts* #369
*The Lieutenant's Lady* #383
*Twice a Bride* #414

## *RAE MUIR*

lives in a cabin in California's High Sierra, a mile from an abandoned gold mine. She is, by training, an historian, but finds it difficult to fit into the academic mold, since her imagination inevitably inserts fictional characters into actual events. She's been a newspaper reporter, has written and edited educational materials, researched eighteenth-century Scottish history, run a fossil business and raised three children in her spare time.

She loves the Sierra Nevada, Hawaii, Oxford and San Francisco. Her favorite mode of travel is by car, and she stops at every historical marker.

To the Memory of Dorothy V.
and the Future of Dorothy JoAnn

# Prologue

Will stripped off the clean shirt he had just put on, hung it on the bedpost and dug in the sack of dirty linen for the one he had worn yesterday. No sense ruining the day's clean shirt in the furnace heat of his father's study. He took the stairs two at a time, stopped in the hall for one last gulp of cool air and opened the door narrowly to avoid letting in a draft. Sure enough, a fire blazed on the hearth, despite the fine Indian-summer dawn.

"You wanted to see me?" he asked. His father turned, and Will's heart lurched when he saw the anger in his eyes.

"Shut the door," he said, and abandoned the fire for his desk. His father glared from beneath his thick gray brows, and shoved a roll of papers toward Will. "What is this?"

No need to unroll the sheets, no need to read the title. But how had his father found the manuscript, secreted deep in his high boots?

"*A Sportsman's Adventures in the Mountains of Pennsylvania,*" he replied. "An account of hunting trips. Nothing of consequence," Will said, dismissing the work of months with an airy wave.

"This purports to be an account of a single trip." The papers crackled as his father spread them flat. "A lengthy journey I cannot recall you ever taking."

"I thought...I thought the stories of my...hunting trips would be of greater interest if strung out as a journal. Of a single expedition."

"So you've written a lie." His father sat down and damned the manuscript by flicking it with his fingers.

"No. Not lies, but a technique to rouse interest."

"Whose interest?" The fat was in the fire now. His father could certainly see that this was the fair copy, destined for a printing house.

"Whose?" his father demanded. He rose to his feet. "You are a clerk in my office. I pay you to learn the business. I do not pay you to spend your time writing lies, preparing them for printers who will encourage you to include filth—"

"There's nothing immoral in what I write and I did not write it in the office," Will said.

His father sorted through the papers as if searching for something specific. "Your memory has been selective, to cover your sins. No mention of Sabbath duties neglected. No mention of the slut on the Clarion River."

*My first reader,* Will thought wryly, *my harshest critic.*

"You should have mentioned the girl. So your readers learn the immoralities that result from a sportsman's life. To the discomfort of one's immortal soul."

Will arranged his face into what he hoped was resignation; he stared at the painting hanging above his father's head. His mother, in angelic pose. Should he deny the accusation of sexual misconduct? But he'd denied it many times, always to be met by caustic disbelief. His father could not conceive of an innocent walk with a woman.

"You will go to your room."

"But the manifest for *Pittsburgh Lady!* I'm not half done, and she leaves for Louisville tomorrow morning!"

"Another clerk will handle the job. You'll spend what remains of the day contemplating the enormity of your error. I'll not allow my son to join the ranks of scribblers, corrupting the youth of the nation with notions of individuality and selfish ambition. Robert's coming to sort your books, for the maid informs me your reading material is unsuitable for a Christian gentleman."

The maid! His father had set her spying on him! His legs quivered, like the skin of a horse bothered by flies.

"It's my fault," his father said. "While you were young I did not pay sufficient attention to the literature that silly French governess allowed in the house. Novels and travel narratives. All the more reason for me to be strict now. Another incident of this nature—" he shook the papers until they rattled like autumn leaves "—and I shall order you from the house and disinherit you."

He turned to the fireplace, arm raised. The curled sheets sailed through the air and scattered in the flames.

"No!" Will cried.

"Better they in the fire than you," his father said. He gripped the poker like a sword and lifted the papers that had caught on the brass fender, shoving them into the heart of the flames. They caught at the edges first, bending in agony. Will discovered his hand pressed to his heart, clawing his damp shirtfront. He stared at the portrait to avoid his father's triumphant eyes. His mother would not like being displayed in a dress already two or three years out of fashion.

"Thank heavens your mother did not live to see this!" his father said, looking at the portrait, too.

Will had to get out of the room, because he teetered on the edge of self-control. "Thank you." He turned on his heel. The tears started when he mounted the stairs. He wiped them away with his sleeve, shook his head to banish them. He locked his door behind him, stripped himself to the waist and threw open a window to let in the warm breeze.

"Half a year of work," he shouted. He gripped the window frame, leaned out, daring himself to look the full three stories to the front steps. "I will do it again," he yelled to a carrier wagon passing by, the iron tires rumbling on the bricks. The teamster looked up, laughed and waved.

Will pulled his head in. No sense making a public spectacle of himself. But he would do it again, and again. Because no matter how he tried, keeping ledgers and writing manifests did not satisfy his urge to put pen to paper.

A buggy pulled up at the front steps—Robert, slim in his permanent black, perpetual mourning since his wife died six years ago. He handed the driver a coin. His brother would be up shortly to empty the bookshelf. Will ran his eyes over the titles. Nearly all would go. He snatched his new copy of Frémont's *Report* from the shelf, looked desperately for a hiding place. Not the boots; that security had been betrayed. He thrust the book under the mattress. What else? He grabbed two Fenimore Cooper novels, sure to disappear. A slip of paper fell from *The Last of the Mohicans*.

*Responsibility is the price of independence,* he read. He had copied the words months ago, but from what source he could not remember. *Irresponsibility and independence cannot exist in the same personality.*

"You've always known it would come to this," he said to his reflection in the mirror. "You promised a year in the office after Mother died, but the vow was made under pressure.'' He turned away from the mirror. He had promised because he could not bear the accusations and the guilt. When the news came he had been in the mountains, not at home. His absences had broken his mother's heart. He spun back to the mirror. "*She* was in New York. No matter what Father says, my going off didn't kill her.''

The reflection's mouth seemed to move in a different rhythm. *Leave now, before winter closes the river.*

Will pulled the blankets from the bed, rolled them with two shirts, several pairs of stockings and the books from under the mattress. He hesitated before the bookshelf, selected two more and added them to the bundle. His diary? He dropped it on the rumpled sheets. Nothing from the past year mattered one iota. He would buy a new diary today and start life fresh on the first page.

He unscrewed the decorative ball from a bedpost, with two fingers extracted a leather bag. Every coin and banknote he had hoarded from his pay for the past eleven months. Nearly two hundred dollars, enough to pay his fare down the Ohio to St. Louis, up the Missouri to the frontier towns. Not the time of year to cross the plains. He must find someplace to hole up for the winter. He dressed in the rough clothes he wore in the field and pulled his rifle from under the bed.

Robert's querulous voice drifted up the stairs as Will descended. "His work in the office has been neat and adequate. I have no complaint," he said. "But if you think it best that he not come to the waterfront…'' Robert had neglected to close the door completely. His father must be terribly distracted not to notice the draft. Will leaned the rifle against the wall, pushed open the door. From the threshold he tossed the two keys, with such force they hit the blotting paper on the desk and bounced onto the floor.

"What do you mean by this?" his father roared. "Why are you dressed so shabbily?"

"I'm leaving. I don't need the house key or the key to the office."

"If you leave, I'll send for my lawyer. I'll write you out of my will, disinherit—"

"No, you won't have a chance. I'm disinheriting you. Don't worry." Will pointed to the pile of ashes in the fire. "You'll not see your name on a book of hunting tales." He picked up the bundle, the rifle, and strode down the front hall, his boot heels echoing on the polished walnut.

"You can't leave," Robert said, puffing beside him. "You're not of age."

Will ignored him, opened the front door and stepped onto the narrow stoop. Indian summer, a slight haze in the sky, the colorful leaves drifting to the ground. Perfect weather for hunting. A perfect day to leave Pittsburgh forever.

"Goodbye, Robert," he said, extending his hand. "We'll not see each other again."

"You can't leave," Robert said desperately. "Father *will* disinherit you! You can't possibly make out on your own."

"Then I'll starve to death," Will said, and he bounded down the steps, grinned because his legs did not hesitate or his heart tremble. Down the hill to the wharves along the Allegheny River. Down the hill to every hidden place he would visit and record. The West, the frozen North. Hunting great white bears, tigers in India, elephants in Africa, boars in…he could not remember, and had no time to think about it, for sweating boatmen were lifting the gangplank of the *Bonnie Scot*. He halloed: they waited as he ran the last hundred feet and jumped aboard.

# Chapter One

*Missouri River*
*March 1848*

"We'd make better time walking to St. Joe," growled a man leaning far out to see the side-wheel of the steamboat. Rachel held her breath, afraid he might topple into the river. The tempo of the engine increased, the wheel churned, showering the men near the railing with mud. The growling man staggered back, wiping his face.

Rachel sidled away from the crowd, to the rear of the boat, so she had a view of the riverbank. She focused on two leafless cottonwood trees. Their position did not change. The boat was stuck on another sandbar.

Her father leaned against the aft rail, in the company of a tall man wearing a bulky coat made from a blanket. The stranger had boarded in Independence, and Rachel had noticed him because of his coat. Embroidered leaves and flowers cascaded down the front and vined in profusion around the bottom. A gangly mountain man, bedroll slung over one shoulder and a long rifle in his hand. Perhaps an old friend of her father's, from his years as a trapper in the

Rocky Mountains. But now, seeing him at close range, she realized he was much too young to have been a trapper.

"All passengers for'ard," a man shouted from the pilot-house. Rachel caught her father's eye. He abandoned the stranger with a quick word and a wave.

"Get to your room," he said the moment he stepped beside her. "They'll have the men run back and forth to rock her off the bar." Rachel grimaced, but nodded her obedience, resigning herself to an hour in the smelly state-room. She understood the necessity, with only two women on board, that they share a room, but she had not expected a baby. She opened the door carefully, lest she bump into or step upon the little thing, who was allowed to roam at will. Mrs. Brown cautioned her with a finger upon her lips.

"Merri's asleep," she whispered, pointing to a humped quilt in the middle of Rachel's own cot. Rachel swallowed her protest. Her blankets would be wet again!

"What's going on out there?" Mrs. Brown asked quietly.

"Another sandbar."

"If it weren't for Mary Merrill, I'd walk to St. Joseph," Mrs. Brown said. "I'd make better time. Is something wrong?" she asked, puzzled. Rachel realized she had been sniffing, unconsciously and very impolitely. She relaxed her face to smooth the wrinkles from around her nose.

"Nothing. It's just...I was an only child. I didn't know the...smells that babies bring with them."

Mrs. Brown muffled her titters by spreading her fingers over her mouth. "You'll learn when you have your own."

Rachel almost said she did not want children if they were this much bother, but a shout from the pilothouse interrupted her. "Aft!"

Boots pounded past the door, every man yelling as if

noise alone might dislodge the steamboat. Merri sat up, clutching the quilt.

"Look what they've done now!" Mrs. Brown cried. But when the tumult passed the baby stuck her thumb in her mouth, closed her eyes and lay down, asleep once more. The engines thumped in their accustomed rhythm, the passengers cheered, and the boat rose and fell slightly, a clear sign it was afloat once more.

"I wish the river would rise, to cover the sandbars," Mrs. Brown said. "I can't take Merri on the deck with all this running and shouting. Pity the poor people who have appointments in St. Joe. Will the delay discommode you?"

Rachel shook her head. "A day or two makes no difference. My father's the advance agent for a party from Pikeston, Indiana, friends and neighbors heading for California. They're coming overland, and we'll have supplies waiting when they arrive."

"And you'll go to California?" Mrs. Brown, unlike most of the women on the St. Louis boat, showed no amazement at the destination. Perhaps Mrs. Brown planned to travel west.

"My father's one of the scouts. I always longed for adventure, so I joined him."

"And your mother?" Rachel hesitated, decided there was no need for Mrs. Brown to know the full story. That her parents had not been married, and her mother the wife of another man.

"My mother died a few months after I was born. I was raised by my aunt and uncle."

"And your father has never remarried?"

"No," she said.

Mrs. Brown said nothing for several minutes, then broke the silence. "I'd hoped to make the acquaintance of the men who boarded at Independence," she whispered.

"I'll watch the baby, if you'd like to—"

"Not alone." Mrs. Brown's curls swayed across her cheeks as she shook her head. Every night she painstakingly tied her hair up in rags to create the corkscrews on either side of her face. "Any man who's interested in me must know from the outset that I come with an encumbrance." She smoothed the front of her dull black skirt.

"Father's become acquainted with a young man who boarded at Independence. Shall I ask him to introduce you?"

Mrs. Brown looked doubtful. "Older men are more likely to be searching for a wife," she explained. "The younger ones come to the frontier to sow wild oats." The grim set of her mouth made Rachel wonder—not for the first time—if *Mr.* Brown had ever existed. Perhaps young Mrs. Brown had been the victim of a sower of wild oats. The boat jerked.

"Aground again!" Mrs. Brown cried. Merri sat up, rubbed her tiny fists into her blue eyes, scooted to the edge of the cot and carefully dangled her legs until her toes touched the deck. Her hair, almost white, matted where she had pushed aside her lacy bonnet. She stood, clinging to the edge of the cot.

"Just look at her," Mrs. Brown exclaimed. "Not a year old and able to stand on her own feet!" Rachel had to agree—the child did seem advanced for her age. She only wished Merri had learned the function of the chamber pot.

"Ouw, ouw," Merri said.

"Just listen to her!" the proud mother said. "Talking, and not even a year old!" The baby toddled to the door.

"Ouw, ouw!"

"Not now, dear. The pilot will shout for the men to run and we'd be trampled."

"Ouw, ouw!" Merri screamed.

"Let's go on deck," Rachel suggested, having learned over the past two days that Merri would raise a hurrah until her mother did precisely as she demanded. "Merri should have some fresh air. We'll find a spot out of the way."

Mrs. Brown perched a black bonnet on her curls and tied the ribbon in a jaunty bow against her left cheek. She wrapped Merri in a shawl. Rachel peeked to make sure the deck was empty before they stepped out, then led Mrs. Brown behind a stack of trunks. Most of the passengers jammed the starboard rail, and the larboard wheel churned uselessly in the air. The steamboat yawed, broadside to the current. Mrs. Brown shrieked and clutched Merri.

"Spread out," shouted a voice from above. "Don't all rush to one side, like a bunch of brainless cows!"

The men slunk away from the railing. Rachel glimpsed her father, once more deep in conversation with the man in the embroidered coat. *She* would force the introduction, and relieve herself of Mrs. Brown's constant presence.

"Father," she called. The word rolled strangely off her tongue, but Mr. Godfroy beamed every time she said it, so she used it often.

"You shouldn't be here," he said. "The pilot'll shout for everyone to run." He frowned at the thrashing wheel.

"We'll run, too," Mrs. Brown said brightly. "I need the exercise, and Mary Merrill can't stay cooped up in that room every minute of the day."

Her father's eyes flickered from Mrs. Brown to the stranger. Once more to the stranger, his mouth twisting in indecision. Why was her father hesitating? Courtesy demanded introductions.

"Mrs. Brown, Rachel, this is Mr. Will Hunter." Mr. Hunter lifted his low-crowned hat and sketched a bow.

"Good morning, Mrs. Brown. Good morning, Miss Godfroy." His wavy brown hair matched the suggestion of beard on his jaw. Angular lines dominated his face, level eyebrows, strong nose, unemotional mouth. Square jaw. Young, except for his blue eyes. They shone crisp, icy and cautious.

"How delightful!" Mrs. Brown cried. "This is Mary Merrill Brown, my daughter." She set the little girl on her own feet. Mr. Hunter's eyes narrowed without disturbing the line of his brow. Rachel could see the direction of his gaze—not Mrs. Brown's face, but her bosom, which she exposed above a low neckline inappropriate to widow's weeds.

"The poor child will never, alas, know her papa," Mrs. Brown said. She gestured to the matte black of her skirt. "Say hello to Mr. Hunter, Merri."

"Papa," Merri said. Mr. Hunter's eyes flew open and the level brows curled slightly. The blue changed from icy and intrigued to icy and alarmed.

"Everyone aft," cried the voice from the pilothouse. Mr. Hunter lifted his head toward the man with the speaking trumpet. "On the count, one, two, three! For'ard, fast!"

Rachel retreated farther behind the trunks, afraid she might be run over in the mad dash to the bow, but Mrs. Brown threw herself into the crowd. Merri's screams of delight rose above the baritone shouts of the men.

"I'm sorry," her father said. Rachel started with surprise to find him beside her, supposing he had thundered off with the rest. "Mrs. Brown scared him off. I want you to meet Will Hunter. He has a cabin, a double cabin, near St. Joseph, ideal for us if he'll rent half. We can't stay in a town hostel, for there'd be no place to store the hay and grain I'm to buy for the overland party."

Rachel heard the apology in his words and rushed to reassure him. "I hadn't supposed that we'd waste money boarding. The wagons will arrive in a month. Five weeks at the most. We can manage quite well camped in a tent."

"Spring rain," he said, glancing up at the puffy clouds. "I'm not a lone trapper anymore, to live rough-and-tumble. My daughter needs a roof over her head. Hunter strikes me as a suitable companion. He's looking for a job as hunter for a westbound party. Traders to Santa Fe, or emigrants."

"A hunter named Hunter?" Rachel asked skeptically.

"More than one man changes his name on the Missouri," her father said easily. "And not always to hide a wild life."

Rachel nodded to show she agreed with him, but privately decided Mr. Hunter had a shadow on his past. And so young to have set out on the road of crime!

"Aft! Aft!" shouted the voice from the pilothouse. Once more the baritone shouts, with Merri's shrill scream. A sudden, laughing crowd circled the trunks, had barely caught a collective breath when the voice cried, "For'ard! For'ard!" Mrs. Brown leaned against the trunks, panting.

"Ruh, ruh," Merri said, wiggling against her mother's restraint. Mrs. Brown put the child down, and the little girl ducked from under her arms and set out in pursuit of the men, squealing with delight. Her nose went faster than her tiny boots and she sprawled on the deck.

"Waaa!" The man who snatched her wore an embroidered coat.

"Oh, Mr. Hunter!" Mrs. Brown cried, bustling from behind the trunks. "Thank you. Thank the good man, Merri."

"Papa," Merri said.

"Keep her in your arms," Mr. Hunter said, his eyes simply icy. "She might be trampled." No hint of a smile for the child. No emotion in that level mouth, not even a frown of disapproval for the mother. He turned and walked away.

"Young men are so unsympathetic," Mrs. Brown said,

staring after him. She hugged her baby. "I believe Merri has had sufficient excitement for today." She walked slowly, proudly down the larboard side, ignoring the threat that the pilot might suddenly call "Aft!" But the steamboat slithered and lurched, and with a great slurp disengaged itself from the sandbar.

"She wants desperately to meet the men who boarded at Independence," Rachel said. "I don't understand her. Any husband will do. Love doesn't figure at all."

"Love doesn't figure in many marriages," her father said softly. "You should know that. Your mother and her husband bore no love for one another. Think of Mrs. Brown's difficulties, and be more patient." Rachel stared at her father. He had never rebuked her before, even mildly. "She's alone, a widow with a child. Perhaps she eloped with a man her parents disapproved of, and now she's ashamed to go home, ashamed he abandoned her."

Rachel stared down the river and kept her suspicions to herself, that there had *never* been a husband.

"Mr. Hunter could be a help to us," her father said, resuming the topic of conversation. "I've asked him to join our party. If we hire a professional hunter, the young men have no excuse to waste lead and powder, and tire the horses."

Rachel was not sure why he made these arguments to her. It was his decision, not hers. "If you think it best."

"I won't ask you to spend five or six weeks in the company of a man you find offensive."

"But I've barely met him!"

"How does he strike you?"

"Not offensive. A little cold, perhaps. But it's possible that he pretends to be cold and unemotional to seem older. He's very young."

Her father waved away that objection. "Beyond the Missouri is the land of the young. I was fifteen when I first crossed the river.''

"We'll have separate rooms?" she asked.

"A double cabin. Two cabins under one roof, and we'll have one of them.''

"Then there is no problem.'' She need not associate over much with Mr. Hunter. And after her friends arrived with the wagons, she and her father would move with them to a camp across the river, and stolid Mr. Hunter would be just another hired hand, like the young men driving the oxen.

Will reclaimed his space on the lower deck, rested his head on his bedroll and his heels on a barrel. He had been foolish to expect a job with a trader going to Santa Fe. In Independence experienced trappers and hunters loafed on every street corner. All looking for work, now that the beaver trade had faded. Why should the organizer of an expedition hire a man whose hunting had been limited to the mountains of Pennsylvania and western Virginia?

Will grimaced at the recollection of his first interview, when he had mentioned his experience in Pennsylvania. Between paroxysms of laughter and bursts of tobacco juice, the trader had gasped, "Pennsylvania mountains! You think you seen mountains in *Pennsylvania?*" Will had never mentioned Pennsylvania again.

More than four months in St. Joseph, and he had traveled only a few miles west of the river. He had met no Indians except the tame tribes that came into town to trade and beg. No buffalo or antelope. Four months of close scribbling in his diary, and not more than a dozen sentences worth transcribing in the book he would write.

He could hire one of the old trappers to take him hunting on the plains. But that would be a book by a spectator, not a participant. The thought of traveling on the plains with a guide, like a rich man, stuck in his craw. Besides, hiring a guide would mean caving in to Robert, spending Robert's money, admitting he could not live on his own.

He had not been surprised that Robert had discovered his whereabouts, for the company's tentacles reached all ports on the Ohio, Mississippi and Missouri Rivers. What _had_ surprised him was the money. He should be grateful that Robert did not turn up like an angry schoolmaster, armed with switches and paddles to drive him home, threatening prosecution of the people who had given him refuge. For the first time Robert had tried to bribe him.

"I must have grown up," Will muttered. He closed his eyes against the reflection of the sun off the water.

"Howdy." Will opened his eyes, found a beaded buckskin hunting shirt leaning over him. "This space taken?"

Will dropped his legs against the side of the boat to make room for the man and a young woman with dark eyes and high cheekbones. She wore a dress of multicolored brocade, stylish, except that she had cut ten inches off the skirt to show her high, beaded moccasins. Watery blue eyes examined Will, seemed to find a kinsman, for the man nodded.

"Where you headed?" he asked.

"St. Joe."

"After that?"

Will shrugged. "Wherever the trail forks. And you?"

"Blackfoot country." The man gazed across the river, his faraway eyes focusing on something beyond the water. "When I was young, I lived like you, without a thought for tomorrow," he mused, "but time has seized my bones. I thought to go home to Ohio, take up a farm, but the wild still holds me." He shifted his cud of tobacco. "And my people shunned her." He jerked a thumb at the woman, without elaboration as to her status—wife or concubine, daughter or friend. "We're going to her people, who won't call me a burden, even though that's what I'll be, with the beaver gone. But I'd rather die tomorrow in the Rockies than live a century in this pigsty." He jerked a thumb that encompassed the crowd, the piles of merchandise and the cluster of impassive slaves. He turned his back on them and stared at the river—or some private vision.

Will tried to see what the old trapper saw, but the rays of the level sun blinded him. From this angle, if he squinted, the water resembled thready gold, not brown mud. A snag floated by, a huge tree, torn by winter storms from a forest hundreds of miles upstream. Roots extended upward; his first impression traced malevolent fingers reaching to draw puny humans to a watery grave. But as the snag drifted by, the gnarled roots transformed into an extended hand, begging for rescue. The tree did not want to leave its wild forest. A forest he would never see. Unless he went as hunter with Godfroy's California party.

Will drew his diary from his satchel. The small book fell open on Robert's latest letter. "Return to Pittsburgh in October, to celebrate your coming of age...your duty to an aging parent...Father asks after you daily."

Folded inside the letter had been the biggest bribe so far: permission to draw upon the company's account to any limit. Will had burned the draft, putting temptation out of reach. He would go home on his own account and on his own schedule. He would pay his steamboat fare with the coins earned when he carried game to the hotel. He would travel east with the manuscript, an account of his adventures, ready to be copied fair to submit to a publisher.

October in Pittsburgh meant going no farther than South Pass, the top of the Rockies. Perhaps by that time he would have material for a book. Perhaps he would be eager to leave the slow emigrant train, burdened with women and children, wagons and ponderous oxen. Farmers grousing about rain and heat, never satisfied with their fate.

"I've been offered a job as hunter for a wagon train bound for California," he said suddenly, turning to face the trapper, hoping to catch a reaction. "The scout's by the name of Godfroy."

"Trail?" the trapper asked. His sun-bleached eyes lost their faraway focus. Will was startled by the mysterious question embedded in the single word. "The half-breed?"

Will had not considered Godfroy's race, for every man and nearly every woman on the frontier was tanned brown as a nut. Calling up a memory of Godfroy's face, he realized the man did carry Native blood, probably more than half.

"May be. I hadn't thought about it. He's aboard, with his daughter."

"Trail's got his daughter?" The trapper slapped his buckskin leggings. "By gritty, Trail always talked of his daughter, which is why we called him Trail, because come spring, sometimes before the hunt was over, he'd trail off with his pelts, and we'd not see him till first snow. Is she pretty? He said she was, but we figured he lied."

Pretty. No, nothing so simple as pretty, with her wide mouth and big eyes. "She's quite beautiful, in an unusual way."

"So Trail's looking for a hunter," the trapper mused. His eyes narrowed, his lips pouted out of the bush of gray beard. "What's he paying?"

"I don't know," Will said, glad he had avoided the details of the contract. The trapper toyed with the fringe of his shirt, his eyes thoughtful slits.

*He'll search out old friend Trail Godfroy, and agree to be hunter for the California emigrants.*

Will went cold as his heart skittered away, taking with it his last chance to hunt on the plains and in the mountains. The boat jolted.

"Damnation! Aground agin!" the trapper cried. "We might as well have walked to St. Joe. Well, this child's not running up and down, back and forth. Let them as steer this contraption figure how to get it free!"

"I'll find out what we've hit," Will said, climbing to his feet with some effort, for the deck canted to starboard, and the boat made unpleasant, jerky motions in that direction, as if sliding into an abyss. He got to the upper deck by clinging to the banister.

"Gather on the larboard side!" yelled the voice from the pilothouse. Will ignored the plea and searched for Godfroy, whom he found still gazing idly over the aft rail. He walked to the stern, pretending the orders from overhead did not apply to him. He lounged casually beside Godfroy, stared into the chocolate foam kicked up by the wheels.

"This party of emigrants, how many will there be?"

"From my town in Indiana, maybe thirty, counting me and Rachel, in fifteen, sixteen wagons. My partner, Jed Sampson, he's bringing his kinfolks from Ohio. A few hired bullwhackers. We've got a passel of boys along, but they're of an age to be more trouble than they're worth. Give out under hard work. We need more men."

"If I join you...possibly I'll turn back in July, August at the latest...I have family responsibilities." The final words struck a false note. Godfroy might think he had a young woman in the family way. "My father's elderly."

"So you'd turn for home at South Pass, or maybe Bear River Valley," Godfroy mused. "There's truly not much game beyond Bear River, although on the desert's where a hunter's of most value. He may not bag much, but it tastes better than three-month-old bacon."

Will nodded miserably. When Godfroy learned an old friend was aboard… But—Will straightened up—he held a trump card. The cabin.

"You can use the cabin—"

"Why don't you come all the way to California? There's plenty of work on the coast during the winter. Head east in the spring. California's a magnificent place. The hunting! Grizzly bears and elk, antelope and panthers! Once there, you'd stay for sure. Great, great opportunities for a young man in that country."

"I suppose," he agreed so he did not appear to dispute an older man's opinions. But he could not stay in California, even if he should go all the way with the emigrants. Once the book was written he had to return east—New York or Boston—where he would find a publisher.

The steamboat shuddered, slid sideways and floated free. The passengers cheered, the whistle blared and the boat bucked the sluggish current.

"I'll hire you," Godfroy said, "if Rachel and I can live in the cabin and use the place to gather fodder. The men of the party agreed, before I left Indiana, that they'd make up a purse of fifty dollars for a hunter. You'll stay with us to at least Bear River Valley. You can't say you've seen the Rocky Mountains until you've seen Bear River."

"Fine." Will extended his hand, Godfroy took it, and the twilight, the ending of the day, gave finality to the agreement. He would write Robert and tell him his plans. Robert would gradually learn he no longer controlled his brother's destiny. That to try only created a greater chasm.

The steamboat swung toward the bank and slaves jumped ashore to tie up for the night. Will joined the crew cutting wood for fuel, answered the glare of the white overseer with a glare of his own.

"I'm not accustomed to being idle," he said. The man

nodded, an unwilling acquiescence. Will found pleasure in the heft of the ax and the play of his muscles. Darkness had closed in by the time he returned to the spot he had claimed. The trapper and his woman had left for some more comfortable vacancy. He stretched out in his blankets, listening to the voices of the slaves ashore, cooking their supper. Small waves slapped against the boat. Will lit a stub of candle and in its narrow glow spread his diary. He noted the steamboat's slow progress, wrote of the trapper, his woman, the great snag, of Godfroy, and a mocking account of Mrs. Brown. Eastern readers would be amused by a Western widow's frantic efforts to secure a husband.

The temptation of the plains filled his dream, and a woman, much like the Blackfoot, walked by his side.

# Chapter Two

The stench of unwashed bodies, tobacco juice and caged animals had thickened overnight, driving Will to the upper deck to watch the dawn. A blanket-draped figure stood at the railing like a statue, staring at the dark, silent land.

"Miss Godfroy." She started as if she had just wakened.

"Mr. Hunter," she said after several seconds, and acknowledged him with a nod.

"You're about early."

"Mrs. Brown's baby spent a restless night." She leaned against the rail. "Father says we'll be your guests while in St. Joseph, and that you'll cross the plains with us." No question about her race with the blanket draped over her head and her face illuminated by starlight. Less than half-breed, but an Indian by the dictates of Pittsburgh society.

"I leased a double cabin last fall. There's a separate room for you and your father, Miss Godfroy."

"Please call me Rachel. I'm not...accustomed to being Miss Godfroy."

"Not accustomed?" What a strange thing to say!

"My aunt and uncle raised me as their daughter. I was called by my uncle's name, Ridley. He's a lawyer, and a member of the Indiana state legislature. This winter I learned that Mr. Godfroy...Father is my real father."

"And you came away with a stranger?"

"He's no stranger!" She laughed, the sound of the tinkling of small, silver coins. "Everyone in Pikeston knows Mr. Godfroy. He came summers, all the way from the Rocky Mountains, and camped on the White River. He brought furs, and he lived in a pointed tent he called a tepee."

"How wonderful for you!" He gripped the railing and leaned far back to view the starry zenith. "When I was a boy, I dreamed some Indian chief would knock on our door and demand that the palefaces return his son. Me, of course."

The blanket shifted. He could not read her face, but her posture mocked his fantasy, and he was sorry he had spoken.

"It was not wonderful when Mr. Godfroy...Father came to my uncle's house and told the truth," she said sternly. "Aunt Caroline has a weakness, and for a time her mind failed." Will frowned in sympathy, but blood thundered in his ears. How wonderful if Trail Godfroy had come to the mansion in Pittsburgh, and said, "You are my son!"

"I suppose it caused a sensation in your town, when Godfroy announced that you and he were kin?"

"A sensation to some, and a horror to others, when they realized they'd called me friend and welcomed me into their homes. An honor I didn't deserve." She spoke slowly, choosing the words carefully, but did not bother to disguise her bitterness. "My friend Tildy and her family lived in the most elegant house in Pikeston, and her mother no longer allowed me through the front door."

"A dreadful shock to you," he said.

"A shock? No, not really. All my life I'd suspected my

aunt and uncle lied to me. About who I was.'' Will turned because a spiderweb touched his face. He brushed it away, only to find it at his chest. Strange, that he could feel such a delicate thing through his coat.

"Tell me, Mr. Hunter—"

"Will. If I'm to call you Rachel, you must call me Will." He brushed at his coat to rid himself of the annoyance, but his fingers found no spiderweb.

"When you were a child, did you ever feel the urge to run away?" she asked.

He laughed nervously, because he was not accustomed to confessions. Because she had shown contempt for his fantasy. The thread somehow made its way under his coat, his shirt, and floated against his skin, a line of warmth.

"Run away? Constantly, Miss...Rachel. Not just the urge. I ran away more times than I can count."

"You did!" She turned on her heel so quickly the blanket fell away, revealing dark hair in a braid down her back. "How wonderful, to be a boy, to actually do these things! I wanted to run away, every spring, and when the leaves turned bright in the fall, but I never got beyond the river. The water seemed to talk, threatening me, and every time I turned back, and forced myself to be the girl Aunt Caroline thought proper. I owed her so much, for she took my mother in. Where did you go when you ran away?" she asked eagerly.

"At first, when I was five or six, to..." He slowed to choose his words carefully. If he mentioned servants she would guess more about his life than he wanted her to know. "To a nearby house, to a family I liked, and my brother Robert—he's eighteen years older than I—would be sent to bring me home." The thick rims of the earthenware mugs, his first sips of coffee poured straight from the pot on the hearth, without cream or sugar. And the first words he could remember writing, an awkwardly spelled note of thanks, slipped under the kitchen door in the dead of night.

"And then?" Her question contained all her regret at the expeditions cut short by the river.

"My family visited a man in the hills," he said, stepping around details as he would steel traps. "When I was eight I hitched a ride with a farmer for twenty miles, then walked ten." Autumn, the glory of the hills, the morning chill of the caretaker's cabin. He had turned his back on the civilized mass of his family's country home, pretending it did not exist. His first hunting trip, his first kill, and the guilty shock at watching death overcome living eyes.

"And your brother found you?"

"The man was beholden to my father. He sent a message, and my father missed two days of work fetching me. On the way home he cut a willow switch, and whenever he stopped to rest, he swatted my bottom."

"So you learned to stay home?"

"I learned to go where they'd not find me. I used a different name." *Will Hunter*, he came very close to saying. He must not trust her simply because she was an attractive woman. A woman who had longed to run away from home.

"Look! The morning star!" He followed her hand, to a light hung like a lantern in a leafless tree.

"The hunter's star."

"I've never heard anyone call it that."

"A hunter rises early. Up with the morning star."

The stars seemed to drop closer. Almost as if he might pluck one and hand it to her, to complement the beauty achieved by the blending of races. He turned a little away so she would not see his smile. He imagined his father and Robert emerging from a stateroom, their censorious words when they discovered his companion. His father's pontifical tone flowed from a hidden crevice of his mind.

*Why should I expend my money on missions to the savages? We've offered them every opportunity to better themselves, but they insist upon returning to their pagan ways and dirty hovels. The only thing worse than an educated Indian is a squaw man, a white renegade who knows the teachings of civilization and Christianity, and abandons them.*

The voice of the trapper edged out that of his father. *My people shunned her.* The tiny thread of silk caressed his face. If he married a woman like Rachel Godfroy his family would cut him off forever. His people would shun her, and call him a squaw man. No matter that she had better manners than half the ladies of his acquaintance. No matter that she was graceful and beautiful. No more pleading letters, no more sheaves of banknotes to sway his determination.

Marry Rachel Godfroy because of her race? A silly and trivial reason to take a wife. He had seen men marry to have children, or to gain a companion. Friends only a few years older than he married to get their hands on a woman's fortune. Of course, they prattled about love, until deep in boozy conversation the real motive revealed itself.

Marriage? He'd not thought of it before. But then, he'd never before met a woman who longed to run away and have great adventures. He brushed at the spider silk tickling his neck, but found nothing.

The log cabin smelled of damp and rot. Rachel leaned in the open door, but could distinguish nothing until Will flung open the shutters. Sunlight flooded across a drift of leaves, piles of hides and furs stacked near the door.

"I'll clean it out, of course," he said. Did she hear

shame, at this revelation of his bachelor housekeeping? No furniture, except for a bed in the corner. Only the frame, not even leather straps to support a mattress. No grate or irons in the fireplace, a single pot hook above the scattered, flattened ashes of a long-ago fire.

*I asked for this. I wanted adventure.*

Rachel squared her shoulders and refused to flinch. She had chosen to follow her father. At this moment she might be snug in her aunt and uncle's house in Indiana, protected from the wind gusting through the unglazed window, stirring the ashes on the hearth, skittering leaves across the floor.

"We'll buy a few things in town," she said stoutly. "Irons for the fire, and—"

"That seems a waste," Will said. "You can't take them to California. Instead of fixing this place up, you two move into my cabin. I'll repair the bed here for myself. We can housekeep together for a few weeks." Will looked to her for a decision, not her father. His steady eyes gave no hint of his own wishes. Her legs weakened, that he should look at her in that fashion, and say the word *bed*.

"We won't chase you out of your house," her father said. "This will do fine, won't it, Rachel—" But Will was out the door in two long strides, into the open hallway that separated the cabins. Nothing to do but follow him, helpless. She resented her helplessness, and the openness of her emotions in the face of his self-control. Will had seen her revulsion at the filthy cabin. He guessed she was not the stalwart, daring woman she pretended to be.

The second room proved to be a mirror image of the first, but a few pieces of rough furniture, plus pots hanging from the mantel, transformed the cabin into a home. Four panes of glass had been set in the window to keep out the wind. A buffalo robe on the bed changed it to a comfortable couch.

"We can make another bed," Will said, pointing to an empty space beyond the hearth.

"I don't need a bed," her father said. "My life's been spent sleeping on the ground."

Will nodded. "I'll fetch some wood. The wind's cold." He dumped his bedroll on the floor, hung his rifle on wooden pegs set in the lintel of the door. He smiled at her, and the smile altered his face. No longer a geometric structure, the corners of his brows twisted, one a bit more than the other, and faint lines accented his eyes. The issue was settled. He thrust the responsibility of hearth and home into her hands. She took off her cloak and hung it on a peg by the door, clasped her hands at her waist so Will and her father did not see them tremble. For the first time in her life she was the woman of the house.

"I'll go to the river and haul up our luggage," her father said. The statement excluded her. The woman of the house, left to take up her duties. Rachel knelt by the wood box, selected shavings and kindling, and laid them on the hearth. She found matches in a covered jar on the mantel. The flame caught instantly, and she breathed a bit easier. Behind her Will stacked wood. The bail of a bucket creaked, the door opened and closed. He had gone to fetch water. He would expect coffee, and something to eat.

A large wooden packing crate had been mounted on the wall, and shelves built inside. Flour, coffee, salt, all in labeled tin boxes; a small crock that, when she opened it, emitted a vile odor. She flaked dried brown foam from the rim and studied the dark mass, sunk to the bottom. Yeast. She could not bake light bread until she had healthy yeast.

Will set the bucket on a low stool. "Thank you," she said without facing him. But his presence wafted to her, as the airborne fluff of a cottonwood tree drifts in still air. A delicate caress on her cheek. She spun about to rebuke him, found him standing by the bench that held the water bucket and the wash basin. Staring at her.

Her father trusted Will and had left her alone with him. But did her father know Will had been a wild child who ran away from home, and dreamed of being an Indian? That he used a false name? She was certain of that now. Age had not tempered his wildness. In fact, manhood probably sent it into channels....

The shelves hung very close to the bed, so close he could throw her down. Her fingers fumbled weakly at the tin sugar box. He took it from her and lifted the hinged lid. He wrinkled his nose as he leaned over the crock.

"I never remember to feed the yeast," he said.

"I'll make biscuits." She regarded the fireplace. No oven. She had never cooked on an open hearth before, although she had helped her friend Faith, who managed all the food for a family of six without a cookstove. "Or flapjacks," she added, realizing they would be a great deal more straightforward than biscuits.

If she had come west with the wagons she would be with her friends, not this wild stranger. In pleasant weather she and Faith, Meggie and Tildy would walk to relieve the oxen. In the evenings Granny MacIntyre would instruct them in the art of cooking over an open fire. But she had been too anxious to begin the adventure. She resolved to ignore Will while she scooped flour into the crock, added sugar and ladled in water.

"Do you have a young man, a beau, coming with the wagons?" Will asked.

"No," she said, keeping her eyes on her work. She stopped stirring, would have put her hand over her mouth, but it held the crock. She should have said yes! Will would not make advances if he thought she had a suitor coming.

"Miss Godfroy." She stirred the yeast, her heart pounding because he spoke very quietly and had stepped closer. "Don't be afraid. You're perfectly safe with me."

She did not trust herself to look at him. When she did lift her head, he had taken his rifle from the pegs. "I'll scare us up some meat. Godfroy'll need an hour or so at the river, getting the wagon put together, and finding a team to pull it." She had forgotten the wagon, shipped from Indiana in a huge bundle of puzzling pieces. "You'll feel easier without me around."

She *was* easier without him around. She filled the coffeepot and hung it above the fire. Despite Will's mountain-man dress, his words and actions showed a gentleman's rearing. What must he think of her, trembling at being alone with a man? A green girl, not a woman who turned eighteen last week. Old enough to pick a husband, older, she suspected, than Mrs. Brown, who had already wed, borne a child and lost her husband.

Rachel regretted that she had not been friendlier with Mrs. Brown. She had last glimpsed her climbing the road from the river to the town of St. Joseph, Merri trudging along on her own feet. Rachel poured herself a cup of coffee and resolved, as soon as she was settled, to search out Louisa Brown. She needed a woman friend to talk to.

She scoured the table with a scrub brush. She searched through the packing crate for a tablecloth, but found only two rags the size of pocket handkerchiefs. Another shelf hung over the bed. She knelt on the buffalo robe.

Books. Adventure stories. Exactly what she would expect of Will Hunter. Novels by James Fenimore Cooper. Perfect reading for a boy who longed to be an Indian. She was silly to be afraid of him. Nothing but an overgrown boy. And naturally, Captain Frémont's *Report.*

A shot echoed faintly from the hill above the cabin. Will had found meat. Rachel tilted her head to read the next title, and drew back in surprise. *Pilgrim's Progress.* On second thought, not surprising. A religious book, but still an adventure. And it showed more wear than the Bible propped against it. She patted the shelf until her fingers touched the log wall. No tablecloth.

Her coffee was cold, but she drank it anyway. If her trunk had arrived she would unpack her embroidery, to use her spare moments productively, as Aunt Caroline had taught her. Perhaps she should walk into town and find Mrs. Brown. After days on the steamer, Merri's clothes would need mending. She and Mrs. Brown could sit and sew and chat, the way she and her friends had done in Indiana.

He stood in the door, shoulders broader than she recalled. "Just a rabbit, but it'll do until I find something better." He held the animal out to her. She shrank away. She hadn't the slightest idea how a furry creature was changed into meat in the pot. She put her hands behind her back. Will would know for sure that she was helpless, and his blue eyes would mock her.

"I've never..." she whispered. "The butcher took care of such things," she managed to say in a firmer voice. No reaction, except his level stare, and his composure made her angry. Why should he suppose he could throw game at her feet? Like a savage. He turned without a word, returned a few minutes later with the rabbit skinned and gutted, decapitated so she did not have to face dead eyes.

"I'll make a rabbit stew, or if you'd prefer—"

"Stew's great, and you'll find onions and a few wrinkled potatoes in that corner. Under the planks." He pointed with a closed fist. "Unless some squirrel or rat has found them first. Hold out your hand." She held her elbow against her side. A mistake, for it forced him to come very close to drop a bit of soft fluff into her palm. "The rabbit's left hind leg. That's to carry for good luck. Tonight, I'll string it on a thong and you can tie it on your belt."

He lifted the short planks away from a rock-lined pit. Digging about in a heap of straw, he extracted two onions and three potatoes shrunken to the size of eggs.

"We can't eat your food, Mr....Will."

"We'll settle up later. Your father's on the road from town. I saw him when I came down the hill. He'll be hungry as a bear after taming that team of mules."

"Mules?"

"Hitched to the wagon, and the way they danced about, I don't think they've ever been in harness before."

Rachel dismembered the still-warm rabbit, selected a pot, filled it with water and hung it over the fire. She mixed flour and cornmeal in a small basin for the flapjacks. Will whistled in the hall, the casual sound at odds with his stern demeanor. A faint odor of oil and gunpowder drifted through the open door. Cleaning his rifle. A neat man. A gently reared man who had fallen on hard times, and into moral decay. An educated man.

A threat! Educated gentlemen lived on the frontier for just one reason: trouble. He had fled his home in the East one jump ahead of a sheriff. Or a father who found his daughter seduced. Rachel thought the second reason more likely, for Will was rather good-looking.

A clatter of wheels, the jingle of harness and a frantic yell. "Whoa! Whoa!" Will ran past the door and Rachel dashed behind him. The wagon made wide circles in the clearing. Her father had wrenched the mules' heads far to the right, so they automatically turned, but they did not stop, did not seem inclined to even slow down.

"Run them!" Will cried. "You got to run them first time, till they're so tired they can't lift their heads." He leaped at the wagon as it rattled by, caught the tailgate and hoisted his long legs over the side. "We'll be back," he yelled at her. "Get the stew ready." Both men now tugged at the reins, and on the second circle they had the mules pointed down the track leading to the main road. Rachel stared after them as they disappeared in a cloud of dust. The dust lifted slowly, like a curtain, and revealed a woman walking toward the cabin, carrying a child.

"Hello!" Mrs. Brown cried. "I saw Mr. Godfroy driving this way, and guessed you'd settled here in the country." She put Merri down and let her toddle the last few yards to the cabin. "I found a delightful situation at the hostel Mr. Robidoux built for travelers."

"I'm glad you're already es—"

"Mr. Robidoux is very proud of St. Joseph. He founded the town, you know. He was quite pleased when I remarked how surprised I was! I expected to find a settlement of log cabins, but it's a city. Brick buildings, and lovely houses. And the courthouse! Did you see it? A dome!"

"I saw it. Won't you come in?" Mrs. Brown stopped on the threshold and looked about the cabin.

"This belongs to Mr. Hunter?"

"Yes. He graciously let us move in, since he'll be traveling with us, across the plains. My father's hired him as hunter for our party."

"Oh." Disappointed, Rachel thought. Mrs. Brown stepped inside and walked directly to the packing crate. She examined its contents closely, without picking anything up. She moved to the bed. She was so short she had to climb onto the edge of the bed frame to see the books.

"Very neat, for a bachelor. When do you expect your friends to arrive?"

"I can't say exactly. About the middle of April, so they can rest for a few days before we cross the river."

"You'll be happy to see them, I imagine." Mrs. Brown smiled coyly. "You have a young man coming, I reckon."

Why should Will, and now Mrs. Brown, be interested in her Indiana suitors? "Not especially." She shrugged.

"No young man you walk out with! Why, I'd supposed they flocked about you like flies around a honey pot." She returned to her examination of the shelf. Rachel steered Merri away from the fire. Merri grabbed the rabbit's foot and stuck it in her mouth.

"Don't!" Rachel cried, snatching it from the baby. "Will...Mr. Hunter, I mean, killed that rabbit not an hour ago and the foot's not been washed."

"He gave you the rabbit's foot?" Mrs. Brown asked. She frowned, her chin nearly on her chest. She looked through the top of her eyes, and Rachel felt accused of a gross sin in accepting the charm.

"Yes. He said it brought good luck." Mrs. Brown sighed, sat down and pulled Merri onto her lap. "Would you like a cup of coffee?" Rachel asked.

"Now, that's very kind of you. I would, indeed. Would you have a bit of cracker or biscuit that Merri could chew on? She's teething."

"There's no bread of any kind in the house." Mrs. Brown sighed more deeply. "But I'm peeling potatoes for stew. She could chew on a slice of potato." Mrs. Brown nodded. Merri snatched the potato and gummed it energetically.

"Has he got money?" Mrs. Brown asked suddenly.

"Who?"

"Why, Mr. Hunter, of course."

"I shouldn't think so. He's looking for a summer job as a hunter. Why should you think he has money?"

Mrs. Brown shrugged. "The thought came to me. He's tall, and looks a bit like a man I met in Na—in a river town. That man scattered money like chicken feed."

Had Mrs. Brown meant to say Natchez? That would account for her soft drawling speech, the accent of the rivers.

"Just because he *spent* money, doesn't mean he *had* money," Rachel reminded her.

"I wonder what Mr. Hunter's real name is."

"Why shouldn't his name be Hunter?" Rachel asked, outwardly calm, but inside she prickled at Mrs. Brown's suspicions, then wondered why, when she had her own doubts.

Mrs. Brown tucked Merri beneath her arm, marched to the bed, stretched upward, almost spilling her bosom over the top of her bodice. She sat Merri on the buffalo robe, pulled the Bible from the shelf and opened the front cover.

"That's not proper," she said, slamming the book shut.

"What?"

"Writing a joke in a Bible, that's not proper."

It's not proper to look in Will's books without his permission, Rachel said to herself. But Mrs. Brown had aroused her curiosity. What shocking thing had Will written in the Bible? Something indecent, since Mrs. Brown pressed her lips together and frowned.

I'm living with him, Rachel rationalized. I should know what he's capable of. Mrs. Brown opened the cover again, and this time Rachel reached her side before she closed it.

*Awarded to William Shakespeare for perfect attendance.*

"A man who'd write a joke in a Bible's not worth a woman's effort," Mrs. Brown said. She dropped the book, and it bounced slightly on the buffalo robe. Merri reached for it, but her mother snatched her up. "I best be getting back to town. It's time for Merri's nap." The little girl had masticated the potato into a fistful of pulp, which she now smeared on her mother's shoulder.

Rachel considered asking Mrs. Brown to stay for dinner. But there was only one rabbit for three people, two of them hungry men who right now wrestled with a team of wild mules.

"Do call again," she said. "Next time I'll have more provisions, and you can stay for dinner."

"Thank you, but I'll meet more suitable men by dining in town." She hesitated on the threshold. "Are there any single gentlemen coming west with your friends?"

"There's Pete MacIntyre, who makes wagons and carriages. The wagon my father drove, Pete made it and packed the pieces so we could bring it with us on the steamboat."

"Money?" she asked. What a vulgar woman, coming to the point so ruthlessly!

"His father's a farmer. Or was before he sold the farm to head west."

"How old is this Pete?"

"Twenty-two or twenty-three."

Mrs. Brown shook her head so emphatically her curls swayed across her nose. "Younger men tend not to be sympathetic. Any older bachelors or widowers?"

"Mr. Tole's a widower. His daughter Faith keeps house for him and her brothers."

"What does he do?"

"He's a blacksmith."

"How many boys?" Mrs. Brown asked.

"Four. But Kit, the oldest, he's seventeen, and the youngest is ten, so there's no tiny ones to care for."

"They probably eat like horses, and the woman who feeds them's stuck at the fire day in and day out. But—" she brightened "—please introduce me to your friends when they arrive. Maybe I'd like California. Do call upon me in the city,'' she said grandly.

Rachel put the Bible back on the shelf, next to *Pilgrim's Progress*, but not before taking one more peek at the inscription. A joke. In fact, a double one, and Mrs. Brown had not noticed, because she knew little of Will Hunter. The name was not nearly as funny as the notion that Will sat still long enough to have perfect attendance at anything. Anything so proper as to award him a Bible, that is.

## *Chapter Three*

⸙⸙⸙⸙⸙⸙⸙⸙

 W ill tied the mules to a tree with a doubled rope. Their
legs buckled, their chests heaved, their heads hung to their
knees, but he trusted wild mules no more than a wounded
bear. He had seen mules take off when their owner feared
they were dying.

He sank to the ground, his chest heaving, his shoulders
screaming with pain. He leaned against a tree near Godfroy,
who had thrown himself full-length on the ground.

"Thanks," Godfroy gasped. "I knew you were a good
man."

"You did? A little early for judgments, isn't it?"

"Why, that cute gal with the baby, you sent her packing
without so much as a smile. A man who can be firm with
a buxom woman's going to be firm with everything else."

Firm? When it came to women, more like scared to
death! Now that he thought back, no one had ever called
him firm before. Robert and his father called him weak and
vacillating. Perhaps he had been, until the day he watched
the fire curl the edges of his manuscript.

"I should drive those mules to the waterfront before they
get their second wind," Godfroy mused. "Rachel's trunk's
still at the landing, and I'd best pick up provisions."

"There's provisions enough for dinner. Rachel's making rabbit stew."

Godfroy licked his lips, and Will found himself repeating the gesture. Breakfast on the steamboat had been hours ago and meager, and his stomach twisted in sudden anticipation of a decent meal. "I suppose, if we each hang on to a bridle, we could head the mules to the cabin," he said.

The mules resisted, determined to regain the freedom they had lost two hours before. One finally yielded, protesting loudly. Luckily he was the larger of the two, and he dragged his obstinate companion along.

"Thank you for giving us shelter," Godfroy said. "Rachel was raised in a fine house. Not that she can't cook and sew and keep a garden. Her aunt taught her, for her mother died when she was a baby."

*And she did not know you were her father until this winter,* Will thought, giving Godfroy a sidelong glance. He could ask, flat out. But mysteries had a way of clearing themselves. No need to push the man into revelations that might be painful to admit to a stranger.

"In California I'll make my fortune and Rachel will be a belle, with her pick of men."

"You'll let her pick her own husband?"

"I'll make suggestions, but Rachel gets huffy about parents choosing husbands. Her mother married the man her family picked. He lacked male power, which was why she came to me." Part of the mystery cleared already! Rachel's mother had been the wife of another man when Godfroy got her with child. "And this past winter," Godfroy continued, "the father of one of her friends—he shut the girl away till she agreed to marry a fat Yankee."

"Poor girl!" Will recalled his youngest sister, shedding bitter tears on the morn of her wedding day, and his seven-year-old lack of understanding.

"It all ended well," Godfroy said. "The Yankee proved a scoundrel, and the girl married the man she wanted, Matt Hull. You'll meet them when the wagons arrive."

"Who will you recommend to Rachel? What should she look for in a husband?" He hurried the question because they had turned off the road, onto the track leading to the cabin.

"You want to be considered?" Godfroy asked with a twitch of a smile.

"She's beautiful," Will replied, evasive, unwilling to be drawn into a courtship until he weighed the implications.

"On the steamboat men clustered about her, city fellows traveling on business, plantation owners with a hundred slaves, every sort in the world. I told her, make sure a man's firm and determined." He winked, ascribing these attributes to Will. "That he sticks with one thing long enough to be good at it. If a man shifts from farming one year to storekeeping the next, you're sure to find hungry babies in his cabin. Worldly goods don't bring happiness, that I know, but without a sufficiency of worldly goods, a woman faces hunger and cold. So I tell Rachel, find a man who has money enough to make you comfortable." He turned away from the cabin, toward a grove of trees where they could tie the mules.

"But that's my own selfishness," he said after a quick glance at the cabin. "Rachel's my only child, and my blood passes on only if she has children. I want my grandbabies cared for. These mules might behave better next time if I rewarded them with a bit of grain. Got any corn or barley?"

"Not a thing but cornmeal and flour. The hunting's so good around St. Joe, I haven't bought a horse."

"We'll have grain tomorrow," Godfroy said. "There's five dozen oxen on their way from Indiana, depending on me to have fodder waiting. I'll start looking this after-noon.''

They trudged to the cabin, with several wary, backward glances at the restless mules. Godfroy, Will decided, was a man he could work with. A practical man, who faced reality. Someday he might tell Godfroy why he wanted to go west with the emigrants.

His tin plates lay on the table, with spoons and knives in proper position beside them. The cabin smelled of rabbit stew, a definite odor of onions grown strong in storage. And another faint odor, a feminine presence he could not iden-tify. Perfume? He sniffed discreetly. Not perfume.

She placed the pot in the center of the table. ''I couldn't find a serving basin, so we must—''

''I don't own one. The pot's fine.''

She took her seat at the table, which struck Will as odd, since flapjacks puffed and bubbled on the griddle and would need turning in less than a minute. He reached for the ladle sticking out of the stew pot, noticed Rachel fold her hands just in time to snatch his hand away.

''Lord, we thank you for this food. Thank you for the success of our journey, and bless all at this table, especially those who provided.''

''And those who prepared,'' he added, remembering the servants' gracious acknowledgment of the cook. He joined her in the ''Amen.'' She smiled and nodded her thanks.

''Help yourself,'' she said, rising, returning to the flap-jacks. Will shoved the ladle in Godfroy's direction. He stared at Rachel, then about the cabin. No possession of hers in sight, except the cloak hanging near the door. Yet the cabin was different, as if everything in it had shifted slightly. But nothing looked out of place.

Cooking and cleaning were women's jobs, and he had assumed Rachel would take over the moment she walked

through the door. Only men without women willingly hung
a pot on the hook or lifted a broom. She bent over the low
grid, lifting the brown flapjacks from the griddle. Not a
very big woman. Yet her feminine spirit filled every crevice. She arranged the flapjacks on a wooden tray. Pretty.
Neat. Homelike. When he made flapjacks, he put them directly on a tin plate, or sometimes right into his mouth.

"I couldn't find your pitcher," she said, placing a tin
cup on the table beside the flapjacks. She had warmed the
molasses so it poured in a thin stream.

He had not foreseen this complication. A woman took
over, spiritually as well as physically. Of course, the house
was a woman's natural sphere, and in his own home his
mother had reigned supreme, when she bothered to be
there. But he had not expected, in an hour or two...

He took a large bite of flapjack, started chewing, stopped.
Sugar. She put sugar in her flapjacks. That strange feminine
odor—browning sugar—came from the griddle. The smell
grew stronger with the flapjack in his mouth, and the taste
overpowered the flavor of the stew. After dinner he would
tell her he did not like sugar in the flapjacks. If he wanted
something sweet he would ask for cake. Although, with a
second bite, knowing what to expect, it did not taste half
bad. If a woman brought this much change so instantly, he
would think very carefully about taking a wife. Why de-
clare his independence from his family, only to be ruled by
a wife?

She spooned more batter onto the griddle, and the odor
embraced him. Her voluminous skirt and layers of petticoats did not completely disguise the flare of her hips. He
closed his eyes against her, but could not shut off the sweet
fragrance flowing like warm molasses. Rachel, her skirt and
petticoats rising to the height of the Blackfoot woman's
dress, exposing ankles, the swelling of her calf. He opened

his eyes. Why should he think of Rachel in that sensual way? She did nothing to seduce him, not like Mrs. Brown, with her ridiculous display of bosom. Rachel was an innocent. Alone with him, she had been afraid. Perhaps even an innocent woman could be a temptress, to a man ready to be seduced. And lately, like early this morning on the steamer... She invaded his cabin, his secure retreat.

"Do you know a farmer with hay or grain to sell?" Godfroy asked, his voice far off. Will delayed his answer with a spoonful of stew, which wiped out the flavor of flapjacks.

"About a mile east, a man named Perry has haystacks behind his barn," he said after a long swallow. Rachel leaned over the table with the tray piled high, the aroma bathing his nostrils. He thought he had left the pesky spider on the boat, but its thread wound about his throat and emphasized his pulse. The silken thread came from her! She stood so close he might reach across the table and grasp her waist. Her bodice outlined her bosom. The high collar circled a slender throat, and somehow the modesty was ten times more exciting than bulging white breasts.

"Would you like to walk to this farm with me, Rachel?" Godfroy asked. "Perhaps there's a woman you could visit."

"No, I have the washing up to do. And we must not eat all Mr. Hunter's food. I'll go to town and find a store."

"Don't go alone," Godfroy said. The last bite of flapjack stuck in Will's throat. Godfroy would ask him to escort Rachel to St. Joe! They'd be together, without a chaperon to interfere if his self-control failed.

"I'll drive in and pick up your trunk as soon as we're done with dinner," Godfroy said. "While the mules are too tired to fight. I'll buy what we need." Will swallowed and sighed. With relief, he thought. The disappointment caught him by surprise. He had to get out of here.

"I'll find us better meat than a rabbit." He shoved with all his strength to push the bench away from the table, forgetting that he shared it with Godfroy, and nearly spilled the older man on the floor. He grabbed his rifle. "Don't wait supper," he called over his shoulder as he plunged the length of the passageway, into the dooryard.

*Lust!* Not like the girl on the Clarion River, when he had thought it daring to hold her hand. Nothing like this had happened to him, at least not wide awake. His heart pounded as if he had already made the climb to the crest of the hill. He tightened his grip on his rifle, for his hands and fingers weakened as strength concentrated in his loins.

He forced his legs to stretch out, conquer the slope of the hill. Forget her. Godfroy had put it plainly. His son-in-law must be a man well fixed in life. Perhaps Godfroy was right. Only a settled man deserved a wife and family. Clerks at the office had joked about the women of the waterfront, women who took money to ease the swollen organ, the fiery loins. Will had never before felt the need...a sinful thing to consider.

He found a concealing thicket overlooking a deer trail that led to the river, eased in carefully so he did not tear his trousers on the thorns. Before he sat down he slid his diary and a pencil from his pocket, preparing for an extended wait. Nothing to be expected until near sundown.

He had never written of sexual feelings before, and the vulgar words, set down in black and white, were grossly obscene. None of this could go in his book, naturally, but writing it down would help bring order to his personal chaos. The deer walked by his hiding place before he found euphemisms to replace the filthy slang of a boy's world, the only words that came to mind. The need to concentrate, to focus on the game, overruled his obsession with his heat.

Will gutted the deer on the hillside, staggered under its deadweight and had to rest on the rise above the cabin. The mules stood picketed in the small clearing, nuzzling at the dried grass of last year. Not much for them to eat, until Godfroy hauled in hay. Through an opening in the trees he spied Godfroy trudging along the road, heading for the cabin. His shoulders were bent as if he carried a weight greater than the deer.

"Perry refused to sell his hay," Will said aloud.

Godfroy was a hunter of wilder game than hay and grain. Wandering from farm to farm gave him no satisfaction, Will thought. Just as entering figures in ledgers had hobbled him. He and Godfroy had a great deal in common.

Smoke rose from the chimney in languid curves, reminding him of the nymph who had taken possession of his cabin. The sugar smell reached him even at this distance, and faint stirrings of longing wrapped about him like a spider's silk.

Rachel poked her finger through the hole in the sack of barley, eyed the trail of grain leading down the hall and outside. A rat or mouse had discovered the bags. She struggled with the heavy sack, rolling it onto its side so the hole was on top. At least no more grain would spill, and every ounce was vital, since her father had not found a single farmer willing to sell hay. From her sewing kit she selected her largest needle and strongest thread. When Will or her father came home, she would suggest that the sacks be moved inside, perhaps into Will's cabin.

No, better if she found room in her cabin. She and her father gave Will enough worry. In the past days she had decided that he regretted offering them his home. His un-

happiness showed in wary eyes, in his cold attitude to her.
He spoke only when necessary, absented himself every day
and found excuses to leave after supper. She went out of
her way to be kind to him, cooked the best meals she knew
how over an open fire. Yesterday her father had brought a
reflector oven from town, and she had actually baked a
cake. Will had not noticed. He had gobbled his supper in
a minute or two, then fled to the hillside with his rifle.

"Hello. You must be Godfroy's daughter. He said you
could sew." The woman blocked the sunshine lighting Rachel's work. "I'm Hester Perry."

Rachel scrambled to her feet, leaving needle and thread
in the last stitch and her scissors in the dirt. "Please come
in. I'll make us a cup of tea." Rachel did not understand
the disagreement between Mr. Perry and her father, except
that Mr. Perry refused to sell even one of his stacks of hay.
She would be very nice to Mrs. Perry. Sometimes women
could come to terms more easily than men.

"No time for tea," said Mrs. Perry, shaking her head.
"Your pa wants to buy two of our haystacks."

"Yes. He's quite anxious, for we have friends—"

She waved Rachel to silence. "I know. He told us about
the California emigrants. It's got nothing to do with your
pa and what he is. But he doesn't understand Mr. Perry,
who's loath to let go anything he owns. Now, I don't be-
grudge Mr. Perry his pride in plentiful stacks of hay, but I
need a woman who can sew. My daughter's getting married."

A wedding wardrobe. "I can do plain sewing, and set in
sleeves, and I helped my friend make flounces—"

"Alice can manage her clothes, but she hasn't finished
her wedding quilt. Mr. Godfroy said you knew quilting."

"I've pieced three quilts of my own, and my friends and
I quilted eight," she said. "Together," she added, so Mrs.

Perry would understand that she had not done one by herself.

"That's what your father said. You come to my house every day, finish that quilt, and I'll give *you* the hay. My husband'll never notice it's gone until he starts mowing this summer. Maybe not even then."

Rachel clutched her hands under her apron to restrain herself. She must not be childish and throw her arms about Mrs. Perry. If she quilted every hour...if Mrs. Perry would accept a rather simple design...she could finish in less than three weeks. Rachel squatted at the barley sack to take the last knotting stitch and clip the thread. She must remember to carry along her small scissors, check that she had her tiniest needles...how relieved her father would be... thimble, her small pincushion.

No, she could not leave the cabin just this minute. She had spitted a venison roast over the fire and it must be turned often. Biscuits still to be mixed, rolled out and cut, to go in the reflector oven.

"But I can't spend my days at your house!" Rachel said. "Who'll fix dinner and supper for Father and Wi—Mr. Hunter? That's my first responsibility, you see, for we've taken over Mr. Hunter's cabin, and I owe it to him, to fix him decent meals, that is." Mrs. Perry frowned and her eyes tightened, saying this was the last chance to get hay. "I could bring the quilt here, and the frame—"

"There's room in this cabin for a quilting frame?" Mrs. Perry asked doubtfully.

"Do come in. Let me make us a cup of tea. What pattern is the patchwork?"

"A Star of Bethlehem, but Alice calls it Lone Star, because her sweetheart's from Texas." Mrs. Perry blocked the door, surveying the room. "If we shove everything over, I suppose there'd be room, but you have no proper floor.''

"The quilt won't be on the floor."

"But you'll drop the thread, or your needle, and carry dirt to the quilt."

"Mr. Hunter has skins and furs. If I spread them under the frame…''

Mrs. Perry scuffed her toe on the floor and sniffed. "Let me see your work. I don't buy pigs in pokes."

"I didn't bring my quilts on the steamboat, for they'd be in the way. But I have my embroidery."

"Pretty useless, embroidery, for a girl of your type," Mrs. Perry said airily. "Well, let's see it."

Rachel opened her trunk, wondering what type of girl Mrs. Perry thought she was. She unfolded the white paper from around her threads and ribbons, the strip of fine linen that would one day be pillow covers for her best bed. Mrs. Perry merely glanced at the top of the decorative work. She turned the fabric over and studied the back.

"Very good." She pointed to Rachel's trunk. "Take that tray out." Rachel thought it a very curious order, but lifted the shallow tray from the top of the trunk, exposing her clothing arranged in careful piles.

"Neat enough. I'm always suspicious about trusting a breed. You look and talk proper, and you keep the cabin clean—'' she scuffed at the floor again ''—but the tendency to savagery and slovenliness always lurks in the blood.'' Rachel's breath stuck in her lungs.

Slovenly? Savagery? Mrs. Perry accused her father, herself…*that* kind of girl! Rachel sprang to her feet, lifted an arm to put emphasis behind the words ordering Mrs. Perry out of her house. Just beyond the open door lay the sack of grain on its side. Only grain. No hay. And the hungry oxen already on the road. She lowered her arm.

"My father is the grandson of François Godfroy," she said, trying to balance the fine line between pride and humility. "A chief of the Miamis, and Chief Godfroy's father was French, descended from the king of Jerusalem."

"No need to get huffy," Mrs. Perry said. "I wouldn't have guessed if I'd seen you alone, but your pa's a dead giveaway. Has that Injun slyness about him. You'd be better off away from him. Find a nice family to take you in and you could pass for white."

"I did that, for years." Unhappily. "I'm bound for California with my father."

Mrs. Perry shrugged. "Won't be remarked upon there, I suppose, for they're mostly half-breeds themselves, I dare say. I'll have my son Lem..." She looked at the floor, twisting her mouth in thought. "Mr. Perry'll bring down the frame and quilt when he gets in from the field. No sense exposing Lem to the temptation of you, I guess. He'd be panting about your doorstep every day after his work's done. I'll send the thread along, but no pins and needles. Those you must find yourself. Give a hired woman pins and needles, and you never see the half again, if that!"

"The hay? When can my father start hauling the hay—"

"When I see progress on the quilt, and my bones feel sure you'll finish what you start."

A spatter of rain on the roof threatened another shower, then faded to a faint patter. Perhaps the storm was over. Rachel leaned far over the quilting frame, her eyes on the faint chalk line marking the pattern. She followed it with small stitches, the fingers of her left hand tracing the same path on the underside to catch the point of the needle. The clouds let through only a gray light, but she dared not stop quilting. A week gone already. The faint plop of a drop of water reminded her the kettle beneath the leak must be dumped. If it ran over, the floor would turn to mud.

The raucous protest of a mule heralded the arrival of another load of hay. Her father would smile and chatter at supper, happy that the haystack beside the cabin grew daily. This morning she had heard him whistling while he hitched the mules. Adequate reward for her hours of work.

A murmur of male voices. Will must be helping fork the hay from the wagon. They would come in wet and hungry, ready for supper. She left her needle at the edge of the quilt, stoked the fire and put the remains of the carrot pie on the hearth to warm. A poor excuse for a pie, but she had found nothing else to use except dried apples. With bread and cold venison it would make a supper.

Quilting left precious little time for cooking. Only when it got too dark to see the chalk did she stop. Then she spent hours peeling, mixing, boiling and roasting—meat, potatoes and bread, a pudding that kept her standing over the fire, stirring every instant until it thickened. Food of a sort to warm up for fast dinners and suppers. Tonight she would boil the last piece of venison with an onion and the rest of the carrots. Tomorrow at dinner she would dress it up with a quick batch of dumplings spooned over the top.

To her satisfaction she heard the snap of coats being shaken. Twice her father and Will had come in covered with grass seed and straw, forcing her first housewifely order. "Brush yourselves off before coming into the house." To her amazement they had accepted the command like sheepish boys, and since then cleaned themselves very carefully. She turned and smiled when the door opened. Will held out a large fish, his finger hooked through the gill.

"No hunting today, but I had some success in the river."

Rachel nodded and gulped down her dismay. If she objected, Will would resent her presence even more. But a fish to cook! On top of everything else! A greasy, smelly skillet to scrub!

"You keep us well supplied," she said. She broadened her smile, hoping he read sincere gratitude, not anguish. It would be nice if he smiled back, but his face remained stiff. He stood, his back to her, and held his hands over the fire. Her father squatted close to the flames, pulling off wet gloves, and she noticed he had to stop for a moment because his whole body shuddered.

She shoved the cold roast on the shelf and dared a groan of exasperation while her back was turned. The fish was far too large to fit in the skillet. And she had used all the lard making the pie crust, which meant frying salt pork to get drippings to cook the fish. She lifted the skillet with her left hand, dropped it noisily on the grid because the handle pressed on her sore fingers. Will moved away. She glimpsed him from the corner of her eye, staring at the quilt in his level, sullen fashion. *I suppose now he'll start pointing out what I've done wrong.*

Will's anger, her weary arms and nearly raw fingers, the unwanted fish! She blinked back tears and screwed up her face. *You asked for adventure. It comes with hard work.*

"Is all the hay moved?" she asked when she could say the words cheerfully. Will did not respond, and her father seemed absorbed in getting warm.

*Will goes out all day, hunting or fishing.* Another way of saying he plays, she sneered to herself. It rankled that she quilted all day, purchasing the hay, and then got no help at all with the cleaning or the food. Her anger and self-pity nearly boiled over, despite her resolve.

Her father cleared his throat. "The first stack's done." He coughed, a hacking cough. "Almost came to blows with Perry when he found us there. Poor man, with a wife who makes bargains and doesn't tell him. Tomorrow we'll finish, if the weather clears." He must be chilled to the bone.

"I've one more row of quilting before the frame must be turned around so I can reach the other side."

"Mrs. Perry asked how you were coming," her father said.

Mrs. Perry did not seem to understand how long quilting took. And Alice had insisted on sprays of feathers in the border. Thank heavens for the rain! It kept Mrs. Perry from stopping by every day to lecture on diligence.

She chopped the salt pork at the table, and Will returned to the fire. Water dripped from the fringes of the men's hunting shirts, the drops rolling to the lowest places in the rough stone. A good thing she had rubbed the hearth with lamp oil on the first wet day. She knelt to dump the salt pork in the skillet, felt dampness beneath her knees, penetrating her skirt and petticoats.

"I'm in your way," Will said, and turned abruptly. She heard the latch lift, the door of the cabin open and slam shut.

# Chapter Four

"Father." He huddled near the fire, nodded to show he was listening. "I think we should find a place in town to stay. Will is so aloof, and I know he resents—"

"Hard to find a place big enough for the quilting frame."

"I'll be done with the quilt in another week if I work every daylight hour," she said.

"I'm gi…giving Will a job. Hu…hunter for the party." He rubbed his forehead, shook his head as if to clear raindrops from his eyes.

"You're shivering, Father. Put on dry clothes." She busied herself at the table, slitting the fish down the middle of one side, lifting out the spine and ribs, cutting it into chunks to fit in the skillet. He stripped before the fire, warmed himself, clad in nothing but a breechcloth. By the time she had rolled the fish in cornmeal he squatted before the fire in a wool shirt and trousers.

"Will doesn't mind you having the cabin. He's pleased to make you comfortable." This statement amazed her so much, she nearly dropped a piece of fish into the fire.

"But he hardly speaks to me! He's cold and indifferent, and doesn't eat enough to keep a bird alive, grabs a bite and runs off, although I cook the very best I know how."

"He's not indifferent. He's at the age when a man thinks of women, and he finds it hard to be near you. You haven't noticed? He spoke to me."

"Spoke to you?" They had talked about the cravings of masculine flesh? Mentioned her...as a female? Her skin crawled, as if a slimy animal had touched her.

"Will thought I might notice. He promised he'll do nothing improper. With you, I mean."

"With one of the women in town?" she asked faintly. Mrs. Brown. Would she allow a man in her bed, and let him do whatever it was that men did to a woman after they married?

"That's none of our concern. Young men sow wild oats."

Wild Will Hunter. She imagined him with Louisa Brown, but the vision progressed only to a kiss, for Rachel was quite unclear as to what came next.

"Will's a man grown, a fine man, who avoids a respectable woman who rouses his passion. That's proper. I expected you to praise him, not complain."

"Yes, Father." She slid the fish into the skillet, piece by piece, jerking her hand away to avoid the spitting fat.

"Pay no special heed. Give Will food and let him be."

"Yes." Of course she would, now that she knew! She turned the fish, spattering fat into the fire. She would not smile at him, or look at him more than necessary. The fish curled, brown around the edges where the hot grease bubbled. Men must boil in turmoil much like this, burning the women they drew to their bed. Had it been that way between her parents, this strange father and the mother she never knew? Him, seething, churning with need? Her charred by his heat as they came together. Was that grand passion?

She could hardly breathe, remembering her proud announcement to the sewing circle that she would marry only in the grip of grand passion. How silly! She had confused passion and love. Passion was not grand, not loving, but fiery. Its flame rose from sordid lust, not pure sentiment.

The door opened, admitting Will and a gust of damp wind. He had changed his clothes. The thought of him being naked at the same moment she thought of passion...she averted her face so he would not see her flush.

"Supper will be ready directly."

He examined the quilt again, tracing the unfinished line of quilting with a finger she hoped was clean. She put the last of the fish in the skillet and managed to turn in his direction, wash the mess off the table and put out tin plates and cups without catching his eye.

"Hunter's star," he said, tracing the myriad diamonds that formed the central design. Did he expect an answer? He had not asked a direct question, so she ignored him. She set out the bread and the crock of butter. She sliced a bit of cheese very thin, and arranged it on top of the warm pie. Keeping her eyes off him was a strain. She had not been aware how often she looked at Will. Had she, with some innocent gesture, suggested that she would welcome his attention? Mrs. Brown's revealing dress and coy manner were open flirting, but perhaps there were subtler gestures in the game of sex. Gestures she did not understand. Her sense of guilt disappeared in a flare of anger. Will had no right to fault her, when he did not tell her what she did wrong!

They ate in silence, Rachel only nibbling at her food. Her stomach rebelled at the taste and smell of the fish. And she must scour the unpleasant skillet, and go to the work of shaving soap in hot water to wash the stench from the plates and forks. Her father shoved his plate away, half full.

"By Jove, I can't seem to get warm." He pulled himself

to his feet, grabbed at the table, slid down as if to reseat himself, but missed the bench and landed on the floor.

Rachel cried out in alarm, but by the time she rounded the table, Will had him in his arms, lifting him to the bench. Will laid a hand on her father's forehead.

"You're burning with fever. Godfroy, why didn't you say you were sick? I'd have finished the last load of hay."

"I'm not sick, I'm cold." He shivered violently.

"You're feverish. You've got the chills of a fever."

"I don't have the ague. I don't get fevers." He shook his head, but his brow furrowed and his eyes questioned her.

"Help me put him to bed," Rachel said. She pulled back the blankets on her bed. "Lie down, Father."

"No, just spread my bedroll in front of the fire. I need to warm up and sleep. I'll be fine in the morning."

Will steered him to the bed in the corner, none too gently. "The bed, you fool! You're sick."

"I don't think so. I'm ju…just cold. Working in the rain." Will shoved him onto the bed, Rachel knelt and pulled off his moccasins, and Will lifted his legs and stretched them upon the blanket. Her father struggled for an instant, then sank back upon the pillow with a sigh.

"I'll make you a cup of tea," she said. "With sugar."

"You think I'm sick?" he asked.

"Yes." She shoved the teakettle over the glowing coals.

"Wild critters, when they're sick, they curl up in a warm place and drink water," he mused as if speaking to himself. "Put my blankets by the fire, and a jug of water."

"You'll stay where you are," Rachel said.

"I'm not sure water's best," Will said. "Feed a cold and starve a fever, or is it starve a cold and feed a fever?"

"The first, I think," Rachel said.

"Bring me water," her father ordered. "Spouting old

wives' tales, at your age! I've seen dogs eat grass when they're sick, but I'm not sure what kind to eat.'' He managed a little laugh.

"Grass?" Will asked.

"Grass!'' Rachel exclaimed, delighted to find something logical to think about. "Granny MacIntyre, back home, she collects herbs and prescribes for sick people—''

"Granny MacIntyre's not here," her father reminded her. "Nor her collection of herbs. They're both with the wagons.''

"But I remember—for a fever tea of willow bark.''

"We don't have willow bark.''

"There's a whole riverbank of willow out there," Will said. "I'll get some.''

"You'll get soaked to the skin," Rachel objected. "Don't you hear the rain on the roof?''

"I'll put my wet clothes back on.'' He was out the door before she could protest further.

Rachel sprinkled tea leaves in the bottom of a tin cup and filled it with boiling water. She wished she had a teapot to make more than a cup at a time, for Will would come home cold. Putting on wet clothes would chill him before he stepped out the door. She quaked before the image of clammy trousers and shirts stretched over warm, strong limbs. She covered the cup while it steeped, then fished most of the leaves out with a spoon. Her father sat up when she approached, turned pale and fell backward with a groan.

"My God! I didn't know!'' he whispered.

"What?''

"What it feels like to be sick. I'm afraid I've never had proper sympathy for sick people. Once I yelled at my partner, told him to stop whining. Oh, my God! If he felt this way, no wonder he wanted to lay by a day!''

She put an arm behind his back to help him sit. He managed to wrap his fingers around the cup and take three sips of tea. He pushed it away and shook his head.

"Leave me alone," he said. "Hovering doesn't help."

She kept herself busy with the washing up, scoured the skillet with sand before she put it in the soapy water, flaked the leftover fish into a small bowl and tucked it on the back of a shelf. Where was Will? She poked the fire and brought it to a satisfying blaze, refilled the coffeepot, ready for morning. Twice she brought water to a boil for the willow bark tea, but Will did not come and the rain rattled on the roof, heavier than ever.

"I'm going out, Father. To empty the kettle under the leak." He nodded. The kettle was not full, but it gave her an excuse to stand at the end of the hallway, gazing into the curtain of water running from the roof. Nothing.

She sat beside her father, stroked his burning forehead, tense with the strain of listening. She jumped when the door opened and a disembodied hand held out a clump of dark vegetable matter.

"Here. Don't want to drip all over the floor."

She nearly laughed at Will when he rejoined them, because he looked like a long-haired dog that had fallen into the river. Her father could not hold the cup steady while she supported him. Will helped without being asked, and coaxed an entire cup of tea down her father's throat.

"I'll undress him," Will volunteered.

Rachel put a handful of bark in a basin and covered it with boiling water, gave all her attention to the fire, until she saw, from the corner of her eye, Will pull the covers tight to her father's neck. He was panting, his face gray from the effort of removing his clothes. She slumped to the floor beside the bed, stroking his forehead, reaching under the blanket to hold his hot, dry hand.

"Get on your feet for a second," Will said. She did as

he ordered. He spread a fur on the floor, and wrapped her father's buffalo robe about her.

"Thank you." Will could be thoughtful when he tried. She leaned against the bed frame. Her father tossed and moaned, waking her if she dozed. Will spread his own bed-roll near the hearth, but she did not see that he slept. Whenever she turned in that direction she found him looking at her. Occasionally he got up to tend the fire and fill the kettle, pouring cup after cup of tea, thrusting his arm behind her father's back to bring him upright, so she might spoon the liquid into his mouth.

She fell asleep near morning, but later wished she had stayed awake, for she dreamed Mrs. Perry stood in the door, demanding the quilt. And somehow all the stitches had unpicked themselves, and the entire thing was to be done over again. She woke damp with fear.

"Rachel?" Her father's whisper barely penetrated the fatigue that enveloped her. "Where's Will?" he whispered.

She closed her eyes, opened them again. The blankets near the hearth had vanished. The water bucket was gone. "He's gone for fresh water." Her father nodded slightly, swallowed with an effort, and closed his eyes. The moment the door opened he tried to sit up, thought better of it and merely lifted his hand.

"Come here," he said breathlessly. "Will, what's your real name?" Will, occupied in putting the bucket on the bench, turned his head in surprise. By the time he walked to the bed, his face was serene.

"My grandfather's name, when he came to America from Germany, was Jäger. It means hunter. I translated it."

"Why did you change it? You in trouble with the law?"

"No. I think an English name's more appropriate in

America. I'm not an escaped criminal, no lawman's looking for me and I abandoned no woman. I swear.''

"I'm dying."

Rachel cried out as she dropped to her knees. She laid one hand on his forehead, and with the other wiped sudden moisture from her own cheeks.

"I don't want...Rachel to go to her aunt and uncle. Marry her."

The ground heaved beneath her, but somehow Will stood against the quake, erect and strong. His hand cupped her chin, he lifted her head until their eyes met. Pale eyes, hardly blue in the dim light, expressionless. No, a question, a hint of concern. Marry him?

"I'll go to town and get a doctor," Will said. "A doctor knows what to do for fever."

"No, I don't need a damned doctor." From somewhere her father summoned the energy to lift his head and raise himself on his elbows. "Robbers who take money for killing me. I can die on my own. You get a preacher, bring him here, so I can see that Rachel's taken care of." He tried to lower himself to the pillow slowly, but had spent his strength and simply collapsed. His eyes rolled back in his head, his mouth opened and his chest rose and fell erratically, in a struggle to breathe. Rachel tried to speak to counter his words, but nothing came out but a sob. She laid her ear on his chest, listened to his heartbeat—steady—felt the uneven lift with each breath.

"I'll not do it unless Rachel agrees," Will said.

"Daughter?" he asked, barely audible.

"Yes. Yes. Of course!" Anything! Nothing mattered, except she must ease the twisting pain of his face, the fear in his eyes. "Yes, I'll marry anyone you say."

A rattle in his chest. A death rattle? "Hurry, Will."

Will hung over her, his hands on her shoulders, lifting her off her father. She shoved him away.

"Go. Get the preacher," she said without looking at him. The weight of his hands disappeared and the door slammed. Off on his errand, unless he was running away. Why shouldn't he leave? Take a wife on the whim of a dying man?

"Would you like for me to pray, Father, or perhaps read from the Bible?"

"Water." Scrambling to her feet, she caught her toe in the hem of her skirt. She knew without looking that she had ripped twelve inches of hem. No time to think of repairs. She dripped weak tea into his mouth, squeezing it from a rag. He swallowed tiny gulps, choked with exhaustion. She dropped the rag into the pan, knelt beside him and clasped his dry, hot hand in both of hers.

"Our Father—"

"It's up...to you, Rachel, the hay and the feed."

"Don't talk, Father." He regretted his duty, undone.

"I should not...have brought you." And he regretted placing her in this situation, the daughter he had tempted from a safe home, to the frontier without friends or family.

"I'll have everything ready when the wagons get here. I promise you," she said as brightly as possible. "And by that time you'll be well." He attempted a smile, but it distorted into a grimace.

"Will...help you...the money..." Where? She could not buy supplies without money.

"Where?"

He took two shallow breaths. "Boot."

"In your boot?" He nodded weakly.

He managed a deeper breath. "You leave me...die." He spent several seconds arranging the next words. "Get on with...quilt."

"No. I couldn't take decent stitches this morning." She laid a hand on his burning forehead. If she could cool him... She searched for a rag, but they had all been dirtied in the washing up the night before. Her father moaned. Find something! She lifted her skirt, stripped off the innermost, flannel petticoat. She dipped a long strip of the bottom ruffle in the water bucket.

"Good," he whispered as she bathed his face. Aunt Caroline, she recalled, had put cold compresses on her forehead when she had the measles. She grasped the edge of the ruffle with both hands, tore to the seam, then destroyed hundreds of carefully made stitches by ripping a yard of the fabric away. She folded the wet cloth to fit her father's forehead, making sure the dripping ends did not touch the pillow. She laid one hand on the compress to keep it in place, and rested her head on the blanket.

*Our Father, forgive him, he and mother did nothing wrong. They simply fell in love. And if he could meet her, step into heaven and find her there...*

A man cleared his throat. Will ushered in a short gentleman with a full, unkempt beard. He wore a swallowtail coat and a vest spotted with grease. In this weather, she reminded herself, few people in St. Joe could wash themselves, let alone their clothing.

"Reverend Kraft," Will said.

"This is the bride?" he asked. Rachel nodded and stood up. "Take off your apron, girl. You don't intend to get yourself dressed up for the ceremony?" She had one decent gingham dress, at the bottom of her trunk. But her father's half-closed eyes and raspy breathing decided against it. She shook her head. So different from the brocade dress Aunt Caroline had planned, the veil edged in gold.

"Wait!" She found the square piece of cloth of gold in the tray of her trunk, fabric so thin light shone through it.

She folded it diagonally, tied it about her shoulders. "It belonged to my grandmother," she explained, "and my cousins in Virginia sent it to me for my wedding dress."

"Is there a ring?" Reverend Kraft asked.

"No. There's been no time," Will explained.

"Yes!" They all turned at the single, breathy word. "Possible bag."

She let Will search through the leather satchel in which her father stowed his personal gear. After much digging he drew out a leather pouch, loosened the drawstring. A gold band fell into his palm. Her mother's? Her father had bought a ring in those weeks of waiting, while she matured in her mother's womb? Planning for a wedding that never happened, because her mother already had a husband.

"Dearly beloved," began the preacher.

*What am I doing! This is what Mother did, married a man the family wanted her to.*

She shuddered beneath the golden scarf, paying no attention to the promises she made, for the rasping breath from the corner drowned out any other sound.

"Say 'I do,' girl," Reverend Kraft prompted. She said, "I do." The ring slid coldly onto the third finger of her left hand. Will said the words, so familiar they might be an echo in her head.

"I now pronounce you man and wife. You may kiss the bride."

Will's hands clasped her shoulders, his lips dropped against hers, soft and mobile, only for an instant. But she had time to realize that this kiss—her first one—put an irrevocable end to girlhood. She was now a wife.

"You want me to fetch Dr. MacDonald?" Reverend Kraft asked. He spat tobacco juice into the fire. "This man needs a pint of blood took off, and a purge. That'd ease his breathing."

Her father rejected the suggestion with a jerk of his head, and the compress slid onto the pillow. Rachel knelt to replace the cloth. The heat of fever had dried the rag, so she wet it once more. The twisted cloth no longer covered his forehead, and the ends dripped water.

"No doctor," he whispered.

"I won't let one in the cabin," she promised.

Will knelt beside her, took the rumpled cloth from her hands and refolded it in a compact rectangle.

"You just gonna let that man die? Without a doctor?" What was Reverend Kraft hanging around for?

"He doesn't want a doctor," she said too loudly. Will jumped up and she heard the jingle of coins. He had forgotten to pay Kraft for the ceremony. The door slammed.

"Godfroy," Will said when they were alone, "would you let me bring an Indian woman? A wise woman of the Pottawatomi? The folks here call her the Gray Woman."

Her father closed his eyes and his fingers rubbed the blanket. Was it true that dying people picked at their blankets? She grabbed his hand, noticed with surprise the glint of gold on her finger. His rough fingers were limp in hers. She steeled herself to bear the moment when his hands and heart stilled. His lips worked. Finally he simply moved his head, a motion that might be an affirmative.

"I'll get Gray Woman. You hold on for two hours, Godfroy. Two hours, you hear, because she's across the river. I'll have to send the ferryman to fetch her."

Rachel stared at the ring. She did not want to be married to Will Hunter, whoever he was. She had seen dogs mating, the bitch struggling, trying to escape the grip of the male. Was that how it was with men and women? Will might feel passion for her, but her heart held nothing but fear. She left her father to dampen the compress and stumbled over the bottom of her skirt. She had been married in a dress with half the hem out.

## Chapter Five

A breeze redolent of spring hugged the ground. Leaf tips feathered the willows and a one-winged maple seed in wobbly flight glanced off Will's shoulder. Spring. Bitter, that Godfroy should die on such a day.

"Are the Pottawatomi camped on the other side?" he asked the owner of the ferry.

"Aye," said the man from the corner of his mouth, not shifting his pipe. Will slid two coins from his belt.

"Cross the river and ask for the medicine woman they call Gray Woman. Trail Godfroy's sick."

"Doc MacDonald's just up the bluff," the man said, but his eyes focused on the coins, torn between profit and a desire to loaf in the spring sunshine.

"Godfroy doesn't want a white doctor. He says they just charge to kill a man faster."

"None of my darkies speak the Pottawatomi lingo," muttered the ferryman, but he motioned to the slaves, who climbed on board to man the sweeps. He pocketed the coins before he clambered onto the flat boat.

Will watched the boat glide through the quiet water near the shore, into the buffeting current, the men straining at the huge oars. An hour at least before they returned, and only if the Pottawatomi camped near the landing. A one-horse buggy swung around the curve leading to the ferry landing. The driver cursed when he caught sight of the boat, now a speck on the brown water a quarter mile away.

The ferry was handy for the people of St. Joe, Will thought, but a bother for emigrants, who must drive their animals through the middle of town. He would suggest to Godfroy that his party use Parrott's Ferry, north of town.

Will noted that the water was higher than a week ago. The snowfields of the high plains and the Rockies melted under the spring sun. This summer he would see the remnants of drifts clinging to the northern faces of the peaks. See buffalo and antelope over the sights of his rifle.

*I'll go all the way to California!* Rachel Godfroy was now Mrs. Hunter, and Will Hunter could not go home. Not in October. Never. He must write a letter to Pittsburgh. Now, while he had an hour to wait. Robidoux could offer more privacy than the cabin. He trudged cross-lots, following the creek that led to Robidoux's brick hostel. If he and Rachel should ever return to St. Joe, they would find lodgings here. Perhaps a few years from now he and Robert would meet in St. Joe, no longer elder brother who ruled and younger brother who rebelled. He imagined the stiff opening words of the conversation. He would buy Robert a drink, wait until they both relaxed before mentioning his book, his publisher, his plans for a second journey. More exotic this time, India or China. Robert's eyebrows would curl into the arrogant question marks that marked his disdain.

*My wife, Rachel.* Would Robert be so stuffy he would refuse to acknowledge her presence? They might have a child by that time. Will skidded to a stop on the brick-paved yard. A child! A handicap. A burden to a man who meant to shoot tigers in India. Perhaps he could leave Rachel and the child behind with Godfroy. Godfroy's dying.

The act of engendering a child, no longer a dream, a wife of flesh and blood lying in his bed. He made a wry face. Considering Rachel's innocence, and his own, their wedding night would be more fumbles than fulfillment. Rachel, torn by losing her father…his own heart pinched at Godfroy's death, and he had known the man only two weeks. Out of consideration for Rachel he'd postpone the ritual until her mourning eased. Perhaps until they were out on the plains, when the painful memories of St. Joe lay behind her. Wait until he screwed up his courage. He smiled at his unconscious pun, and the smile calmed his nerves.

"Hello, Mr. Hunter." Mrs. Brown leaned from the open window of one of the apartments. He took off his hat and inclined his head slightly, enough to be considered a bow. "I hope you're well."

"Fine. But Mr. Godfroy has a fever, and there's little hope for his recovery." Her white bosom pushed high over the black lace of her bodice.

"And you've come to town for the doctor," she said.

"He refuses a doctor. I've sent for the Pottawatomi healer, Gray Woman."

"An Indian!" she cried. She shook her head, clasped her hands beneath her resplendent breasts. Then her mouth formed a rosy O, expressing sudden understanding. "But then, Godfroy's a half-breed, isn't he, so it makes sense."

Will could not follow Mrs. Brown's logic. Perhaps the display of white flesh distracted his mind. He lifted his eyes resolutely to her face, but peripheral vision, and the rise and fall of the bulging mass with every breath…

*Mrs. Brown's an experienced woman, trying very hard to attract a man. Perhaps, for money, she'd teach me how to make love to Rachel.* To have sex outside of marriage was a sin; to have a wife and lie with another woman was adultery, a greater sin. But shouldn't he have experience before he climbed in beside Rachel?

"I have...business with Robidoux," he stammered.

"But I'm pleased to see you're well." She smiled broadly.

He begged a pen and paper from Robidoux, who cleared a space at his own table. The letter turned out far shorter than Will had envisioned. Sentences announcing one's marriage should extend for many pages. But here lay the blunt truth, covering only half a sheet. He had married a young woman named Rachel Godfroy, whose father was half French, half Miami Indian. She was beautiful, with large brown eyes and dark brown hair. She had been raised in a cultured household by her aunt, a white woman. She would not disgrace the family in any way. Will folded the paper twice, on the outside carefully wrote his brother's name, and addressed it in care of the company in Pittsburgh, Pennsylvania. He finished with a dab of wax.

From the post office he glimpsed the ferry on its return trip, dashed toward the landing, wanting to shout at every passerby that he had a wife. In three or four weeks his family would hold a secret meeting. They would agonize over the black sheep son, but in the end would write him off as ruined goods. Robert would withdraw the invitation to return. That letter would never reach him, of course, for by the time it arrived in St. Joe, he would be on his way to California. With Rachel, who was beautiful, adventurous and set his blood thumping every time he looked at her.

A huge woolen shawl of black and green enveloped the woman's head and shoulders, and a red flannel skirt peeped from beneath it. A civilized Indian from the mission, Rachel thought, until Gray Woman dropped the shawl. The red flannel petticoat was belted high under her arms. Rachel pretended the fire needed her attention, so she did not stare. From the corner of her eye she watched Gray Woman fold the shawl neatly and tuck it in the notch between fireplace and wall. A great mane of gray hair hung loose, far down her back.

Gray Woman joined Rachel at the fire, extended bent and gnarled fingers toward the warmth. She loosened the narrow belt holding up the petticoat and it slithered into a heap at her feet. Beneath it she wore a plain doeskin dress that reached just below the knee, the leather dark with age. Leggings and low moccasins encased her feet and legs.

Gray Woman poked through the pots and pans on the hearth. Rachel wondered if she should offer her something to eat. Gray Woman picked up the pot of willow bark, sniffed it, made a universal face of disgust and disapproval. She turned away without a word, stood over the bed, said something Rachel did not understand. Her father shook his head, so the words had meaning for him. Gray Woman threw back the buffalo robe, exposing his nearly naked body.

"No!" Rachel cried. "He must be kept warm."

Gray Woman did not so much as turn her head. Rachel stepped toward the bed, but Will grabbed her hand and forced her to stand beside him. Gray Woman leaned close to her father, ran her nose the length of his body, sniffing, from his mouth and ears to his feet. She poked and prodded, turned him over and thumped on his back.

"I'm sure she knows what she's doing," Will whispered.

Gray Woman straightened her father's limbs, covered him neatly and crossed his hands on his chest outside the blankets, a posture horrifyingly reminiscent of death. She knelt by the bedside, muttering.

"Is she praying?" Rachel whispered. Will shrugged his shoulders. Gray Woman wrapped her crooked fingers around her father's wrists, felt his arms, his fingers, then spread a hand across his face. She sat back on her heels, apparently done with her examination.

"Goddamn not die, maybe," she said.

Rachel, tense with anxiety born of ignorance, shook her arm to dislodge Will's hand. "Get her out of this house!" she said. "Tell her to leave. Find the doctor."

"She's trying to help," Will said, his fingers tightening. He spoke in a tone he would use to calm a fractious baby. He would not treat her like a child, no matter that she had married him! She began peeling his fingers from her sleeve, one by one.

"Didn't you hear! She wants him dead! She cursed because he might live." Will grabbed her with both hands, so she had no choice but to face him.

"Goddamn?" he said in a low voice. "That's no curse. Not to the Indians. They call white men goddamns."

"God—" She stopped, unable utter the second syllable.

"I'm afraid those are the words they hear most often on the streets of St. Joe."

"So she—"

"She meant there's a chance."

Rachel sagged against Will, not realizing she used him for support until she felt the texture of his shirt on her cheek. She would move away, to show she did not depend upon him, but later. After she had recovered from the shock. When her breath came at an even pace.

Gray Woman picked up the remains of the willow bark drying on the hearth. She shook it in Will's face, made a hacking motion with her hand.

"She wants me to get more, I suppose. We've been doing the right thing after all!'' He grabbed the hatchet from the kindling box and headed out the door.

Gray Woman dumped all the bark in the pot and moved it to the hottest part of the fire. She mimed dipping a finger into a basin, licking it, smiling. Something good to eat? Rachel opened the sugar tin, but the woman shook her head. Molasses? Rachel showed her the jug and Gray Woman grabbed it. She poured a large dollop into the pot of willow bark, and with gestures indicated that Rachel should stir the mixture. She donned her shawl and left the cabin. Rachel bent over the fire with a long spoon, but stared after Gray Woman. Was that the extent of her doctoring? She wouldn't know when the willow bark was ready. Rachel dropped the spoon and started toward the door, but her feet tangled in Gray Woman's red flannel petticoat. Certainly Gray Woman would not leave that behind. Rachel tossed the petticoat on the table and went back to stirring the pot. When Gray Woman returned she carried five rocks the size of large apples and laid them close to the fire.

"Of course! I should have remembered. Aunt Caroline put a warm brick at my feet when I had the measles."

Gray Woman smiled, the smile of one who does not understand, but wishes to please. She pulled a squirrel pelt from beneath the quilt, threw the fur over her shoulder while she studied the patchwork, tracing the lines of quilting. Rachel held her breath. She had seen the woman's nails, rimmed with dirt.

"You?" Gray Woman asked, pointing at the quilt, then at Rachel.

"Yes, I'm doing the quilting."

Gray Woman, in the manner of the elderly, leaned back to see better. She traced one of the corner stars, smiled, lifted her hands, moved her fingers to mimic twinkling.

"Yes," Rachel said, nodding, smiling in relief that they had achieved even this minimal communication. "Stars."

Gray Woman took two steps, laid her hand on Rachel's chest. "Star," she said.

"Star," a husky, breathless voice repeated. Her father watched them from the bed. He had named her Star at her birth, a name unknown to her until he came last autumn to claim her. Rachel dropped the spoon and bent over the bed.

"How did she know? Did you tell her you called me Star?"

He shook his head, spoke, but in so wispy a voice that Rachel had to lean close to hear. "Wise woman." He closed his eyes and took a ragged breath. "She knows…without seeing…we don't understand."

"You shouldn't talk, Father," Rachel begged, "but I'm glad you told me. I'll trust her, and do what she asks."

Gray Woman took a smaller pot from its hook and made gestures of pouring water. She untied a leather bag from her belt, sorted through packets of thin leather and paper, selected one and poured part of the contents into the small pan. She pointed at the fire, so Rachel placed the new medication on the grid.

"Is this enough?" Will asked from the door. He had carried along a gunnysack, and he dumped it, at least half full of bark, near the hearth.

"Blanket," Gray Woman said. Will ran into the other cabin and returned with one of his own. Gray Woman pointed to the shelf, outlined with graceful gestures a canopy hanging over the bed. Will nodded, grabbed the hatchet once more. Rachel watched from the window as he cut two saplings and trimmed the branches. Bedposts, to support the blanket on the outer side of the bed. The shelf, she decided, could hold the upper end.

Standing on the bed frame, Rachel laid the blanket across

the shelf. She wished Will had left his books. She could use them as weights. But several days ago he had taken them to his own room. The blanket smelled of Will, the aroma that surrounded her when she stood beside him. She finally secured the blanket with two earthenware basins.

Will thrust the poles through the door, maneuvering them carefully to avoid the quilt. Rachel helped him lash the supports to the bedstead. Twice their hands touched, twice she pulled away. Gray Woman signed for more furs, and Will crawled beneath the quilt, holding each out for her approval. She wrapped the warm rocks in the furs and tucked them at her patient's feet and along his legs.

"Too hot," he gasped.

"The heat brings perspiration," explained Will. "To end the fever."

"Let me die...in peace."

"You can't die," Will snapped. "Too many people depend on you. Gray Woman thinks you'll recover."

Gray Woman's cackling laugh echoed off the stones of the fireplace. Rachel backed away from the sound, as far as the quilting frame permitted.

"All men...die, die!" Gray Woman said. She pointed to Will's rifle above the door, strutted about as if holding a weapon, the posture and walk of a proud young man. Gray Woman bent her body nearly double, pressed her hands against her stomach, groaning. "Die, die," she whimpered.

Rachel stifled her laugher out of respect for her father. His condition was much too serious for merriment. But Gray Woman's pantomime reminded her of her uncle when he had eaten too many oysters at the tavern, and was certain he had been poisoned. Aunt Caroline had gone into hysterics and was useless, so it was Rachel who had sat by his bed as he dictated his will. She had written the document in her straggling, misspelled, ten-year-old scrawl, he had signed it, and then he had promptly sat up and eaten a bowl of mush.

Gray Woman balanced the small pot on the end of the bed. She said a few words, accompanied by gestures, and Will lowered the blanket to enclose the bed under the curtain. She pulled the red petticoat over her feet, belted it above her breasts, wrapped the shawl around her head and shoulders, and curled up near the fire. Her fingers beat steadily on the hearthstone, accompanying singsong phrases in the same rhythms. Unintelligible, as one might imagine the incantations of a witch.

Rachel leaned to Will's shoulder. "What's she doing?"

"Praying, I suppose. After the doctor's gone, we pray, so I imagine an Indian does the same."

"But it would be...an infidel god!" Rachel protested.

"Perhaps." He shrugged.

"Does she intend to stay?"

"I think so. Perhaps she's telling us to rest while we have the chance. You should go to the other cabin, climb in bed for an hour or two."

Bed! She was Will's wife. She must go to his bed in the other cabin, and he would come and claim her. When their fingers had touched putting up the canopy, she had sensed the power of his hands. Had he touched her accidentally, or had he been hinting at what would come?

"No, I've got to quilt. Mrs. Perry expects me to be done in a few days. I can't waste such a bright day."

She stretched her hands and flexed her fingers. She threaded three needles and plunged them into the edge of the quilt to save her from the interruption of rethreading. If only she and Gray Woman could talk to each other, she would ask her to explain exactly what Will would do in bed. Girls in Pikeston went to Granny MacIntyre. Rachel regretted she had not, but last winter the necessity had seemed distant. She might ask Mrs. Brown, but she could not leave her father to go to St. Joe. Perhaps Mrs. Perry. But that vulgar woman would laugh at her ignorance, and gossip around town. All St. Joe would know Will had married a silly ninny.

Who else? Her father, if he were strong enough to speak, and if she knew *him* better. But he had been her father for such a short time.

That left Will. When the time came, she must confess her ignorance.

Someone tunneled into a hillside, right against the wall of the cabin. The wrong place to dig a grave, Rachel thought, and she tried to explain, but the man paid no heed. She tried to grab his muscular arm, but her fingers passed through the flesh, no more substantial than a cloud.

"Rachel," the digger said. She wavered from side to side, and his arm, now solid muscle, seized her, dragged her into the pit.... Will's arm, she realized, for the odor of him wafted between the dream and waking. Will could not be here, for he was digging her father's grave.

"Father's dead," she said.

"No, he's asleep. And so were you, right on the quilt. Gray Woman needs our help." The blanket had been raised and Gray Woman knelt by the bed with a cup. All Rachel saw of her father was the back of his head. "He wants to die. She thinks he might drink the medicine for you."

Rachel leaned against Will for a moment, her head spinning. "You were digging his grave," she said.

"Not yet. Tell me when you can stand alone." She stiffened at his words, pushed him away and walked to the bed. Gray Woman handed her the cup.

"Please, Father," she said to the tangle of dark hair.

"Remember, we're going to California together, and it won't do for the scout to ride all that way in the wagon."

He turned his head into quarter profile. Gray, wasted, angular. "No." He struggled for breath. "Will's wife."

"It makes no difference that I'm Will's wife. We'll all go to California. I won't leave you." She hoped that was true, but when she'd said "I do," she had promised also to go where her husband led, and that might not be California.

"I'm going to California," Will said, "with you." Her father shook his head. Will thrust his arm behind her father's shoulders, and lifted him. "Take your medicine, Godfroy," he said, suddenly angry. "Your daughter's fretting, and she'll be sick from the anxiety."

Rachel put the cup to her father's lips. Will's rough treatment had worked, for he took small sips of the dark liquid, thick as syrup. When he finished Will lowered him gently to the pillow and Gray Woman pulled down the curtain.

"Now you're taking a nap," Will said, grasping Rachel's hand and pulling her into the hall. A faint breeze touched her hair and caressed her face. It smelled of spring.

"Wait!" She ran to the dooryard. "It's spring!"

"Finally. I noticed when I went to the river, but forgot to tell you. Grass is sprouting."

"And leaves?"

"On the willows. The maple seeds are flying."

"Walk out with me. I want to see." In this private moment before he took her to bed, she would tell him the truth. Will offered his arm, and she tucked her hand in the crook of his elbow. The brilliance of the sun surprised her. Spring, with summer close behind. She must remember to wear a sunbonnet, or she would be burned as dark as Gray Woman. A rounded bush exploded into a yellow cloud, and as far as she could see a green haze spread beneath the trees.

"Will," she said. He swung in front of her, a barrier. "Why did you marry me this morning? To be kind to Father?"

"No. It's been in my mind for a long time."

"That's impossible! We haven't known each other for a long time. Only two weeks!"

"On the steamboat, when we saw the hunter's star, I nearly asked you at that moment."

"Why?"

He looked at the ground and scuffed with the toe of his boot. He smiled when he looked at her, but his eyes still reflected the old wariness. "Can't a fellow decide on a whim? Isn't that how Cupid operates? One twang of his bow, and the arrow's in your heart."

She looked over his shoulder. "Cupid didn't hit me, Will. I don't love you."

"You married me because your father asked you to?"

"Yes. If I could help him live, or make his...death easier, I would say 'I do' to the devil."

"I hope you don't think of me as the devil."

Did she? A man who used a false name, who had been running away since he was little more than a baby?

"I don't know who you are, Will. Hunter isn't your real name, is it?"

"I told Godfroy the truth. My grandfather came from Germany, his name was Jäger, and in German the word means hunter. I've never been married. I've committed no crime, beyond wanting to live a free life. If it will ease your mind, I'll take an oath on the Bible."

On that pristine Bible, with the joke on the flyleaf.

"You've run away?"

"I guess you could say that."

"Why? Thousands of men come to the frontier every year and they don't run off and change their names."

The toe of his boot moved nervously. She looked down, found him tamping a clump of snow-flattened grass deep into the soft spring soil.

"My father lays down rules for the family. I don't like them. I hated his restrictions when I was a child, and, try as he might, he could not break me. I suppose I love my family as well as the next man, but when I look to the horizon, I want to walk on the other side."

"But this morning you took a wife! The horizon never ends, Will! Even if you've gone all the way around the world, there's always a new hill, north or south, east or west." His arm slipped around her waist.

"Now I have a companion. You told me you tried to run away, but stopped at the river. In a few weeks we cross the Missouri, and all rivers between here and the Pacific."

"But Will, a woman..." How to explain the difficulty of following a will-o'-the-wisp with a baby in tow? She thought of Mrs. Brown in the cramped cabin of the steamboat. How much worse in a wagon on the prairie? The baby brought her full circle, to her necessary confession.

"Will, when you take me to bed, what will you do? I never had a mother to explain, and Aunt Caroline wouldn't speak of it." The breeze cooled her cheeks. His arm across her shoulders drew her closer to him and his lips gently touched her eyes, closed the lids.

"Sweet wife, I'm as uncertain as you. Do you suppose I experiment with public women in the river towns?" he asked.

"I didn't suppose anything." His mention of fallen women shocked her to anger. "Will, I don't know what you'll do."

"Rachel, we won't share a bed until we've stood like

this many days. After we've learned to kiss. Do you like my arm around your shoulders or your waist, higher or lower?''

Did she like it? She leaned back and found the sense of protection very pleasant. Her uncle's arm had felt this way the first time he had lifted her onto a horse.

"I like it around my waist."

"I kissed you this morning. Did you like that?"

Had she liked the kiss? "I don't remember. I was thinking about Father being sick to death, not you. Oh, Will! That's a terrible thing for a wife to say."

"I forgive you." He chuckled in his throat, and she felt the sound through his arm. A little like the vibration of holding Merri when she cried. But more pleasant.

"Let's do it again," he said. "'I pronounce you man and wife. You may kiss the bride.'"

His lips skirted hers, then settled into place. Silken, and the special smell of him clogged her nostrils.

"Put your arms around me," he murmured against her cheek. She lifted her arms, spread her hands lightly against the back of his blanket coat. She followed the raised threads of the embroidery. One hand touched the hilt of the knife thrust in his belt, and the fringe had much the same pressure as his kiss. His hand tangled in her hair, drawing her face into the notch of his neck. His coat smelled of wood smoke, not of horses. That was the difference!

"Don't be afraid of me, Rachel. After we get to know each other, when we're comfortable together, then we'll talk about bed." She had not meant to sigh with relief, particularly such an explosive sigh. He would laugh again, but this time laugh *at* her. Instead he kissed her forehead.

"Will you go to bed now? Get some sleep?" She nodded, moving her face against the flannel of his shirt, where his coat hung open.

"We'll do well together," he said as they walked back to the cabins. "I understand Cupid's very active in the spring, and I already like you."

"I like you," she said, but the words had no sincerity. "I must check on Father before I rest." He let her go, and that pleased her.

Gray Woman snored softly, curled up near the hearth. Rachel lifted the corner of the blanket. Her father's eyes turned toward the light. A familiar sweet scent mixed with the disagreeable odor of sickness. Cherry! Gray Woman had used cherry bark and dried cherries to clear his lungs. Exactly what Granny MacIntyre would prescribe!

"I should have remembered. Granny MacIntyre used cherry bark to help us through a cold. From now on I'll pay more attention to what she does, so I'm not helpless when my family gets sick." The pot on the end of the bed had grown cold. "I'll put this on the fire to heat."

Will poked at the fire, shoved two small logs beneath the grid and moved the coffeepot. As she leaned beside him, his hand brushed her hip. Her petticoats buffered the touch, but she remembered the texture of his hands from their embrace. Rough and strong, she thought. She had enjoyed walking through the spring wood, her hand on his arm. Someday his hand would touch her naked. Would she enjoy that? She would try to be a good wife to him. If he could wait, she would have time to talk to Mrs. Brown.

"Nothing will change while you sleep an hour or two," Will assured her. "When the pot boils, I'll put it under the curtain."

"If there's a change, for better or worse, wake me," she ordered. He nodded, his eyes alight with a glow of friendly concern, and she thought being married to Will might not be too bad, after all.

# *Chapter Six*

Rachel moved from day to night, only intermittently aware of the angle of the light. Steam from the boiling pots fogged the window and dampened everything she touched. The idle needles accused her of sloth, but the endless nursing took every waking moment. Increasingly Gray Woman did nothing but sit near the fire, chanting in a monotone. Rachel lined the hearth with rocks, alternated the pans of cherry water from fire to bed. Will helped her coax tea down her father's throat, and kept the pot full of water, willow bark and molasses, until the very air she breathed cloyed with its sweetness.

Periodically her stomach growled, and she assembled a disorganized meal, handing Will and Gray Woman plates without even setting the table. It seemed unfair that the demands of everyday life should occupy her attention, when her father's life hung in the balance.

Night again. A shadowy movement. She had not undressed for days, but had simply wrapped herself in a clammy blanket and stretched out on a fur beneath the quilt. Gray Woman moved silently between the hearth and the bed. Will knelt by the bed, his hands clasped, and Rachel's heart skipped a beat. Will dropped his head on pleading hands.

*Father's dead. Will's afraid to tell me.*

She knelt beside Will, brushing her hand across his shoulders to let him know she had joined his prayers. Her husband. She had sworn to obey him, this man her father had given her. His last act on earth. She would do her best.

"The fever," Will whispered. "It's broken." With his guidance she touched her father's forehead. Damp, cool.

"Rachel! Rachel!" Will shook her, her head wobbled, out of control. Something wet on her forehead. She pushed it away and clung to Will, buried her face against his shirt.

"Heavens, daughter!" said a weak voice. "You faint when you hear I'm getting better. What might you do when I die?"

She groped toward his voice. Will held her in a tight embrace, sitting on his knees. "You're not dying, Father." A branch on the fire dropped, and shadows leaped around the room. She took it as appropriate reflection of joy. "Gray Woman said, from the beginning, that you wouldn't die."

"Not now, perhaps, but someday. Anything that lives dies. With luck, we'll see California and I'll make a fortune for you before the devil's claws find my heart."

"You'll live to see your grandchildren grown," she said forcefully.

"You two married?"

"Yes. Day before yesterday, or the day before that, I've lost track," Will said.

The shadows of his sunken eyes, the haggard cheeks showed the skull beneath. He closed his eyes, dropped his head to the pillow, panting from exertion. "I thought... such a memory," he said weakly. "But I've had strange dreams."

\* \* \*

A bee hummed around Rachel's head, landed on the quilt and investigated the bright colors. Finding nothing of interest, it flew off, buzzing through the open door. She hated to see it go, for it brought springtime to her ears, even though the quilt occupied her hands and eyes.

She shifted her stool to a more comfortable position. She would stop at the corner, because the needle had pricked her left fingers almost raw. She would give them a rest while she mixed biscuits for supper. A figure in the door, but she did not look up, knowing it was Will, returning from the first trip he had made into the hills for days.

"You're not done!" Mrs. Perry cried.

Rachel dropped her needle, lifted a finger to her lips and pointed at her father, snoring quietly in the corner. She shoved Mrs. Perry into the hall before she spoke. "My father's been very sick," she said quietly.

"Sick?" Mrs. Perry hissed. "Cholera?"

"No. A fever. It broke early this morning."

Mrs. Perry tiptoed across the floor to the quilting frame, as if the light scuff of her shoes on the packed earth would wake the sleeper. She studied the quilt. Rachel started the long curve of the next feather pattern, even though she had reached the end of the chalk marks and had to sew free-hand. Mrs. Perry must see her hard at work.

"Nice," Mrs. Perry said, "but I'd expected to carry it home. Alice must fold it in the bottom of her trunk. Nothing in the way of clothes can be packed till it's in."

"She's leaving Missouri?" Rachel asked with surprise.

"Of course. To Texas with her husband. He says Missouri's too sickly a place to settle."

"I'll work every minute there's light enough."

Mrs. Perry stared at the bed. "You called out Doc Mac-Donald, I suppose, and he's sure it's not cholera?"

"No, Father wouldn't let me bring a doctor."

"Be on his feet by now if he had," Mrs. Perry said scornfully. "Savage superstitions, I suppose. A surfeit of blood brings on a fever. The doc would bleed him. Too much wild meat, living with this hunter fellow."

Rachel ignored Mrs. Perry's opinion. She had reached the end of the curve and must begin the scallops that created the feather illusion. Those she had to sketch with chalk.

"Let me know when it's done. You want this door closed? Open, it lets bugs in."

"Leave it open. There's more light."

Rachel looked at her father to be sure he still slept. Sleep was the best medicine now. His chest rose and fell evenly. She arranged her chalk, scissors, thread and needles on the bit of shingle that served as a tray for her sewing things, massaged goose grease into her fingertips, and placed the reflector oven before the embers. The earthenware bowls nested inside one another. She lifted the top one out so precisely she made not the slightest clink.

The flour made soft plops as she spooned it from the sack, and rose in a white fog to the rim of the bowl. She would mix in the lard with her hands, to avoid the scrape of spoon against the pottery. As she dipped her fingertips into the flour, she noticed the ring. It seemed a shame to get it greasy and dirty. She slid it off, laid it behind the jar of matches on the mantel. When she turned back to the table she found her father looking at her, his dark eyes big in his wasted face.

"I'm sorry, I woke you."

"You didn't wake me. Mrs. Perry did, but I pretended to be asleep. She'd hover and get that quack out here." He lifted himself on his elbows. "I could use a drink."

He reached for the cup, but his hands shook too much to hold it by himself.

"I'm weak as a newborn rabbit," he said, falling back on the pillow. "You'll have to help me." She assisted him with a hand behind his back, put the cup to his lips.

"Gray Woman showed me how to make a broth from venison. Perhaps you should have some."

He nodded. She gave him one spoonful of the barely warm soup, watched him swallow.

"Good," he said. "Did you pay the Indian woman?"

"Yes."

"You got the money from my boot?"

"She didn't want money. I gave her something of mine."

"What? A petticoat or a—"

"My cloth of gold. It was in the tray, on top when I opened the trunk. You wouldn't believe, her eyes actually bugged out of her head." *And her hand closed around the cloth before I could snatch it away or utter one syllable.*

"No! That was your grandmother's!"

"What will I ever do with cloth of gold?" She laughed so he knew the gift was negligible, although deep down she ached for the loss. She had nearly jerked it out of Gray Woman's hand, until she recalled that cloth of gold had no value measured against her father's health. Her prayers and Gray Woman's strange appeals had been answered. And she was Will Hunter's wife, who would live on a series of frontiers following her husband. *What do I need with cloth of gold?*

"Do you want anything else? I must mix the biscuits, and my hands will be messy."

"Nothing."

Her hands were in the flour and lard before she remembered that she could use a spoon.

Her father's eyes stayed on her. He loved her, had loved her since she had been born in Aunt Caroline's upstairs bedroom. Summer after summer he had ridden the hundreds of miles from the Rockies to Indiana, just to catch a glimpse of her. He kept his fatherhood and his love a secret, a sacrifice, so she might be raised by her mother's sister, in a proper house provided by her uncle, the only lawyer in Pikeston, Indiana. Cloth of gold was trash beside love of that kind.

"Hello. Anybody home?"

"Low, low," piped a baby voice, and Mary Merrill toddled in the open door, her white lace bonnet askew, her hands and face covered with dust. In one hand she clasped a long rock, narrow enough to fit in her tiny fist.

"I'm sorry, my hands are all messy, so I can't welcome you properly, or put on the kettle for a moment. But do come in, and find a—"

"No trouble," Mrs. Brown said, pulling a bench from the table.

"Low," Merri said. She dropped the rock, and now her small fingers grasped the edge of the bed. She stared at the face on the pillow. "Low."

"Why, Mr. Godfroy!" Mrs. Brown cried, jumping up. "What are you doing in bed in the middle of the day?"

"Would you please hold Merri?" Rachel displayed her sticky hands. "He's been ill and she'll bother him." Mrs. Brown snatched Merri into her arms, and stepped to the door.

"Cholera?" she asked, terror distorting her features.

"Not at all. A fever. It broke early this morning. He's on the mend."

Mrs. Brown's face relaxed. She took the seat farthest from the bed, the stool beside the quilt. Merri twisted in her arms and leaned toward the colorful patchwork.

"I wondered why you hadn't visited me in town, but now I understand. Mr. Hunter's not at home?"

"He went into the hills," Rachel said, returning to her biscuits. "To hunt."

"I guess that's his job. Well, I'll ask the two of you." She shrugged, and the slow drawl of her voice said she did not expect them to be of any help. "Do you know about the Englishmen who came on the steamboat two days ago?"

"Englishmen? No," Rachel said. Her father shook his head.

"Well, these Englishmen are in St. Joe, two of them. I should say four, but they don't count their servants as people. The way they treat them, Lordy! Worse than any Missourian treats his slaves. And them being white!"

"If that's so, they won't stay servants long," Rachel said. "They'll ask for their wages and set themselves up in business here in St. Joe."

"May be," Mrs. Brown drawled, and she tilted her head, the gesture saying she had not considered that possibility. "Anyway, one Englishman's called 'mister,' like an American, but with two names. Mr. Brant-Reid. The other one, everybody says 'sir' when they talk about him, or to him. And the servants bow. Sir Anders this and Sir Anders that, and he struts around like a turkey cock."

"I remember Sir *William* in the West some years back," her father said, his weak voice barely carrying from the corner.

"Don't tire yourself, Father," Rachel said.

"Don't hover, daughter. I'm mending. This Sir William, back in Scotland he was a lord, richer than a St. Louis storekeeper."

"What does it mean? Sir?" Mrs. Brown asked.

"I don't know. That he's the man in charge, I expect."

Merri had twisted and climbed so now she dangled over her mother's shoulder. "Sir Anders says he has a castle back in England," she said. She pulled Merri onto her lap, then set the wriggling child on her feet. "Of course, I don't believe that. It's 1848, for heaven's sake! There's no more knights and dragons! And those are just fairy tales."

Rachel wiped her hands on a rag and washed them in the basin next to the water bucket. "You've talked to him?" she asked, looking over her shoulder. "Come here, Merri, and I'll wash your face and hands."

"No," Merri said. She ran to the bed and leaned against the frame, daring the women to make her obey.

"Sir Anders and Mr. Brant-Reid have taken rooms at Robidoux's. And doesn't old Robidoux scrape and bow, and if they mention wanting something, he orders it set out. Anything they want. Hooper comes—"

"Hooper?"

"Sir Anders's servant. He comes with a packet and says, 'Sir Anders drinks only this tea that's brought from his land in Ind-ja,' so the pot gets emptied before the rest of us have drunk our fill, and the kettle put on, the water freshened just like Hooper says."

"Sir William wasn't like that," her father said. "He made do as the trappers did."

"Low," Merri said, staring at the face on the pillow. She unwrapped her hand from the bed frame and tentatively stroked his cheek. Mrs. Brown made no move, and Rachel hesitated to discipline a child not her own. She found a crust of bread on the shelf and held it out to Merri.

"Than oo," Merri said. She sat down on the floor, studied the crust, then stuck the end in her mouth. Rachel stared in astonishment.

"Thank you?" she gasped.

"Doesn't that child beat all?" Mrs. Brown said proudly. "Not a year old until tomorrow! But what I need to know, are all English sirs rich? After all, he could be lying about the castle. Did this Sir William have a castle?"

"I don't know."

Rachel turned away so Mrs. Brown did not see her gaping mouth. She swallowed her laughter. Did Mrs. Brown seriously believe that an Englishman would marry her and take her home to his castle?

"Why is he here? In St. Joe? It seems a strange place for an Englishman," Rachel remarked, cutting the biscuits into squares because she did not have a biscuit cutter.

"They intend to hunt on the plains. You should see the guns they've brought, every kind you can imagine, and some with silver and gold, and the wood parts carved with hunting scenes." Rachel finally looked up, drawn by the excitement in Mrs. Brown's voice. Mrs. Brown's eyes and curls danced, lost in admiration of the Englishmen's weaponry.

"When do you expect Mr. Hunter?" Mrs. Brown asked. "I believe—" she leaned forward as if sharing a secret "—Mr. Hunter was raised a gentleman, and he'll know something about English gentlemen."

"These Englishmen, they're looking for a guide for their hunting trip?" her father asked.

"Yes. I mentioned Mr. Hunter to Sir Anders. Sir Anders tried to hire an old mountain man, a friend of Robidoux's, but he didn't like how they spoke. It's a howl, hearing them talk, harder to understand than a New Englander. Anyway, the mountain man didn't give them the time of day, so they're still without a guide."

"Mr. Hunter's already hired," Rachel said, interrupting her father so he would not tire himself. "He's hunter for our party to California." *I hope, I hope Will meant it when he said he would go all the way to California,* she thought.

*If he turns back, I'll have to leave my friends and go with him, and live among strangers.*

"Please don't speak of this to Mr. Hunter," Mrs. Brown said, gathering her skirts around her, rising from the stool. She brushed roughly at her dress, scooped Merri into her arms. "You see, I'd like to be the one to give him the news. Good day. Better health to you, Mr. Godfroy."

Rachel politely escorted her to the yard. Mrs. Brown took two steps beyond the open hall, then turned around and beckoned for Rachel to follow her.

"Don't say a word to anyone," she said when Rachel stood beside her. "You see, Sir Anders has...made advances—" Rachel gasped, laid her fingers over her mouth "—but I've turned him away until I know for sure. I've tried asking Hooper, but he won't say more than two words and usually I can't understand those. But if I can find Sir Anders a guide...he might conclude I'm a useful sort of woman."

"Yes," Rachel said. Useful sort, but did that mean he would marry her?

"He's an ugly little man, but a woman in my position can't be picky."

"Yes."

"It's too bad Mr. Hunter's so cold. I think I could like him. He reminds me of a...friend."

Her "husband," Rachel thought. The man who had seduced her, then scuttled off before he could be convicted of fathering Merri. She recalled that her father had ordered her to be patient with this woman. She would do penance for her evil thoughts by reading First Corinthians, to remind herself of the love due a fellow Christian.

"Sir Anders is very proud," Mrs. Brown whispered. "Prouder than any man I've ever met. You'd think he stood

on a mountain, and the rest of us scuttled about like mice."
She bit her lip, and a shadow crossed her face.

"Perhaps he's only seeking a mistress," Rachel said
harshly. Mrs. Brown clasped Merri so tightly she cried.

"Women must be terribly careful," she said. "If you
hear anything about Sir Anders, you'll tell me? I mean, if
you hear he's said things like this to other women?"

"Of course. But the only woman I see is Mrs. Perry, and
I doubt she'd interest Sir Anders. She's built on the order
of a cemetery monument." Rachel laughed at her own wit,
but Mrs. Brown glowered and set off down the path.

Rachel found her father half-sitting, leaning against the
log wall. She got her Bible from her trunk. "Would you
like me to read to you, Father? I can't do any more for
supper until Will comes."

"Yes. Sit here, beside me." She moved the stool from
the quilt to his bedside, and as she opened the book, she
thought of the other Bible, now in Will's room. She had
married the man whose pen had defaced it. She found the
verse she sought.

And whether one member suffer, all the members suffer with it; or one member be honoured, all the members rejoice with it.

She must not condemn Mrs. Brown, but offer support to
her in her sufferings. All Christians suffered when one did.
She must have charity.

Charity suffereth long and is kind...thinketh no evil.

She must not even *think* that Mrs. Brown had sinned with
a man not her husband.

Charity rejoiceth in the truth.

"But what *is* the truth?" she asked, staring over her father's head at the chinked log wall.

"Don't ask me impossible questions, Rachel."

"Mrs. Brown's a city girl, I'm sure of that. She talked about the wood parts of guns, not the stocks. A city woman, looking for a husband on the edge of settlement? I bet she never had a husband!"

"Rachel!" Even weakened, his reprimand stung, but she had throttled her suspicions too long, and words poured out.

"And this Englishman! Any man can claim to be a sir, and no one here would know the difference. Will says his name is Hunter, from his grandfather's, but in his Bible he wrote William Shakespeare, a fake name if I ever heard one, so I don't know who he really is! And I'm married to *him.*"

Her father's stare was part astonishment, part anger, but the expression vanished quickly, for emotion could not compete with weakness. He took her hand.

"Shakespeare?" he whispered.

"Yes." She was shamed by her outburst. "I'm sorry Father. I should not have said—"

"Rachel, Will's a good man. I trapped in the wilds of the Rockies, and I know the signs of evil and of good. Will's a bit young, that's all. You treat him kindly, he'll do the same for you. Have charity, like the Book says. Now, read me the part about the Hebrews going out of Egypt. Many's the time, standing on the bank of a raging river, I wondered how they talked God into parting the waters."

"The troops of pharaoh breathed down their neck."

"And once the Blackfoot were so close I heard their yells," he said, "but the river kept on rolling."

\* \* \*

Will strained at the reins to keep the mules walking. He dared not take his eyes off the team to look at Rachel in the wagon behind him. She clutched the quilt, fearing that a disaster would occur in the mile between the cabin and the Perrys' farm. He regretted they were not walking, but the quilt frame had to be returned, and the last of the hay hauled to the cabin. No chance for a private conversation, for he could not even glance over his shoulder, lest the mules take it into their heads to shy at a bough or a bird swooping down to warn intruders away from its nest. From the top of the rise he glimpsed a flash of white far away, the unmistakable arcs of white wagon covers.

"Wagons coming," he sang loudly, so Rachel would hear. The wagon shifted slightly as she knelt behind him.

"Stay down," he warned. "If the mules take it into their heads to dash off, I don't want you thrown out." She crouched, her chin resting on the edge of the wagon bed.

"Where?" she asked. "I don't see anything."

"You will when we round this curve. I saw just a spot of white from the top of the hill."

One of the mules dragged its feet, protesting the indignity of harness. The second mule interpreted the uneven strain as a signal to stop. Will lashed out with the whip. It seemed an eternity before they rounded the curve, and came face-to-face with three yoke of oxen and a wagon cover so white Will knew it had been in use only a few days. He dragged at the reins, prepared for the mules to rear in fright, but they stopped immediately and acted as if they had met oxen and wagons every day of their lives.

"Whoa," yelled a man walking beside the front team.

"Whoa, whoa, whoa," the cry echoed down the line of wagons.

"Where you bound?" Will asked.

"For today, we're aiming at St. Joe."

"You're nearly there. And later?"

"Oregon," the man said proudly. "We're looking for a place to turn out our cattle. And buy hay and grain. You know of a man who could furnish that? We asked at a place half a mile back—" he jerked a thumb in the general direction of the Perrys' "—but the woman said they'd already contracted for their hay. Some of us want to buy fresh teams, too. You know of—"

"Ask in town," Will said. "How far have you come?"

"From the Mississippi. Near Hannibal."

"We're expecting a party from Indiana led by a mountain man named Jed Sampson. Have you crossed paths?"

The man shook his head, but he shoved back his hat and his eyes brightened. "Jed Sampson, you say. I've heard of him. Heading for Oregon?"

"No. California."

"Makes no matter, we could travel together for a big part of the way. We've got no guide and would like to join a party that's hired one."

"You might speak to—" Will began, but Rachel poked him in the ribs.

"Don't mention Father," she said in a low voice. "They'll interrupt his rest."

"See Sampson, or the captain of the party. Now, I'll lead these mules off the road to let you pass, but be patient. Two weeks ago they were wild as lions."

He climbed out of the wagon, was surprised that Rachel followed him. She stepped to the head of the right-hand mule. Her skirts brushed the mule's leg, and Will had a horrible vision of the animal rearing, the thrashing hooves knocking her down and trampling her.

"Rachel, get back in the wagon."

"It's better if both mules have hands on their bridle."

In the shade of her bonnet he saw confident brown eyes, like her father's. Will pointed to a rutted turnout. The wagon jolted, and the quilting frame rattled without Rachel's steadying hand. The mule he led jerked its head in alarm. Rachel talked to her mule, a singsong of nonsense words, and the animal followed her obediently.

"That's all right, boy," he imitated her. "It's just the wagon making that infernal noise, not the devil behind you."

Whips cracked and one by one the wagons rolled by. Women waved at Rachel and called out hurried questions. "Have you heard news from Oregon this spring? Is the grass on the prairie grown enough for pasture?"

Will envied women who could display their worries openly. These men showed a brave facade, but inside lay a core of fear. At night dark care settled like a suffocating cloud, and they fretted over dangers lurking beyond the horizon. The men had made the decision to go to Oregon, but women and children would suffer for their foolhardiness. A cluster of boys and girls brought up the rear, driving milk cows. One of the girls balanced a small child on her hip.

"Oregon," Rachel said in a low voice. "How many will make it to Oregon?"

"Are you afraid to set out?" he asked.

"Not for myself. I have Father to take care of me, and he's traveled the road before, and knows the dangers." Her face brightened with a new idea. "And you! I have you. But children. So much can happen to a child. Even though their mothers take special care."

"We'll take special care," he said, although he was ignorant about safeguarding children on a journey. "Godfroy and Sampson, they know what they're about. Godfroy coming ahead to arrange for feed. That was wise."

"When we left Indiana, I didn't understand why I should leave my friends and come by steamboat, but after the trouble we've had getting hay—"

"Getting oxen will be worse. The army's advertised to buy a thousand yoke at Fort Leavenworth. That'll drive the price up. I'd better go into St. Joe tomorrow and buy the mules your father needs."

"And vinegar," Rachel said. "Father told our friends not to carry the weight of pickles and vinegar from Indiana, for we'd find plenty for sale here."

"We'll ask Mrs. Perry," he said. Rachel's skirt and petticoats swung out with each step, lifting a few inches, and twice he glimpsed her ankle. A trim ankle.

"You're good with the mules," he said.

"My uncle taught me to ride when I was four years old. Living in town, we didn't keep a horse, but I rode Meggie's pony, when she'd put a saddle on it."

"Who's Meggie?"

"Margaret MacIntyre. Her folks and brother and grandmother were the first people in Pikeston to agree to the trip. She's...she's..." Will thought Rachel blushed a bit, but he could not be sure. "Meggie rides bareback, with a leg on either side of the horse, and hitches her skirts up, and some men call her a wild woman, but really, she's quite moral, and can be a lady if she has a mind to. She and her cousin Tildy, and Faith, the blacksmith's daughter, we had a sewing circle."

"When they get here, maybe they'll help you make our wedding quilt."

"I already have one. My quilts are in Faith's wagon, so I wasn't bothered with the luggage on the steamboat."

He would wait until the wedding quilt arrived, so they might make a ritual of their first night. A patch of skin on his stomach twitched and his sex stirred. He would buy a tent to carry in the wagon, so they had privacy at night.

He imagined Rachel on the overland trail, walking beside the wagon. No, his wife should not walk. He saw himself leading a horse to her. He must buy two or three horses for himself. Why not one for Rachel? He hoped the wagons hurried with the wedding quilt.

## *Chapter Seven*

$$\sim\!\!\infty\!\!\sim$$

$W$ill tied the mules to the rail fence bordering the row of
haystacks. "You grab the quilt," he said, balancing the
quilt frame on his shoulder.

Rachel smiled at him, and regretted the mules took so
much of his attention. If they had walked, he might have
put his arm about her, and kissed her. She no longer shuddered at his embraces. In fact, she anticipated them with
warm shivers.

Rachel lifted her hand, but Mrs. Perry must have heard
the thud of the quilt frame against the wall, for she opened
the door before Rachel knocked.

"Well, it's about time!" Mrs. Perry cried. She grabbed
the quilt. "You wait until Alice sees that everything's suitable. Alice!" she shouted over her shoulder.

Rachel watched through the door while Mrs. Perry and
a young woman spread the quilt on a table. Did they expect
her to stand on the doorstep and listen to their comments?
She stepped away, toward the haystack, to show her contempt. Rather than pitching hay, Will was staring at her,
the fork clutched like a spear. He thrust it into the stack
with the strength of anger, took a long step toward the

house. *Will doesn't understand about Mrs. Perry!* She ran to meet him.

"She doesn't invite you in?" he asked with tight lips.

"You don't understand. Go back to the hay."

"I understand. Mrs. Perry insults my wife—"

"If you say one word, I have no chance of buying vinegar and pickles. Get to work on the hay."

"Just stand still and let this pass? Let her keep you standing outside, like a common—" Rachel put her hand over his mouth.

"Yes. Mrs. Perry says I should leave Father. That no one guesses what I am until they see him." His lips moved against her palm, warm, sensual. A different kind of kiss. "Please, Will! I must bear it. For now."

He heaved a great sigh of resignation. "Just for now. But after this, any man or woman who dares to treat you like an outcast, I'll—"

"The hay, Will. Please."

He nodded, turned away from her, a stiffness in his back and legs she had never seen before. Mrs. Perry was leaning against the door frame; Rachel ran back.

"Alice says it'll do. She likes the feathers."

"We'll finish the hay today," Rachel said. "Father wants to know, could we buy a barrel of vinegar? Or pickles?"

Mrs. Perry twisted her mouth. "Just might," she said coyly.

"We need a whole barrel of vinegar, to divide among six or seven families. If you'll tell me how much—"

"Don't want money," Mrs. Perry said. Rachel waited, noticing the pleasure in Mrs. Perry's eyes as she maintained the suspense. "You might do some work for me," she said.

Rachel waited. Mrs. Perry waited for her to ask. *I will not humble myself any more.*

"I got another patchwork top." Rachel let out her breath in a gust of relief. Just more quilting. Not some despicable, demeaning job.

"You'll do it?" Mrs. Perry asked.

"Yes."

"I'll wrap it up. You come here after the hay's loaded and it'll be ready." Rachel nodded and headed across the barnyard to the wagon. Another quilt! At least her father was mending, so her nursing chores didn't keep her up half the night. *This one will go faster,* she assured herself.

"Is there another hay fork?" she asked Will.

"You don't have to pitch hay. That's a man's job."

"If I help, we get back to the cabin sooner. Father shouldn't be left too long alone."

"Just inside the barn door," he said.

Rachel hefted the heavy fork doubtfully. She had never pitched hay before. But she had never cooked on an open fire before, and after two and a half weeks felt like an expert. She thrust the fork into what remained of the stack, found that the dry grass came away in light tangles. Easy. Except that tossing the hay into the wagon used a set of back muscles that she had never noticed before. After a dozen heaves she stopped to rest.

Will leaned on the hay fork. "Tonight I'll clean out the wagon. Maybe Godfroy can explain how I make storage compartments out of that pile of boards. And put in the false floor."

"Pete MacIntyre, who made the wagon, thought storage compartments in the bottom would be convenient to keep things out of the way."

"Very convenient. Does Mrs. Perry have vinegar?" he asked, scooping up the very last bunches of hay.

"Brush me off," she said, backing up to him, giving him an excuse to put his arm around her. "Mrs. Perry won't sell her vinegar, but she'll trade if I quilt another top. Is there room to get the frame back in the wagon?''

"We'll put it along the sides." She brushed the fragments of hay from the front of her dress. He ran his hands across her shoulders, down her back, using more pressure than necessary. He stepped very close to her; she felt a trifle of his weight. His lips touched her ear.

"You're a wonderful wife, Rachel. Not many women would help with the hay."

"Why shouldn't I?" she snapped. "Father's alone, and without someone to watch, he'll get out of bed. A man recovering from a fever must stay very quiet."

"Not every woman would see the necessity," he murmured.

"Necessity? Necessity makes a woman's work last all day…and half the night." His hands curled over her shoulders, pushing her down, exhausting her, the weight a man imposed upon a woman. "I do everything—quilt all day, and cook dinner and supper, and now there's laundry to be done, so much, with Father being…sick." She tried to swallow the sob that bubbled upward. "And you bring home fi-fish and hand it over like to a kitchen maid, and now another quilt because—" She covered her face with her hands, appalled by what she had said, sobbing both in shame and from weariness. He would walk away, or yell at her, the way her uncle yelled at Aunt Caroline.

His fingers tightened and he turned her to face him. He touched her cheek and bits of grass scratched as he brushed them away with the tears.

"I'm sorry, Rachel. I didn't understand," he said weakly. His fingers explored her back, found the ridge of vertebrae. His hands slid to her waist, lower, until his palms rested on her hips. Her legs wavered.

"You're exhausted. You haven't slept a night straight through in ever so long."

"I slept last night." She gulped.

"On the floor," he said. "Godfroy's still in your bed, and I went to my bed last night, and let you sleep on the floor. Please forgive me. Tonight you'll sleep in my bed, and I'll sleep on the floor. It makes no difference to me. Sleeping out, in tents, even in the open."

"Father and I chased you out of your house," she protested in uneven words that ended with a hiccup. "We shoved you into a makeshift bed, and you'll give it up—"

"You're my wife. It's my responsibility. I believe Mrs. Perry has something for you."

"It's the quilt." She wiped her face with her sleeve.

"I'll tie the mules to the gateposts and fetch the quilting frame."

Rachel pulled her sunbonnet as far forward as it would go, so Mrs. Perry would not see that she had been crying.

"How long?" Mrs. Perry asked. Rachel cleared her throat.

"Two or three weeks." If only she had help. If only the Oregon-bound wagons had been her friends! "My friends from Indiana will come any day," she said. "They'll help me, when they come."

"Do they quilt as well as you do?" Mrs. Perry asked suspiciously.

"Oh, yes! And Tildy's better, she makes the tiniest stitches you ever saw." From the corner of her eye she saw Will balance the quilting frame on his shoulder.

"I don't want to see that top quilted with long toenail-catching stitches."

"Of course not!" Rachel ran to the gate, where Will stood with the mules. Toenail catchers! As if Meggie and Tildy and Faith were sloppy seamstresses. Never in her life had she been so insulted…yes, she had. Mrs. Perry found every possible way to insult her.

Will fit the poles along the sides of the wagon box. There was no room for the quilt. She had to carry it, eliminating any chance for an embrace along the road.

"Rachel, I'm sorry I've not…helped you more. I didn't know. Please, from now on, when you're tired and overworked, tell me, so it doesn't come to this."

She longed to hug him, and tell him he was the most wonderful husband in the world.

Rachel rolled out the piecrust with a bottle, for she had no rolling pin. No sense spending money on a rolling pin when they would leave in a week or two. Every ounce in the wagon was an ounce the mules must pull.

The Oregon emigrants had camped a quarter mile beyond the cabin, just off the St. Joe road. Remembering the milk cows, she had walked to their camp and bought a pint of cream. Yesterday Will had robbed a duck's nest at the river, so she had all the ingredients for a sugar cream pie. Something special for him, because he had been kind when she broke down and cried. Before he left for the river, with both fishing pole and rifle, he had whispered in her ear— she still felt the tickle of his moist breath—"If I catch a fish, I'll clean it and bone it out."

She glared at the patchwork top. She should never, never have agreed to quilt it. Mrs. Perry, so fussy about the work of others, had put the nine patches together higgledy-piggledy, so the colors formed no pattern at all. The pieces varied in size, and she had forced them together, with pleats and gathers.

"Not a pretty quilt," her father said. He sat propped against the wall, furs cushioning his back.

"And so poorly made!" she said. "It hardly seems worth the time and effort. Except for the vinegar."

Rachel fit the crust into the shallow pan, crimped it over the edges so it would not shrink. She mixed the egg, cream and sugar, and grated the last of the nutmeg. She carefully slid the pan onto the rack of the reflector oven.

"I hear horses," her father said. "Someone's coming. Maybe it's the men of the Oregon party you spoke of." She pulled her head from beneath the chimney in time to hear the shod hooves in the clearing. Had Will told the emigrants where to find Father? After she'd asked him not to?

"Hunter! Hunter, are you there? Will Hunter!" Whoever it was, she must get rid of them. Her father was in no condition to receive visitors. Will would probably stay at the river until sunset. Whatever these men wanted, they could discuss it tomorrow.

"Sounds like the Englishmen," her father said.

"Hunter!" She ran down the hall, stopped short at the sight of the two men mounted on elegant horses, with braided manes and tails. Other men, on less magnificent steeds, led two strings of mules carrying empty pack saddles.

"You Hunter's woman?" asked the closest man. He wore white buckskin leggings and hunting shirt, with long, long fringes dangling from the yoke and from the seams of sleeves and leggings. The fringes undulated with every shift of the horse. The tops of his tall moccasins were embroidered with glass beads that sparked red and blue in the sunlight.

Hunter's woman? She lowered her eyes, cautioned by the implications of the words.

"Mr. Hunter will be here directly," she said, evasive, hoping they concluded Will was just around the corner.

"Robidoux told us Hunter might be for hire. To guide us to Fort Laramie for buffalo."

Rachel found it hard not to smile at the man's speech. *Buff-ler.* The ugly, overbearing man must be Sir Anders. His hair grew low on his forehead, his narrow nose barely separated his eyes, and his cheeks sagged in blue jowls.

Sir Anders lifted a commanding hand. "Hooper, Tibbels, let the mules eat of that hay. They've been under saddle all day and should be rewarded."

"Stay away from the hay," Rachel warned. The men leading the mules looked to Sir Anders for orders.

"Do as I say!" he snapped. "Must I tell you twice?" They tugged on the ropes, kicked their horses and headed toward the haystack.

"No!" she screamed. She lifted her skirts, ran to block their way, but Sir Anders rode between her and the mules.

"We're training those mules to carry pack saddles. Now is their time to eat."

"Not of my hay," she cried, and tried to dodge around his prancing horse.

"Never fear. I'll settle with Mr. Hunter," he said.

"Money? But money's of no use, when there's no hay!"

Where was Will? Why must he be gone just now, when she needed him desperately? He would level his rifle and show these Englishmen…rifle, her father's rifle! She ran to the cabin, nearly tripping over the threshold.

"What is it, Rachel?" her father asked. He sat on the edge of the bed, his scrawny legs bare. His rifle was propped in the corner beyond the foot of the bed, where he had left it days ago. She grabbed it, checked the load, sighed with relief to find it capped.

"These Englishmen won't get my hay!"

"Rachel!" he cried behind her.

"You get back in bed," she yelled, and flew out the door.

The two lead mules munched contentedly, and their companions crowded around the stack, pulled bunches out, dragging more in the dust than they ate. She raised the rifle to her shoulder and took sight on the nearest mule.

"Get them away from that hay, or I'll shoot."

Sir Anders raised his short whip and spurred his horse. He would hit the rifle and disarm her, unless she pulled the trigger in the next two seconds. A mule jerked on a critical stem, brought down a huge clump and the top of the stack collapsed on its head. She tightened her hand.

The air roared about her ears, a great blow to her shoulder sent her tumbling backward. She crashed into the wall of the cabin, felt her rear end bump down each rounded log until she landed on the ground.

"My God! She's killed it!" A new voice. At last someone other than Sir Anders had spoken.

"You bitch!" Anders was off his horse, grasping her arm so hard the pain of it blotted out the ache of her shoulder and bottom. "You'll pay for this. I bought the best mules to be found in this primitive hole, and you've killed one."

Near the haystack a mule convulsed on the ground, while two others, roped to their companion, screamed and kicked randomly in their effort to stay on their feet.

"He wouldn't be dead if you'd kept him away from my hay," she yelled. She would fight this arrogant Englishman as long as her breath held out. She would tell Mrs. Brown what a sot he was, for he smelled of stale whiskey. She regretted the rifle, which she had dropped when she hit the wall. She struck at Sir Anders with her free hand, tried to kick, but her skirts got in the way.

"Rachel! Leave her alone. I'll pay." She twisted against the tight fingers, wondering how far she could turn before her arm broke. Her father clung to the wall of the cabin, but even with that support, he bent almost double.

"Who's she to you?" Sir Anders snarled, pulling her feet off the ground so only his grasp kept her upright.

"My daughter. I'll pay for the mule. Let her go!"

Rachel managed to get her feet beneath her, gathered her strength to spin out of his grasp, but at that moment Sir Anders grabbed both her arms and drew them behind her back. She gagged from the odor of whiskey and tobacco.

"Your daughter, old buck?"

"Yes." Her father's knees buckled and he sank nearer to the ground.

"Indian? What tribe?"

His knees touched the ground and his head dangled; he was exhausted. No way he could answer. "Miami," Rachel said as calmly as she could. "My father is the grandson of François Godfroy, a chief of the Miami in the days when they ruled Indiana. And *his* father was a Frenchman, descended from the king of Jerusalem."

Sir Anders pressed her elbows together, and Rachel heard the bones in her shoulders creak. She bit her lips so she did not cry out. "Should your antecedents impress me?" he sneered. "*I* am Sir Anders Trout. *My* father fought with the Great Duke at Waterloo, and together they defeated Napoleon. Unlike your father's pitiful ancestors, who let themselves be driven off their land."

He shoved her forward, until he could touch her father's bare thigh with the toe of his boot. "What coin do you propose to pay with, savage? Your ridiculous pride? I'm taking your daughter to St. Joseph, where I'll present her to the magistrate and charge her with slaughtering my mule."

"No." Rachel barely heard her father, for he lacked the strength to raise his head.

"Or perhaps we might avoid the law." He jammed his knee against her rear, right where she had hit the logs. "You'll serve me until you've repaid the cost of the mule."

The pain vanished from her left shoulder. Her arm was free, for a moment! Rachel swung at him, but he dodged and laughed. He dragged her toward his horse.

"Hooper," he called.

A new sensation about her numbed elbows. Rope! She fought the bond, but had no chance against two men. Sir Anders grabbed her about the waist, and she screamed as her feet left the ground. She found herself on the rump of his horse, facedown. She kicked, aiming blindly for his face. Strong fingers closed about her ankles.

"Sir Anders." A cultivated voice, quietly troubled. "They'll hear of this in town, and—"

"She's Indian. No one in St. Joe cares about a squaw."

"She's wearing a wedding ring." Who came to her defense? The second man?

"Help me," she begged. Perhaps he was a gentleman.

"A ring? Probably stolen. Chopped off some poor, tortured devil." The strong fingers transferred themselves to her hand. She curled her fingers into a fist. He would not get the ring. Not the ring her father had bought for her mother, had carried so long, unwilling to give up his dream.

"But Sir Anders, if the ring should be hers, given to her by some man who cares—"

"I care!" Like welcome thunder in her ears.

"Will!" she screamed. She managed to turn her head far enough to see him step from the undergrowth, his rifle level. Tall, handsome, grim.

"Untie her, set her on her feet, or someone dies." The rifle swung from one man to another, came to rest on Sir Anders. The hand ceased prying at her fist.

"She shot my mule."

"Untie her, set her on her feet, or I put a hole in your chest."

"Disarm him," the haughty voice commanded.

"It makes no difference to me which of you I kill."

The cord loosened and fell away. Sir Anders jerked her off the horse without care, and his hands lingered no longer than necessary about her waist. Rachel grabbed at the stirrup to keep her balance.

"Go to the cabin, Rachel," Will said. "Help your father inside." She gave him a single glance, hoping it conveyed her gratitude. With strength born of panic she grabbed her father beneath his arms and pulled him to his knees.

"Hold on to the logs," she commanded. He leaned into the wall and stayed on his feet by clinging to the crevices.

"I can't walk," he panted.

She dragged him into the hall, amazed by the power in her expanding veins. She took his weight on her shoulder, guided him to a bench. She laid a hand on his forehead. Cool. But he must be tucked into bed, given some broth, covered well lest the fever return.

"If you get sick again, I'll kill Sir Anders." If she could shoot a mule, she could shoot a man.

"Get those mules away from the haystack," Will ordered. Men hustled about. Will needed her, for he stood alone against four men.

"Stay here," she whispered to her father.

The Englishmen huddled shoulder-to-shoulder. Greenhorns, she sneered to herself. Even she knew safety lay in scattering, because Will had only one ball, only one chance to kill. She grabbed the rifle she had dropped, unloaded, but if necessary she could brain Sir Anders.

"Are you Mr. Will Hunter?" Sir Anders walked toward him, holding out his hand as if nothing untoward had happened. "We wish to hire you as our guide on a hunting expedition across the plains. We intend to go as far as Fort Laramie.''

"Go to hell!'' Will shouted. "You send your mules to eat my wife's hay, you abuse my wife when she defends her property, and just because she's part Indian, you think you can carry her off to be your temporary hussy!''

"Your wife? Your wife's hay?'' Sir Anders's voice weakened considerably and rose into a squeaky range.

"My wife owns the hay, and has every right to say who eats it and who doesn't,'' Will said. "Get out of here, and don't come back.'' He backed into the hall, his rifle still level. "Throw some ropes on that carcass and take it with you.'' The horses moved slowly out of the clearing.

"Everyone still alive?'' Will asked with a gaiety Rachel found unsuitable.

"You may think it funny for a woman to have her hands tied behind her back and be flung—''

His arms were around her, rifle still in his hand. It pressed on the spot where she had hit the wall, but she could not tell him it hurt, because his lips had found hers. The odors of him seeped into her lungs.

"I'm sorry, but I feel light-headed,'' Will said when he ended the kiss. "They looked so pitiful trailing off. Like beaten dogs. And you're safe!'' He did not let her go. The glow in his eyes took her by surprise, made her captive once more. Trapped by a newly lit fire, a flame lit by danger. Danger to her! His shout echoed in her head. *I care!*

"Put the rifles away,'' he said. She took his rifle. The stock was warm where his hand had lain. He lifted her father and carried him into the cabin, she following behind.

"What smells?'' he asked. The odor of browning flour and lard, of cooking eggs and cream.

"The pie,'' she cried. "It's ruined.'' She did not stop to hang his rifle on the pegs over the door, but dashed to the hearth. Shove the shrunken, black mass away from the heat before it ruined the pan, she thought. The custard crinkled around the edges, only slightly brown, and the crust was turning golden. The pie had barely started to cook! She sat down beside the water bucket and would have held her head in her hands, except that she stared stupidly at the rifles.

"I thought the pie would be burned to a crisp. I thought I'd been out there for hours," she said. "But it was only a few minutes."

Will hung his rifle over the door and propped her father's near the bed. All his movements seemed slow, beyond reality. His fingers closed on her shoulders, hurting the right one where the gun had kicked. She remembered the pleasure of his arm behind her back.

"Put your arm around me," she said. A fold of his heavy coat pressed on her shoulder.

"My shoulder hurts, where the gun—"

"Rachel, Rachel," he whispered. He kissed her forehead, her cheeks, nuzzled his face in her hair. One hand dropped to her hip and closed the gap between them. No question what he wanted. Men, she learned at that moment, became swollen in their lust, like animals.

"I've made a sugar cream pie," she gasped, just before his mouth caught hers. Not just his lips, but his tongue, and a burning thread coiled within her. She twisted away.

"Sugar cream pie can wait," he said in a husky voice. Her father, who must have been exhausted and should have been lying down, smiled broadly.

"The pie," she begged.

"Just one thing, Rachel." Hands encircling her hips, restraining her, keeping her close. "When you confront men with a rifle, you have only one shot. Threaten, don't fire! Letting go with that one ball disarms you."

"Thank you. I'll remember. Now let me go, because the pie!"

It was not ready, of course. She moved the oven needlessly, fluttered about the wood, shifted pots. She remembered the mating dogs on Pikeston's streets, and how Aunt Caroline had hustled her past the spectacle. That's what Will wanted of her, and she must let him, because he had thrown himself into danger to save her. He said they would wait, that she might sleep alone. But what if Sir Anders should return? Will must come to the bed, for she needed a protector.

# Chapter Eight

**W**ill noticed Rachel press her left hand against her right shoulder. The kick of Godfroy's rifle could break a collarbone. "Let me see your shoulder," he said. He touched the button on her neck band, and felt the pulse of his own blood in his fingertip.

"No." She clutched her hands at her throat, winced, spread her fingers on her shoulder.

"You're hurt. Please, I must see." She loosened the band, released the top button of the placket and folded back two inches of cloth. He worked at the next button.

"Will, don't." Another. A vein in her throat fluttered. If only her heart pounded for him. He could see a redness in the shape of the rifle's butt. Before morning it would turn the color of raw liver.

"Put a cold compress on that and go to bed."

"I have supper to fix." The leather thongs had left dirty marks on her sleeves, near the elbows. "Besides, if you make me go to that cabin alone, I'll cry and shiver under the blankets, and remember what that awful man tried to do. I'd scream at every little mouse noise."

She was right. She should stay busy. But her hands seemed to tremble as she sliced the bacon, maybe nothing more than the shadows of the setting sun. He took the knife, anyway. She poured a mug of broth for her father and stood over him, hands on her hips, until he drank it. Godfroy was definitely stronger, despite his foray to defend Rachel.

"The Oregon men want to join another party," Will said after he had finished his first helping of bacon and bread. "Eighteen wagons." Fill the silence, distract Rachel's mind. "They don't care that we're bound for California. We'll be on the same trail to beyond Fort Hall."

"We'll look at their equipment," Godfroy said. "If they're hauling broken-down wagons with poor stock, they'd be a drag. Not fair to the men from Pikeston who went to the trouble to buy new wagons."

"I'll go into town tomorrow and look for mules. People are swarming in, all wanting outfits. You won't be going to town for a day or two." More like two weeks, but Will saw no need to depress Godfroy with the truth of his recovery. The man would start the trip as an invalid in a wagon.

"No mules," Godfroy said. "I'm tired of the skittish creatures. Get me four yoke of oxen."

"No trouble," Will said, but he thought of the army's order for a thousand yoke. "I'll take care of it tomorrow. I need two or three horses, and Rachel tells me she rides. She should have a horse. I'll see what the Iowa or the Pawnee have."

"The Pawnee? Just so the original owner doesn't spot his animal under your saddle." Godfroy laughed. "The Indian ponies are best. Look for the ones with spotted rumps."

A knock rattled the door against its latch, and a tin plate clattered from Rachel's fingers. The jangled state of her nerves showed plain in her wide, anxious eyes.

"I'll get it," Will said, keeping his eyes on Rachel. She

circled the table as a shield. The man at the door wore a leather hunting shirt and, incongruously, a tall silk hat, which he removed with a slight bow.

"Pardon me for interrupting your evening." The second Englishman, the one who had tried, however ineffectually, to interfere with Anders's abduction of Rachel.

"I told you to get the hell off this place and not come back," Will said. He slammed the door.

"Please, Mr. Hunter, I've come to apologize." The planks muffled his voice, but the shame came through. "I fear you may suppose I countenance such behavior as occurred today." Will opened the door, but blocked the entrance.

"Don't apologize to me. Apologize to the lady." He pointed to Rachel, and realized too late that the gesture invited the man across the threshold. Rachel backed into the corner of the hearth. The Englishman must have seen the fear on her face, for he stopped after two steps and held his hat before his chest.

"Mrs. Hunter, I offer an abject apology, and acknowledge how ashamed I am that I did nothing to thwart the actions of...Sir Anders...who was—"

"Drunk," Rachel said. Will changed his mind. She was not terrorized, but angry. Also cautious. A fine set of characteristics in a woman setting off on an adventure.

"Not exactly drunk, no, madam, although he had indulged to the extent of a full bottle at dinner."

"Why isn't Anders here apologizing?" Will asked.

"It is correct and polite to speak of him as *Sir* Anders," the Englishman murmured. "He is a baronet."

"Title doesn't mean I should be polite to him," Will said. "He's shown himself to be a brute, not a gentleman."

"Sir Anders is, I believe, quite ashamed of himself, and would have accompanied me...except—"

"He'll spend the evening drinking with renegades and liars in some tavern," Rachel snapped.

The Englishman gulped and nodded. "I understand how you can think only ill of him."

"Unless he's tempting that lovely lady, Mrs. Brown, to submit to his...to his disgusting embrace."

The Englishman reared back, just the top half of him, as if a wasp had buzzed close to his face.

"Who might you be?" Godfroy asked. The Englishman seemed to notice, for the first time, the man propped up in bed.

"I'm dreadfully sorry I did not introduce myself. Brant-Reid, of Henley-on-Thames, your servant, sir. I hope you've suffered no ill effects, being forced from your sickbed."

"Probably did me good. A man stays abed too long, his legs weaken. How many in your party?"

"Myself and Sir Anders, our personal servants, one each, and we intend to hire muleteers and camp servants here. Perhaps six men."

"I gather you plan to go as far as Fort Laramie."

"Exactly, sir. Will you tell me whom I have the honor of addressing?"

"Trail Godfroy." Brant-Reid bowed.

"Mr. Robidoux mentioned you as a possible guide, but we learned that you and another mountain man by the name of Sampson have already committed yourselves to escorting settlers to the far West."

"You could go with us," Godfroy said. Rachel gasped so loudly Brant-Reid noticed and briefly shifted his eyes in her direction. Will stepped between them. *The fever's weakened Godfroy's mind,* he thought.

"We'll pass Fort Laramie, and you'll be sure to find

some Indian or old trapper camped there, anxious to make a few dollars as a guide,'' Godfroy said.

"You must pardon my astonishment, sir. I had hardly expected, in light of the day's events, such a generous offer. What would you charge?''

"The emigrants—each man—pay me and Sampson ten dollars for the summer. You and Anders would do the same. The servants would go free, seeing you're not traveling the full distance. But you and Anders must promise, on your honor, to stick with us every step of the way. No deciding when we reach the Platte River that you want to cut ahead.''

"I...I will, of course, consult with Sir Anders," he stammered. He stared around the cabin, focusing on each person. His eyes stayed on Rachel for a long moment, and Will was delighted that she glared back, unflinching.

"Mrs. Hunter, would our presence cause you distress?''

"My father and my husband will be along. As you learned today, my husband's very jealous, and protects me from the attentions of other men." She laughed. "You and Sir Anders received his warning today, I believe, if Sir Anders bothered to listen.''

Brant-Reid reared back again. His hands clasped and unclasped on the brim of his hat. Rachel had insulted him. He opened his mouth, closed it. He managed to wring his hands, even holding the hat.

"Mr. Godfroy, Mr. Hunter, I must in good conscience tell you...a confidence a gentleman does not normally reveal in reference to friends. But you might find Sir Anders a difficult companion on such a lengthy trip.''

"Is he such a monster?" Godfroy asked. "He'll tie up all the women and heave them over his horse?''

Brant-Reid's heavy lids drooped over his eyes. *He's not accustomed to people who meet him head-on,* Will thought.

"Sir Anders expects to be the man in charge. His father was an officer in His Majesty's—"

"He mentioned that," Rachel said dryly. "Something about Waterloo."

"And Sir Anders holds a commission as colonel in one of Her Majesty's regiments, although he does not play an active role. I understand, from what we've been told in St. Joseph, that overland parties elect their own leaders. Suppose the men of your party choose one of themselves, not Sir Anders, to be their general?"

"Captain," Godfroy said. "The leader of an overland party's called a captain."

"Why the hell should Americans elect a fat-bellied John Bull to lead them?" Will exploded.

"Sir Anders, being a baronet, holds a rank far higher than any man in St. Joseph, I believe."

Godfroy let out a subdued guffaw. "His title means nothing here. A man's judged by how he handles himself, and Anders doesn't show well. When I left Pikeston the men talked of electing Lieutenant Matt Hull, a young man just home from the war with Mexico. He fought in real battles, not sham ones. And this winter he made himself a lawyer."

"I'm afraid Sir Anders would be deeply offended, under the command of an American officer. And only a lefftenant!"

"But you'll mention my offer?" Godfroy asked.

"I will. Tomorrow I'll suggest we weigh the advantages of traveling with you. I shall send word of our decision." He bowed, and when no one spoke, he turned to leave.

"Does Sir Anders have a castle?" The words burst from Rachel like water from a flume. Brant-Reid swiveled with the precision of a band major.

"He does, Mrs. Hunter. Lindenlore Castle. Although only the new wing, built in the past century, is habitable.

The older buildings stand largely in ruins. So the Trout family, I'm afraid, must make do with constricted apartments, not more than forty or fifty rooms."

"Forty or fifty rooms!" Rachel exclaimed.

Brant-Reid's mouth twitched at the corners, and Will saw he was torn between amusement at Rachel's innocence, and the need to treat Godfroy's daughter politely. Manners won.

"For an English family of the rank and wealth of the Trouts, the accommodations are quite small. Sir Anders speaks of demolishing some of the medieval walls, and erecting a modern wing of equal size to the present house."

"I see." She turned her attention to the steaming kettle and dirty plates. Brant-Reid bowed his way out the door, repeating his apologies, and his thanks for Godfroy's offer. The moment the door closed Rachel whirled from the hearth.

"Father!" she cried. "How could you?"

Will stepped to her side in support. "I don't want those men about," he said. He could not rid himself of that first terrifying view—Rachel bound, draped over the horse, and Anders trying to wrench the ring from her finger. "What can you mean, asking them to join us? Anders attacked Rachel!"

Godfroy held up his hand. "Four Englishmen, who'll hire five or six men as camp-swampers and mule skinners? A small army. Every man who's coming from Indiana has a family to care for. We need single men to pitch in—"

"I don't think Anders will pitch in to anything but trouble," Rachel said, scowling. Rachel might back into a corner, Will thought with admiration, but she would have a knife behind her back. Perhaps he should buy her a knife as well as a horse, and a fringed sheath to carry on her belt.

Godfroy spent half a minute adjusting the buffalo robe

and squirming into a more comfortable position. "I've seen men like Anders before. He'll stand up to someone weaker than he is, but collapse like a tent with the poles drawn out when he faces a strong man. Today, for the first time since he got to this country, someone stood up to him. Beyond the Missouri he'll learn a new lesson every day, and then he'll follow along and take orders like a lapdog. This Brant-Reid's a weakling, but he's not vicious. The servants are accustomed to doing what they're told. The mule skinners, they're the ones we want. Men who know plains travel. Now, Rachel, I need another cup of that sickly broth, but this time with a bit of bread."

"After a fever you must stay on a low diet," she protested. "Until you're completely well."

"Bread and broth's as low as I want to go. My stomach could hold all a cow's ribs, plus the loin."

While Rachel satisfied Godfroy, Will scoured the plates and knives. He lifted the skillet from the hearth.

"Leave that," Rachel said at his elbow. "In the morning I'll fry the rest of the duck eggs in the bacon grease. You shouldn't be doing dishes."

"You helped with the hay. It's only fair."

He held his breath waiting for her reaction. Thanks? Or a sharp rejoinder?

"The pie! I forgot about the pie! Mr. Brant-Reid came, and I forgot the pie."

"Don't dirty another plate," he said. "I'll eat the pie with my fingers." She looked doubtful.

"And a piece of that pie," said Godfroy, his spoon scraping the bottom of his cup.

"Absolutely not!" Rachel said. Will wondered if she objected to eating pie with one's fingers, or feeding it to a man recovering from a fever. She cut a large piece, put it on a plate, pushed it and a fork across the table to him. She did not look at her father.

"Please, Rachel. My stomach's all in knots, thinking I died."

"But fresh eggs and milk are bad—"

"So's starving." She fetched another plate, cut a piece of pie, not so large as the one she had given Will.

"If you get sick tonight it's not on my conscience," she said, standing over Godfroy. "Gray Woman's right. Men get a little sick and think they're dying, and then don't pay attention to good sense when they start feeling better."

She shoved Will's back as she passed him. "Sit down. I don't like to see a man eat standing up. It can't be good for the digestion." He sank onto the bench. She leaned next him and cut a piece of pie for herself. "See how pitiful I am," she whispered. "A man pleads a little, and I give right in." Her fingers dangled over his shoulder, played a little tattoo. A bit of custard stuck in his gullet and he could not say a thing.

Will stripped off his boots and breeches in the hall, had his long hunting shirt over his head when he reconsidered. Perhaps Rachel had only meant he might ask for some special dinner dish. Maybe she meant he could ask her to help outside. He pulled the hunting shirt down, dragging on the tail so it reached well down his thighs. If he went to her partially dressed, he could excuse himself, saying he wanted to find out if her shoulder hurt too much to sleep.

He lifted the latch with no attempt at silence, stepped in. She shifted on the bed, and in the last fading light he saw her arm extended toward him. No misunderstanding. He had meant to wait longer than this, until the wagons came with the wedding quilt, but if she wanted...

"Are you hurting?" he asked.

"Just the bruise on my shoulder."

"And your arms?"

"They don't hurt at all. Anders isn't very expert at tying up women. In a minute I'd have had my hands free. How much of the fracas did you see?"

"You on the horse, and Anders trying to get your ring. Thank heavens I didn't hang out at the river till twilight." The thought of her in Anders's hands, what Anders would have done to her, weakened his knees, and he sat down on the edge of the bed. The damp from the floor chilled his legs. "But I was hungry, and thought of your good cooking."

"I'm most grateful." He wondered how long before she invited him under the covers, for goose bumps formed on his legs.

"Will."

"Yes."

"You did what a husband does, protects his wife. And I'm grateful, so I want to…show you I can be a true wife."

"You do that. You keep the cabin clean, and cook, and once these infernal quilts are done, you'll sew for us."

"That's not what I mean." Her fingers rested on his thigh for several seconds, made little walking motions until they reached his knee.

"Please, Will. You're my husband." That, he decided, was the invitation. He swung toward her so quickly he tangled with the blankets, and in the seconds wasted freeing himself, his sex rose, taut and hot. She wore a muslin nightdress. No buttons, but a ribbon at the top gathered its fullness above her breasts. He jerked at the bow, tugged at the fabric until he bared her right breast, and covered it with his hand. She inhaled sharply, and his blood rushed to his belly. He kissed her, to distract himself from the demand of his swollen organ. Worse. Much worse. Some nerve must track directly from lips to loins. He pulled at the bottom of her nightdress, succeeded in getting one side to her knees. He wedged his fingers between her legs.

"Will, please, what will you do?"

He lay still for a moment, fighting the band tightening around his chest, hampering his breathing. Show her. He dragged her hand beneath his hunting shirt, down his stomach, until it touched the insistent shaft.

"I go inside you, between your legs." She pulled her knees together and rolled slightly away from him.

"I thought it was something like that, because I've seen...will it hurt?"

"I don't know." He should have paid more attention, not stalked away when vulgar conversations turned to the mechanics of sex. The boatmen were quite specific. Embarrassingly graphic. He should have mated first with a strange woman, one he did not care for.

"Tell me, how...how you want me to..."

"Just as you are, on your back."

He touched the inside of her thigh with one hand, while the other reached high, searched for her opening. He lifted over her, guided himself to the magic spot, on the verge of losing control. Tight flesh, a resistance. She seemed very small...if only he could hold himself in check. A yielding...a closure...

"No!" She screamed, pushed at his weight and slid from under him. A violent surge, and his seed spilled uselessly, painfully, racking his whole body with the spasms. He grabbed the tail of her nightdress, wanting her beneath him, but his arms had no strength.

"It hurts, it hurts." She moaned. "You hurt me." She lay crumpled against the logs at the head of the bed, weakly tugging to pull her feet free of his chest. He grabbed her ankles, kissed her feet. At least she could not run away.

"Is that what a wife lets a man do?" she asked.

"Yes," he gasped.

"Well, I don't want to."

"But we're married. It…it will get easier."

"How do you know? You said you'd never done it."

"I haven't. But men talk." *She's small, and I get too big.* Damn his father's morality! Damn all his preaching on chastity! *If we had tried this out ahead of time, we would have known we're not suited for each other.* With a decisive jerk Rachel pulled her legs free and swung them over the edge of the bed.

"Where are you going?" he begged.

"To sleep on the floor in front of the fire." She pulled the buffalo robe from the end of the bed.

"Ouch." She moaned. The latch made a single click.

He crumpled onto the bed, sprang up when his stomach hit the stickiness of his ejaculate. He pulled off the blanket, slung it over his shoulders, collapsed on the floor. Every time he had run away, he had defied his father's rules. Why had he obeyed him in the matter of sex? Because the Bible says, quite plainly, that fornication is a sin. If he had gained experience… He was as ignorant as she. And today, in the flush of her gratitude, this might be his only chance! From now on she would shrug off the lightest touch. Too late. He should have waited for the wedding quilt.

Not too late, he thought. He had been so impatient, the moment Godfroy closed his eyes… St. Joe still rollicked in lamplight. He had time to find someone who could tell him what he had done wrong. He would wake Rachel, hold her in his arms, explain his mistake, and with a little gentle persuasion she would try again.

His coat and boots lay where he had tossed them. His rifle? Hanging over the door of the cabin. He lifted the latch carefully, opened the door a few inches, reached upward until his fingers closed about the long barrel. He could not lift it free of the pegs, standing at this awkward angle. Simply step very quietly inside.

A ghost dragging a buffalo robe careened past him, out the door, and its keening cry echoed in the hall. "No, Will! For God's sake, no!" He followed a second later, stood in the dusk, his heart pounding, his eyes trying to distinguish shadow from substance. Something white fluttered near a tree.

"Rachel?"

"Don't shoot. I'll do anything you want."

"Rachel! You can't think—"

"You've got your rifle!"

He leaned the rifle against the wall and held up his hands. "I don't have it now."

"Yes," she agreed, but without enthusiasm. He walked toward the tree, guided by the fluttering ruffle of her nightdress. He stopped five feet away.

"I'm going into town." She made no reply. "I don't like to walk that distance at night without my rifle."

"Yes."

"I'll find out what I did wrong."

"I wish Granny was here." A little sob.

"The herb woman who's coming with the wagons?"

"Yes. She's Tildy and Meggie's grandmother, and she delivers babies and treats sick people. She could explain. I should have asked her a long time ago."

"She's not here. I'll find another woman."

"Ask Gray Woman. She'll understand."

"She's on the other side of the river, and I can't speak Pottawatomi."

"I don't think you need to speak the same language to—"

"Rachel! I don't intend to get in bed with another woman. Just…ask some questions."

A long silence. The white flutter grew larger and Rachel stepped from behind the tree. Her hands clasped her shoulders to warm herself, which told Will she was not thinking straight, because the buffalo robe lay in a heap at her feet. He picked it up, and she let him wrap it about her.

"Will, back in Indiana, my friends and I talked about who our husbands might be. I told them I'd marry only in a grand passion of love. But then I married you, because Father was sick and asked me to. What happened tonight, it's my fault, because there's no grand passion."

Grand passion? He respected her, but did he feel grand passion? Lust? "You married in grand passion," he said smoothly, "in a passion of love for your father. You sacrificed yourself to give him comfort."

He thought she shook her head. Or perhaps she only shrugged at the weight of the buffalo robe. He threw his arm lightly over her shoulders, guided her to the cabin. "You did nothing wrong. You let me in your bed, trusting me. A man has a duty to his wife, to learn ahead of time what needs to be done."

This time she definitely shook her head in disagreement.

## Chapter Nine

The moon rose, casting a long, irregular shadow before him. Will jogged down Faraon Street, past the courthouse, dark except for the moonlight bathing the dome. The streets near the river pulsed with light and noise. He overheard conversations about the trail, he dodged wagons and an eager auctioneer who put a swaybacked horse through its paces.

Robidoux's place showed up as a line of glittering yellow lamps and candles burning behind the windows. Will picked out the window where he had seen Mrs. Brown. She opened the door at the first tap, a finger across her lips. She pointed to a shadowy corner, a huddle of blankets on a tiny cot. A candle lit paper and pen and ink. He had interrupted a letter.

"I need to talk to you," he said, barely moving his lips.

She wore a loose gown, mourning black except where the candlelight caught the folds it glowed silver-blue. She glanced at the baby, pushed on his chest.

"Under the tree," she said. A sycamore offered shelter to half the yard. He leaned his rifle against the tree.

"Now, why should you be visiting me?" she asked, the words oozing like cold honey. She stood close, her breasts almost touching him. The top of her head reached the middle of his chest. Looking down, he saw only her lacy nightcap.

"I need to know...you're a married...a widow, so you've had experience. With men," he said lamely.

She drew herself up so the puffy top of her cap brushed his chin. "If you suggest that I allow men in my room for carnal purposes, you may leave this instant," she said, but her low, seductive voice contradicted the words.

"Not at all." Nothing to do, he decided, but tell her the entire, embarrassing story. Listening, she did not relax, but squared her shoulders even more, and finally stepped back to look up at him.

"Mr. Hunter! You think so little of me that you come to my room, confess that you threw yourself upon a virgin and caused her pain. And, greatest insult of all, you ask *my* help to tempt her back to you, to complete her ruin!"

"I've not ruined her," he protested. "We're married."

"Married?" The single word carried her shock at the revelation. She took in a deep, noisy breath. Her expanded bosom lifted beneath his nose.

"Yes, we got married."

She let out the breath, shook her head. "I read every issue of the *Gazette,* which publishes a list of marriage licenses, and I haven't seen your name. Or Miss Godfroy's."

"License?" He swallowed to eliminate a small lump in his throat.

"Of course, license. What do you suppose that fancy courthouse is for?"

"There wasn't time. Her father asked us to marry, for he was sick to death—"

"He looked recovering when I saw him."

"He is. He ate a piece of sugar cream pie for supper.

Anyway, I brought a preacher to the cabin, and he had us repeat the words, and I gave her a ring.''

"A nice gesture. I spotted you for a gentleman right away. I do love a ceremony with a ring. But from what you say, Rachel's put out because you fumbled making love to her." The flowing honey returned.

"Yes. And I can't bear the thought of leaving her like this. Hurting. So if you'd tell me—"

"Not here. Other people like to sit under the tree in the dark." He tagged after her, entered her room, his gut churning. She shoved him down on the narrow, soft bed, then untied the bow at her breasts and pushed the dress to her waist. Everything below his belt turned liquid, except for his sex, which tightened and rose. He had to get out of here! The feather bed held him like a soft-bodied monster, surging up on one side when he pressed down on the other. She grabbed his hand and pressed it to her nipple.

"A woman likes to be gentled and embraced. You do that, and soon she'll beg you to come to her."

"I don't think Rachel will let me touch her," he said.

He tried throwing himself sideways, toward the foot of the bed, but the feather bed rose in billows between him and the door. She shoved her garment past her hips.

"Put your hand here."

"Just tell me," he said, swatting at the feather bed.

"Example is better than precept," she said coyly. A familiar saying. He stopped battling the feather bed to consider the source. His reading primer!

Her hand drew his toward her. Her sexual hair was like wire, so different from Rachel's silken welcome. "Touch her here, for that's where a woman feels pleasure." He wrenched his hand away, only to find her fingers wrapped about his arousal. My God! When had she unbuttoned his flap?

"No." He hated the smell of her, an animal odor clinging to the plump folds of stomach and thighs. But his sex lacked the sensitivity of his nose, and surged under her caress. "I'm married," he protested.

"Not really," she said. "No license, remember." She slid over his legs. "I'll be a fine wife for you."

*Cleave only unto her.* And "her" was Rachel. He had taken an oath, license or no license.

"No crying that you hurt me, no silly headaches. You can dive in anytime you have a notion, and I'll teach—"

Hitting a woman went against everything he had been taught. He pushed her hard and she fell away, almost disappearing in the feather bed. He threw himself forward, landed hard on the floor, struggled to his feet and in two seconds felt the grip of his boot soles on the bricks. He detoured two strides to the tree and grabbed his rifle. He was on the street before he wondered if he had hurt her, and nearly cried out from the shame of it. Two women in one night, weeping from what he had done. He forgot his shame on Second Street when a cold wind struck him. His trousers hung open.

He stopped, tidied himself, then plodded up the hill, past the courthouse where no record had been made of his marriage. Did it make any difference? He was near the path to the cabin when a buck, legs high in caution, stepped on the moonlit road, then bounded to the shelter of bushes on the other side. It showed just the nubbins of new antlers. From his position Will saw the deer silhouetted against the silvered road. He concentrated on slowing the pace of his heart until the rifle lay steady in his hands. This was his destiny. A lone hunter. Very obviously he was not a great lover. He squeezed the trigger on a long, slow exhalation.

The effort of half carrying, half dragging the deer uphill drained any residual excitement, and dark thoughts took control. He had no control over his concupiscence. His lust was not for Rachel alone, but came with any woman.

He hung the deer in the passage and went to bed. He would dress it at first light, and carry it to the hotel. He would find Godfroy's oxen, then cross the river and search for horses.

"Rachel." The voice plucked at her unwilling consciousness. "Rachel." Someone dragged her from the safety of sleep. "Rachel, girl, are you sick?" She opened her eyes. Her father sat on the edge of the bed. "The sun's up."

She rubbed her eyes to put off answering him. A patch of sunlight brightened the wall by the chimney. A vile taste filled her mouth. Disgust. She moved her hips, bit her lips so she did not groan. The disaster was no dream.

"I didn't sleep well," she said. She had lain awake for hours, heard Will return, making a thump outside the door. "I'm sorry, you must be starved."

"You say there's duck eggs left?" She nodded. "Well, I want two, cooked in bacon drippings—"

"That can't be good for you, Father."

"Neither was sugar cream pie, but this morning I reckon, if a grizzly crashes through the door, I could put up a small fight before he makes breakfast of the two of us."

She had to start the fire fresh, for she had neglected to bank the embers after supper. Will was probably still asleep, after coming home so late. She knocked on Will's door to summon him for breakfast, but got no answer. She saw the evidence of butchery. He had found game last night, and since nothing hung from the rafter, he must have taken the game to the hotel.

"I'm walking to town this morning, if you don't mind being alone for an hour or two," she said as she placed the eggs before her father, who insisted upon sitting at the table. He should be in bed.

*I'm a pitiful sort. If a man pleads, I give in. I might give in on eggs and sugar cream pie, but never again on marriage! No man will ever make me hurt like this again.*

The ache between her legs worsened with every step, out to the woodpile, from hearth to table.

"Do we need provisions?" he asked.

"No. I haven't repaid Mrs. Brown's calls. It's only polite, before the wagons come and we leave town."

He looked surprised. "I didn't think you liked her."

"I must tell her the truth about Sir Anders. He's made advances to her, and she should know what kind of man he is." He nodded while sopping up the last of the eggs with a bit of not-too-fresh bread. She should stay home and bake.

"Will's gone to see about the stock, I suppose," he said. Of course. She had forgotten he meant to buy horses and oxen this morning.

"I suppose," she said calmly. She thought of mounting a horse, and the pain stabbed sharp as any knife. No way could she ride the horse Will promised, hurting like this. Perhaps Will would not insist on his marital rights, knowing she couldn't walk or ride comfortably afterward.

*I wish I hadn't married him.*

Going downhill was not so bad, but walking uphill made the pain worse. Will had torn something inside her. Why did Mrs. Brown want so desperately to find a husband, when a man caused pain like this? Mrs. Brown should set herself up as a seamstress, or start a school to teach children their letters. She should be happy that Mr. Brown had died.

Rachel plastered herself against the front of a building to avoid a staggering drunk. Three men fought in the street, knocking each other down in steady rotation, until one pulled a knife. She fled into a side street, found a man painting a large display sign shaped like a tooth. A tradesman, hard at work, probably sober.

"Pardon me, sir, but I'm looking for Mr. Robidoux's apartments." He turned from his work, brush poised. She looked into moist blue eyes that topped ruddy cheeks and an untidy beard. "Why, Reverend Kraft, I hadn't expected..."

"Not Reverend Kraft now," he said proudly. "Dr. Kraft. I've decided to set up as a dentist. You got a toothache?"

"A dentist? You've giving up preaching the Gospel?"

"When I got to St. Joe I tried schoolteaching, but the brats hereabouts got hide so tough, a hickory rod don't penetrate. So I tried the preacher route, but there's no money in the Lord. Anyone can read the Bible. I figure among the emigrants passing through there's bound to be a bunch needing teeth pulled. Robidoux's, you go around that corner, then down the hill. Can't miss it, row of brick."

"Thank you," she gasped. She ran until she rounded the corner, every stretch of her legs agonizing. She rested beside an incomplete wall, masons working on a scaffold above her. Kraft not a preacher? But then, were she and Will husband and wife?

*Maybe we're not married.*

She pushed back her sunbonnet and looked up at the tracery of the scaffold, a bit like prison bars against the blue sky. Not married! She stepped into the middle of the street, and the sky shone clear, intensely blue. Not married! She took small steps, each accompanied by the beat of "Not married," until she discovered she was saying the words aloud.

"Hello. I wondered when you'd finally get to town." Mrs. Brown sat on a bench beneath a spreading tree. The new leaves cast spotty shadows on the bricks, and Merri squatted, trying to pick up a coin-sized dot of sunshine.

"Just look at her, turned a year old this week, and jogs about like a French pony." Mrs. Brown looked away from the child. "Well, I hear you and Mr. Hunter got married. Although he confessed he didn't get a license, so I can't believe it's legal."

"You've...you've talked to Mr. Hunter?" she stammered, sinking onto the bench.

"He came to see me last night." Mrs. Brown smirked.

Mrs. Brown! He'd gone to Louisa Brown for advice! Rachel sank into her sunbonnet. This woman knew what had happened in bed last night. The bonnet was not deep enough, even if she bent the sides in. She got to her feet.

"Sit down," said Mrs. Brown. "Nothing to be ashamed of. He's too prim and proper. You'll catch on if he gets a little experience, but right now he's as ignorant as a schoolboy. Are you looking for advice, too?"

Rachel recalled her mission and shook her head. "Sir Anders," she began, but her throat seemed paralyzed. She swallowed, started once more. "Sir Anders came to our cabin yesterday, and behaved abominably. And Mr. Brant-Reid visited last evening to apologize for his friend, and warned us that Sir Anders sometimes...sometimes is unpleasant. Not that Mr. Brant-Reid spoke in an ungentlemanly manner," she added hastily. "I thought you should know, since—"

"Sir Anders paid me a great compliment by dining with me yesterday. He says Merri's a wonder."

"He has a castle," Rachel said. "I asked Mr. Brant-Reid."

"He does! Truly?"

"Mr. Brant-Reid says it's quite small for the wealth and position of the Trouts, only forty or fifty rooms."

"Stars in heaven! And does Sir Anders have a wife in his castle?"

"You mean you don't know!" Rachel cried. "I supposed, since you'd flirted with him—"

"I haven't flirted," Mrs. Brown said firmly. "I've merely let myself be in places where he might appear. In fact, I expected him to walk by this morning, so I brought Merri here to run about before her nap. I wish you'd asked Mr. Brant-Reid if Sir Anders has a wife."

"It didn't occur to me." Pushing up one's bosom, so it looked like two melons poking over the top of a wagon bed—in Pikeston, Indiana, that was flirting!

"My father suggested that Sir Anders and Mr. Brant-Reid travel with us. As far as a place called Fort Laramie."

Mrs. Brown eyed her from under lowered brows. She chewed on her lower lip, a most unattractive habit. She paid no heed to Merri, who whined at her knee.

"These wagons coming from Indiana, there are single women along? Young ones?" she asked.

"My friends, Meggie MacIntyre and Faith Tole."

"They're pretty?"

"Meggie's got beautiful reddish hair. She's more cute than beautiful. But Faith, her hair's golden, and I always thought no woman in the county came close to her."

"Hmm." She lifted Merri to her lap. Did she seriously think that Meggie or Faith would look twice at ugly Sir Anders?

"I must go to my room. Merri will want to nurse before her nap. Are there any families along who would be looking for a maid to care for their children?"

"I can't think of any with children young enough to need a nurse."

"When they arrive, tell all the women with big families that I'm looking for a situation. One to carry me at least as far as Fort Laramie." She turned without a farewell and walked slowly to her apartment. Rachel stared at the closed door. Mrs. Brown still set her cap for Sir Anders.

Rachel entered a store, more out of curiosity than need. She bought a nutmeg, for she had used the last fragment in the pie. She was glad she had no parcels to carry, for the pain between her legs had worsened while she sat with Mrs. Brown. She rested three times on the long hill past the courthouse. No wonder parents taught their daughters to stay virgins until they married. If they knew what was coming, none of them would want a husband!

From the top of the hill she saw the road heading east. A movement, a white line, like a lazy, disjointed caterpillar winding over the crest of a hill. Wagons! *Don't hope*, she told herself, but she ran the quarter mile downhill to the junction, ignoring the pain, and sat on a log to wait.

Matt Hull stood in his stirrups, straining to see beyond the hill. Sampson laughed at his excitement.

"Top of the next rise you'll see St. Joe, Captain Hull."

"Thank God!" Matt said. "We need a day or two of rest." The bickering had started two days ago, the men threatening one another like rutting stags. The moment Matt identified one cause of the unrest, another set of complaints popped out, like water from a rotting India rubber bag.

Even more worrisome, many of the oxen sagged beneath their yokes. They had found only scanty pasture for the past three days, so mired was the countryside from the recent rains.

"I hope Godfroy's got fodder waiting," he said. "We haven't heard a word since Rachel wrote from St. Louis."

"I'll put my money on Godfroy to have everything in fine shape," Sampson drawled. He stopped and motioned for Matt to do the same. "Something moved in the draw ahead, once on the road, then into the bushes." He shifted the rifle that he carried across the front of his saddle. "Can't be too careful, even this close to St. Joe. Stop. Let the wagons catch up."

Matt brought his rifle into position. "Your brother-in-law's lagging behind. Should we send someone to tell him to whip his mules up?"

Sampson shook his head a trifle, without taking his eyes from the spot where he suspected an enemy hid. "I told the Reverend Ludlow—" in his mouth the title slid into ridicule "—his grain-fed mules would sag after eight, ten days, but he's an educated man and knows better than a common trapper. Even found it in the Bible, in the Book of Kings. 'Let my son ride upon my own mule,' or something like that. If Ludlow was robbed of his mules, we'd all benefit, for he'd have to buy oxen in St. Joe." Matt relaxed in his saddle and tried to follow Sampson's eyes.

"Look for the spot of green that's too dark for spring," Sampson said. Matt squinted. The yellow green of new leaves, and yes! A puff too large for leaves, too high for... He threw back his head and laughed.

"What's got into you?"

"It's a calico sunbonnet! Some woman's seen us and is hiding until she knows us for friend or foe." He spurred down the hill. "Ma'am! You needn't be frightened. There's fourteen wagons, nine women in our party."

The sunbonnet dipped, poked through the brush, followed by a flurry of skirts. "Lieutenant Hull! I didn't recognize you! You've grown a beard."

"It's Rachel!" Matt yelled over his shoulder. Rachel lifted her skirts, started running up the road, but thought better of it and stood still, waiting for him. She grasped at his hand as if she needed rescuing.

"Where's Godfroy? Does he have the hay and grain?"

She was panting so hard she could not answer, so he kept the rest of his questions to himself for the time being.

"I have a beard because they elected me captain and there's no time to shave, between making sure everyone's ready in the morning, and settling quarrels at night."

"What does...what does Tildy think of your beard?" she asked.

"Mrs. Hull likes it fine except..." He remembered just in time that Rachel was a maiden and should not know where his mouth sometimes ventured. "Except she says kissing me's like searching for a cow in a thicket."

"Tildy's well? And Meggie and Faith?"

"Everyone's fitter than when we left." Except the oxen and the mules, and he was more anxious than ever to get an answer to his original question. Was Rachel concealing bad news? "Has Godfroy bought the fodder?"

"Plenty. Two big stacks of hay, and bags and bags of corn and barley. And now that the sewing circle's together, we'll quilt the vinegar in no time at all." She threw up her hands and laughed. He shivered, for her laughter verged on hysteria.

"You'll what?" Had the long journey and weeks on the frontier affected Rachel's mind?

"Mrs. Perry won't take money, but she needed quilting done, so Will set the frame up in the cabin—"

"Who?"

"Will Hunter." She stepped back, shaded her eyes needlessly, for the deep brim of her bonnet protected her face from the sun. "Come to the cabin," she said with sudden gravity. "Father will explain everything." She lowered her hand and he saw the glitter of gold. A ring?

"The path to the cabin's at the bottom of the hill and there's plenty of grazing on the hillside beyond."

"Hop up," he said, extending his hand. She put her foot

on the toe of his boot, and he pulled her up behind him. Her hand rested on his shoulder with a feather touch, and from the corner of his eye he again saw the glint of the ring.

The lead wagon topped the hill. Today, by chance of the rotation, it was his own wagon, or rather Granny MacIntyre's wagon that she allowed him and Tildy to share. He took off his hat and waved. Two figures walking beside the oxen waved back. He smiled, imagining the conflicting theories to account for the presence of a woman on his horse.

"Go ahead, Sampson," he said. "Go roust Godfroy out of his luxury and I'll wait here to direct the wagons."

"No!" Rachel cried behind him. "Father's been sick. Dreadfully sick with a fever."

Sampson gave her one long, distressed look, turned his horse and disappeared among the trees.

"Father was terribly sick. He thought he'd die, so I married Will Hunter to ease his mind, so he'd die knowing I had someone to take care of me. But now I'm not so sure we're really married."

Something horrible had happened, and Rachel's mind wandered. "Not now, Rachel. Everyone wants to hear your news, and you want to hear how things have gone with us. We might as well tell the stories just once."

# *Chapter Ten*

Rachel searched in her trunk for a clean handkerchief, wiped the tears from her eyes and blew her nose. She balled the handkerchief in her left hand, noticed her ring, slipped it off and dropped it in the trunk.

"You shouldn't take your wedding ring off," Tildy said. "That's bad luck."

"Bad luck!" Rachel said. She stared at Tildy in disbelief, looked at Faith and Meggie on the other side of the table, appealing for their understanding. "Didn't you hear what I've told you? How can I have worse luck? You tell me. Am I married or not?" Meggie and Faith dutifully curled their brows in thought.

"Did you and Mr. Hunter sign anything?" Tildy asked. "A certificate?" Naturally Tildy would think of papers and signatures, since her husband, Matt Hull, was a lawyer.

"No. Reverend Kraft, who calls himself Dr. Kraft now, didn't write anything. Maybe he *can't* write." Rachel recalled there were no words on the sign. No, just a tooth.

"Witnesses?"

"Father. But after the fever passed, he asked if the wedding had really happened or if he had dreamed it."

Tildy shook her head. "In a court of law—"

"Tildy, don't talk law," Meggie said. "Just because Matt's a lawyer—"

"Why shouldn't she talk law?" Faith said. "She helped Matt study. If women could be lawyers, Tildy would be a fine one."

Tildy nodded her thanks to Faith. "A wedding, to be legal, must be performed before witnesses. A witness in a delirium of fever? I doubt a court—"

"It's my fault!" Rachel moaned. "I should have remembered about witnesses, that the preacher writes a certificate. I should have spotted Kraft for an impostor. I hope no one has a toothache and believes that sign!"

"It's not your fault," Meggie said. "You were flustered as a bumblebee at a pot of hot sugar syrup." Rachel hugged Meggie. Her silliness always made her feel better.

"It's not funny, Meggie," Faith said. She tapped her finger on the table thoughtfully. Through the open window Rachel heard her father talking to Mr. Sampson.

"Father shouldn't be outside, walking about, visiting with everyone. He'll tire himself," Rachel mused. Faith's finger stopped tapping.

"Mr. Hunter can get a license today. We have a real preacher along, Reverend Ludlow, Mr. Sampson's brother-in-law. He can marry you properly."

"But I don't want to be married!"

"But you made a vow and that can't be altered. Not getting a license, a fake preacher, no witnesses, those things make no difference in vows before God."

"Poppycock!" Tildy exclaimed. "She said the words because she thought her father was dying. No marriage is valid when a women is forced. Mr. Godfroy's sickness forced her. Marriage is a civil contract. No license, no certificate, no marriage. Rachel's as free as the wind."

"But she knew what she was doing—"

"I just *bet* Rachel was thinking straight!" Meggie cried. "If my pa lay at death's door—"

"Before heaven—"

"But..." Rachel said, then shut her mouth. She could mention the sex part to Tildy, but not Faith and Meggie. "What do you think of that quilt?" she asked, to change the subject. She pointed at the quilting frame. Faith sniffed. Meggie giggled. Tildy zigzagged a condemning finger across two unmatched seams.

"You've got to quilt this?" Meggie asked.

"So Mrs. Perry will give us a barrel of vinegar."

"Well, let's set to work, then," Tildy said after a moment's consideration. "We'll just stitch along the seams, although they're not very straight. Will she notice if our stitches are a bit large?"

"Yes. She's quite critical of other women's work."

"She doesn't sound like a woman I'd choose as a friend," Faith said, "but I suppose out here, you had no one else."

"She's not my friend," Rachel snapped. "In fact, she won't let me in her house because...because of Father."

"Really?" Tildy asked, her brows lifting. Rachel nodded. "Then I don't want to quilt on her ratty patchwork. We'll buy vinegar from someone else."

"You're not the first emigrants to arrive," Rachel said. "Every man who comes to town wants to buy provisions, and the demand for vinegar and pickles, why, it's beyond belief, and the prices they ask curl your hair."

"We'll get even with her," Faith said. "We'll quilt this so fancy her patchwork shows up as the trash it is. I'll do feathers all around the border and Meggie, you did swags of leaves on my autumn quilt."

"I'll put a burst of tulips in the center," Tildy said.

Rachel doubted that Mrs. Perry would notice this subtle

rebellion, but decided she had best go along with her friends and get the thing done. "I'll fill in the spaces with straight lines. They'll show her crooked seams."

They laughed as they drew the patterns upon the top. They might be in Pikeston, girls together, and Rachel sank into the fantasy. No worry of grain and hay. No marriage to Will Hunter. She had never left home. Except, standing to reach across the quilt, the pain shot so fiercely that she had to sit for a minute.

"Rachel." He returned from a crazy dream she had left in another world. "I bought you a horse. Come see!"

She stood with her needle poised, wondering why she should want a horse, a dreadful expense, and a bother to care for. Her friends looked at her expectantly, waiting for the introduction.

"This is Will. Mr. Hunter." She pointed with her needle. "Mrs. Hull, Miss Faith Tole, Miss Margaret MacIntyre."

"Meggie," said Meggie. "Go see your horse, Rachel."

The polite thing to do, since he had gone to the trouble. She walked beside him, through the jumble of wagons, feeling the eyes of the curious on her back, wondering if the married women knew from her walk what Will had done to her.

"There she is. The spotted one. Not large, but sturdily built. I'll find you a saddle tomorrow."

The horse had cost money, and the saddle would cost more. Presents could tie her more tightly than their wasted vows.

"We're not married, Will. Kraft isn't a preacher. He didn't write out a certificate. We didn't get a license."

"Who told you?" Shock on his face, panic in his voice and an unexpected uncertainty in his eyes.

"I went to see Louisa Brown," she said.

"Mrs. Brown? What did she say?" he asked with sharp insistence, words like razors. Will and Mrs. Brown?

"That you had visited her," she said, keeping her voice low. "She's curious—does Sir Anders have a wife? You could please her very much by finding out," she added.

"I don't want to please Mrs. Brown. I want to please you. My wife."

"We're not married."

"We'll go to the courthouse and get the license."

"No. You married me because father asked, when we thought he was dying. You were forced to it, and a marriage isn't valid unless both man and woman are willing."

"Rachel, we made the vows. Last night we were in bed together. You were my wife."

"It's not you, Will. I won't marry any man. I understand now why the wedding service says 'until death do you part.' Because if a woman didn't promise that, she'd run off. I'm lucky. I had a chance to find out. And I won't be any man's wife. No one will force me to it."

Will tried to take her hand, but she forestalled him by turning to the spotted horse, away from his troubled eyes and the anxious staccato movements of his hands. "The horse is beautiful. Father will pay you what it cost. What's its name?"

"No one said. Perhaps Indians don't name their horses."

Something appropriate to the country, Rachel thought. Missouri. St. Joseph. "I'll call her Josefa. Now, I must go back to the cabin, for my friends are helping me quilt Mrs. Perry's horrid patchwork. I must do my share."

The boys swept the last remnants of supper from the trestle table set up in front of the cabin. Will remembered when he had been that age and was always hungry. A patient stomach must be a sign of growing up. The men clustered around a fire built in the center of the clearing, a dozen tales told at once, impinging on one another, then separating, like a stream flowing around little islands. The women walked an eternal circuit from the cabin to their wagons, hands full of pots and pans, cups and plates. Occasionally he glimpsed Rachel, but she did not look at him. His wife was gone, absorbed into the circle of women.

Godfroy lay propped against a log, talking to Jed Sampson and Captain Hull. Will had expected the captain to be a much older man. Hull was near his own age, perhaps twenty-one or twenty-two.

Will backed into the shadows, feeling out of place. Godfroy had introduced him, but he did not know these people as they knew each other. He could talk about grain, hay and the weather, but their conversations inevitably harked back to life in Indiana. They were his companions to California, he told himself, and this was his opportunity to study them.

Standing opposite, distorted by the heat and smoke rising from the fire, three slender men with family resemblance. The MacIntyre brothers, Ira and James. Godfroy had called James "Jim Mac." And Jim Mac's grown son, Pete. From their easy confidence, the fine quality of their equipment, Will decided these men formed the core of the party. Not far from them lounged Tole, the blacksmith. No mystery about him, an open-faced, thickly muscled man, with four boys who seemed forever tailing in his footsteps. The eldest, Kit, was well on his way to being a duplicate of his father.

On the other side of the fire were two men, Burdette and Marshall. Men who had come because they trusted the judgment of the MacIntyre brothers, and Tole. Men who, without a leader, would have stayed at home. On around the fire, near Sampson stood Reverend Ludlow. A wisp of a man, who wore a black sack coat instead of a hunting shirt, had no knife or pistol in his belt. A man on a mission, devoted to carrying God to the fallen.

"Will." Godfroy twisted his head, looking for him. "Tell everyone the arrangements for crossing the river."

Will stepped beside Captain Hull. "The St. Joe ferry landing is in the middle of town. We'd have to drive the loose stock down amongst the houses and stores. But Parrott's Ferry lies four miles north of town, plenty of open fields on the river bottoms." He said the name as the locals did, French fashion—Pah-row. "He has a fenced pasture to hold the stock overnight."

"Charges extra for that, I wager," Burdette said. "And you took it on yourself to pledge us, without a vote?" Will shrank from Burdette's grating voice. He had expected the men to welcome his arrangements. He looked to Hull for an explanation, but Hull stared into the fire.

"I got sick, Burdette," Godfroy said. "Will and Rachel had to carry the load as best they could. And they did right well. Your oxen seem to enjoy Rachel's hay."

"Rachel's hay? I gave you money to buy hay."

"I didn't spend it." Godfroy pulled a leather sack from inside his shirt. "Rachel quilted for Mrs. Perry to get the hay. Like she's doing now, to earn a barrel of vinegar. So there's money to be repaid to all who put into the fund."

"Some of that money should go to Rachel," Hull said. "For her work."

"Pshaw," Burdette snorted. "What's a bit of sewing, setting around a quilt, jawing with other women—"

"There were no other women," Will said. Burdette glared at him. A man suspicious of all, automatically hostile, a type Will found difficult to tolerate. "Rachel did the quilting herself, at the same time she nursed Godfroy and the hay had to be hauled from the Perrys' farm. She helped with that, too."

The soft chatter of the women fell silent. Skirts parted and Rachel stepped toward the fire.

"If it's causing hard feelings, don't talk about money. I didn't expect to be paid."

"We're not talking about what you expect," Hull said. "We're talking about what's right. And you did the work that got us the hay. As I understand it, if you hadn't, we'd be in a hell of a fix right now."

"Well, the vinegar doesn't count, since I have help. The sewing circle's back together and quilting's fun again."

Burdette stepped toward Godfroy. "I want my share of the cash that's in that—"

"Mr. Godfroy!" The hail came from far down the path, two men on horseback vaguely outlined against the evening sky. Burdette snatched a large pistol from his belt, and his action reminded Will that his pistols were under his bed, unloaded, and his rifle above the cabin door. Burdette would accuse him of being a useless and careless hunter, not having his weapons handy.

"Mr. Godfroy?" Brant-Reid's voice.

"Come on up," Godfroy said. "You've arrived in good time. The wagons rolled in today."

Brant-Reid slid to the ground, but Anders stayed in his saddle. His face worked anxiously. He had come well armed—a knife and pistols in his belt, a rifle hanging from his saddle—but he no longer wore the white buckskins. Some old trapper must have told him they looked silly. Rachel, Will was pleased to see, stared fixedly at Anders, and when he saw her, he lowered his head. Godfroy was right. A few lessons of prairie life and Anders would be meek as a lamb.

Brant-Reid extended a hand to Godfroy, who was struggling to get to his feet. Rachel shoved on the air with her palm, and her lips said "No" without sound. Will stepped forward and laid a hand on Godfroy's shoulder.

"Greet him from where you are," he whispered. "He knows you've been sick." With Rachel distracted by her father, Anders dismounted. He looked about the crowd, suspicious.

"These two gentlemen might travel with us," Will announced. "Brant-Reid, from Henley-on-Thames, and Sir Anders Trout, of Lindenlore Castle. England."

"Keep those horses away from the hay," Burdette said. Rachel burst out laughing, nearly doubled over. Burdette transferred his angry glare to Rachel. "By God, if I'm paying you for your work, no one else gets a share unless they pay up, too. Now, Hunter, you never answered, what's this Pah-row charge for the animals to use his pen and for wagons to cross? You see, I'm no newborn babe, to be tricked into paying too much. I got a copy of the *St. Joseph Gazette* yesterday, from a man riding east, and here's a notice by a man name of Parrott. Can't imagine a man calling himself a comic bird. I'd change it. But this says his rates are fixed by law."

"It's the same man. In St. Joe the name's said Pah-row. It's French." Burdette's eyes flared. A man who hates to be shown wrong; Will filed this fact in his memory.

"I...I am, as that man mentioned, Sir Anders Trout," the Englishman said, raising his voice and hand for attention. "There have been—" he nodded in Godfroy's direction "—misunderstandings between us, which I wish to rectify, for Mr. Brant-Reid and I have concluded that our best opportunity for travel across the plains would be to join your strategically organized party." Brant-Reid studied the ground. Anders must be an embarrassing companion for an honorable man.

"As a gesture of goodwill, and to settle any suspicion that we mean to take advantage of your situation, I—" he paused to give emphasis to the pronoun "—I shall pay all charges for the use of the ferry by the entire party, whether you patronize Mr. Parrott or the boat that departs at the foot of Felix Street."

"Why, now, that's a gentleman's offer if I ever heard one!" Burdette cried. "Which ferry do you—"

Anders silenced him with a wave. "That's for your scouts to decide." He raised a glittering monocle to his eye and directed it at Godfroy and Sampson. The fire reflected in the glass, and Will thought of witchcraft and evil eye. And Anders throwing Rachel over his horse.

"Your scouts have spent more time in this country than anyone around this fire. Mr. Robidoux praises them highly."

At least Anders had the good sense to compliment the scouts, and not undermine their authority. Perhaps Robidoux had lectured him on the realities of western travel.

"Who's there?" Sampson called, springing to his feet. He stared down the path, now deeply shadowed. "Don't skulk about. An honest man calls out. Whoever you are, show your hands." He slid a pistol free of his belt.

"I can't show my hands," protested a female voice. "Merri's asleep in my arms."

Rachel dashed from the fire, and by her quick movements Will knew she took the baby into her own arms. Mrs. Brown pushed back the hood of her cape, gaped, wide-eyed, at the crowd of people.

"So, your friends have come," she said to Rachel. "Not a good time to return your visit. I'm sorry. I didn't know." A strange time of day for a lone woman to be paying a call.

"They arrived a few hours ago. Here, let me introduce

you," Rachel said. She led Mrs. Brown to the cluster of women, who had carried the benches from the cabin and sat in a circle near the door. "Have you walked all the way from town carrying Merri? You must be exhausted."

"She toddled along at first, but then it got too dark to see all the rough spots." A woman vacated a spot for Mrs. Brown, but instead of sitting down, she walked to the fire.

"Good evening, Sir Anders," she simpered. "Good evening, Mr. Brant-Reid." So that's why she had come.

"I think, once we've crossed the river, we should reorganize," Burdette said, recalling the men to the subject at hand. Mrs. Brown, finding herself ignored, flounced to the bench.

"Have new elections," Marshall said. Captain Hull stuck his thumbs in his belt and shrugged his shoulders. Will stood near enough to hear him sigh.

"It's customary, a week or so out on the prairie, to do just that," Sampson said. "Usually at the crossing of the Big Blue River. Sometimes we find our first judgment of men mistaken." Burdette nodded. He edged around the fire, finally got close enough to Anders to stick out his hand.

"Fine to meet you," he said. Anders stared at the proffered hand through his monocle, as if viewing an unknown insect. Brant-Reid tapped his shoulder and finally Anders offered his fingers.

"Our animals need a larger portion of grain tonight," Reverend Ludlow said. Will had helped the preacher hobble his thin, exhausted mules so they did not wander off.

"No," Godfroy said, "there's grazing up the hill. A bit of grain tonight, a bit more tomorrow, a little less each day to ease them onto grass."

"I must object, Captain Hull, and ask for your interference in this matter," Ludlow said. Hull sighed openly. Will frowned, not liking the signs. A bunch of farmers who

would bicker their way west, separating, coming together
in different combinations, so when disaster struck, or even
the normal hardships of the trail… He'd better get his fifty
dollars ahead of time, for some of these bumpkins would
not last to Fort Laramie, let alone California.

"Look, Reverend, those mules of yours are about as
much use as a team of cats," Marshall said. "They hold
up the whole party. Sell them. Get yourself some oxen."

"You criticize me!" Reverend Ludlow cried. "You and
Burdette have five milk cows plodding along, demanding
the efforts of all the boys to push them forward." Ludlow
had a naturally florid complexion, and it flushed redder,
showing more anger than appropriate to a clergyman.

"It was your chickens that bust loose from their coop
this morning, so we hung about camp until two hours after
sunup," Marshall retorted. "And speaking of cats, Mac-
Intyre, that cat shouldn't be along."

"Mr. MacIntyre has chickens, too!" Ludlow said. "Why
should only *my* chickens be criticized?"

Will eased out of the firelight. Rachel had disappeared.
Maybe he should resign his position. Tell Godfroy he had
changed his mind and would stay in St. Joe. Rachel? No
different than any woman. Spoke of adventure, of fulfilling
her dreams, but when faced with the choice between adventure and home, came down on the side of family and
friends.

"What about the leaking barrel?" Burdette yelled.

"Hush!" Will peered around a tree, saw an old woman
step between the quarreling men. Granny MacIntyre,
mother of the two middle-aged men on the other side of
the campfire. Burdette swung an arm, as if he meant to pick
her up and toss her into the fire. He clasped his hands
behind his back and tilted his head in mute appeal to the
stars.

"This is not a woman's place, Mrs. MacIntyre," Reverend Ludlow said as if preaching in church.

"Now you listen to me," she said, turning her back on Ludlow. Her glowing eyes suggested sorcery. "Haven't you learned? Tracking back to find out who did the first wrong always leads to Adam, and he's not around to kick. You blame each other for every little thing. Who saw Ludlow let his chickens out?" She pointed at Burdette. "Did you spot a skulker prying at your barrel?" She swung about and leveled a finger at Ludlow's nose. "Just a bit ago, I spied Mrs. Ludlow carrying a pan of milk from Mr. Marshall's cows. But perhaps I'm mistaken, for my eyes are old."

No one said a thing. Marshall hung his head and Burdette shifted uneasily. Not a specter of the night, but the core of the emigrant party, Will realized. The MacIntyre men would not hold the group together, but their mother might!

"From now on you don't blame anything on each other. You blame me. Because from this instant, I put a curse on this trip!" She lifted her arms, and her dark shawl reminded Will of a bat. He shivered, told himself he was being foolish, but logic didn't stop the shudders down his spine.

"From now on, every wagon on this journey will be cursed with sprung tongues and busted axles. Your oxen will sag under the yoke, and your mules drop dead in their tracks. The milk cows dry up, the horses cast their shoes, the dog get bit by a mad wolf, and the cat get bred by a wildcat. That's what I prophesy, and you remember what I say, and when things go wrong, blame Granny, not each other. Men claim by nature they should be in charge, because it's written in the Bible. If that's God's truth, then men should look to their responsibilities, for if they fall out we'll die on the deserts."

"Tsk, tsk, tsk," said Reverend Ludlow. Burdette laughed

nervously, but stopped when no one joined him. Rachel had said Granny could nurse sick men and animals back to health with her herbs. Was there something more? A magic like Gray Woman's, muttered in endless monotone? A magic that could bind everyone together? Will decided to pay her careful attention, bring her special game, build her cooking fire…perhaps she knew a love potion that would keep Rachel beside him, so the letter in the mail sack heading for Pittsburgh was not a lie.

They *must* be married! He had meant every word he uttered, standing before that scoundrel Kraft. If only Godfroy had remembered that something should be written down. But Godfroy had burned with fever. *My fault!* The groom should be the one to ask about signing.…

Sampson was on his feet again. "This place is busier than a riverfront saloon," he growled. "Come up slow, stranger. Hands wide and say who you are."

Someone threw a dry stick on the fire and flames licked instantly along its length. Will's heart stopped. He closed his eyes. *When I open my eyes, Robert will be gone.* He raised one lid slowly, and his brother stepped closer.

# *Chapter Eleven*

"I'm looking for a man who calls himself Will Hunter."

"Will," Godfroy called. "I thought he was right behind me." Weariness strung out the words, and he coughed.

"Here." Will's boots seemed filled with lead, weighting his feet as he walked toward his brother. "How?"

Robert threw back his head and laughed. "Didn't expect me so soon? Thought you'd escape me, on the road to California? When I'm in St. Louis the postmaster watches for letters addressed to me in Pittsburgh. Get your things. You're coming to the hotel so we can board the steamer early tomorrow. You've shown you can't be trusted."

"He's under contract with us," Sampson objected. "As our hunter to California."

"Contract?" Robert sneered. "He's underage, can't make a valid contract. Where's the squaw you 'married'?" He stared at the women. "I suppose I'll have to pay her off."

"Rachel?" Will said into the darkness. She separated from the rest of the women. He took her hand.

"Rachel. My brother, Robert Shakespeare, of Shakespeare and Company, Pittsburgh."

"Shakespeare," she whispered.

"Shakespeare!" Hull's voice. "Why, the army in Mexico got half its supplies in crates and barrels marked Shakespeare. I didn't suppose it was a man's name."

"My grandfather, Helmut Shakespeare, founded a mercantile establishment in Philadelphia," Robert said proudly. "And as the Ohio country developed, moved to Pittsburgh."

"Grandpa's name was Jäger," Will said to Rachel. "I didn't lie to you. He wanted an English name, and Shakespeare was the best he could think of."

"Shakespeare!" Anders howled. "A colonial tradesman named Shakespeare?"

"Father could have named me something other than *William*. Do you know what it's like, with the neighborhood boys, and your name's *William Shakespeare?*"

The men guffawed and the women tittered.

"How much money to settle this matter?" Robert asked. "I'll deal with her father, if he's nearby."

"I'm her father." Godfroy should be in bed, and now this, upsetting him! "Rachel and Will married—"

"Will can't marry without Father's permission, for he's only twenty. Father will certainly not extend his blessing to a union with a squaw! Besides, he's returning—"

"I am not," Will said.

"You come, or I notify the sheriff. You're wanted for theft. Father reported to the authorities in Pittsburgh, you absconded with blankets, clothing, several books, a rifle and an indeterminate amount of money."

"I took nothing that wasn't mine," Will shouted.

"A minor has no possessions," Robert said. "All belong to the father until he makes gifts at the coming of age."

Rachel's hands tightened upon his. "No!" she whispered.

Robert unbuttoned the top of his coat and hauled out a

folder, opened it to reveal a sheaf of banknotes. "How much?" he asked of Godfroy. "I suppose she was a virgin."

"Does ruining a virgin concern you, Mr. Brown?" The fire gleamed on Mrs. Brown's breasts, but her sparking eyes shone with an energy of their own. She pushed Merri ahead of her, the little girl's face distorted with sleep. She rubbed her eyes with tiny fists, fixed them on Robert.

"Papa," she said.

"Bright as a new penny. Hardly a year old, and can say words," Mrs. Brown said.

"I don't know you, or what you're talking about," Robert said, but the snarl that followed betrayed uncertainty.

"In Natchez, a year and nine months ago." Mrs. Brown's voice dripped poisoned honey. Robert shoved the money under his coat.

"I wasn't in…haven't been in Natchez. Shakespeare and Company hires an agent to handle our business there."

"Except when he died, just about two years ago," Will murmured. Robert caught in sinful, carnal intercourse?

"This woman's a liar!" Robert cried. Several men nodded in agreement. "She's got a bastard, and accuses a man with money and position of being the father. It's happened to me before, all the sluts in the river towns."

"He seduced me!" Mrs. Brown cried. "He said his wife had died and he needed a helpmate, and that he'd build a fine house on the hill. He said he was a slave dealer from New Orleans. I told him I was in the family way, and he vanished like smoke."

"If you did as she says—" Reverend Ludlow began.

"She can't prove a thing," Robert said loftily. "Simply a loose woman from Natchez-Under-the-Hill."

"Oh, can't I prove it?" Mrs. Brown's skirts swayed as she danced in either fury or excitement.

"If you did as she says, you must marry her, make an honest woman of her," Reverend Ludlow said, pointing with a pulpit gesture. "To do otherwise would be to burn in—"

"He has a scar where no woman except a wife or mistress knows," Mrs. Brown said triumphantly. She dodged in under Robert's arms and poked at the buttons fastening the right side of his trouser flap. "The scar's pink, and shaped like the wake of a duck swimming across a still pond."

"Lying slut!" Robert shouted.

"Do help me here," Reverend Ludlow said to Tole, the blacksmith. Tole nodded grimly and grabbed Robert's arms. At the last minute Will tried to push them away. After all, Robert was his brother, and to be saddled with a woman like Mrs. Brown! But Tole's muscles bulged through what would be on any other man a loose-fitting coat.

"Bring a lantern," Reverend Ludlow ordered. "We shall determine the truth, and if the woman lies..."

"We'll stone her, I suppose," Granny said.

Every man except Godfroy, Sir Anders and Brant-Reid traipsed around the corner of the cabin. The two Englishmen gaped in astonishment.

"Aren't you going?" Rachel whispered. Will stared at his hands, surprised to find they still clasped hers.

"No."

"Why not?"

"Because the scar's there. I gave it to him." Mrs. Brown howled with delight, grabbed Merri's hands and swung the little girl's feet off the ground.

"You wounded your own brother?" Rachel said.

"Robert came after me, when I'd holed up with an old Indian. He'd taught me to make a bow and arrows. I got in one shot before Robert grabbed me and started beating."

A lantern bobbed around the corner of the cabin. Robert's clothes hung in disarray.

"You'll stay with us tonight," Reverend Ludlow was saying with the confidence of the righteous. "Tomorrow I'll accompany you to the county offices for the license, and then we'll celebrate—"

"No!" yelled Robert.

"Indeed not!" Mrs. Brown chimed in. "Do you think I'd marry a rogue? Why, he'd settle me in a shack in Pittsburgh and dally with the girls of the river ports, just as before! I'll only marry a man of integrity. And if fate doesn't bring me a husband, one willing to overlook my fault, why, I'll make my own way. And Merri's. Is there any family who needs a woman to look out for the children?" The crowd fell silent. A few women slipped into the darkness.

"You needn't look for work, Mrs. Brown," Will said. "My brother understands your predicament, and will be happy to furnish you the wherewithal to return to Natchez. I'm sure he has cash enough to help you and Merri."

Robert broke off rearranging his clothes and leveled a gaze of malevolent hatred at both Will and Mrs. Brown.

"Perhaps Mr. Shakespeare would come to Robidoux's tomorrow," Mrs. Brown said. "I don't discuss financial affairs in public, but I can say that a one-time payment would be unsatisfactory. I rise early, Mr. Brown. We can meet and you'll still have time to catch the steamboat."

Brant-Reid, Will noticed, grinned in appreciation of the rustic justice. Anders, on the other hand, had a haunted look, as if reminded of something.

"Now, Robert," Will said, taking his brother's arm. "I think we need a private conference. I'll walk you back to town. Wait a moment while I go fetch something."

Will crawled underneath the bed, pried out a section of log and found the packet of money by touch.

Will steered Robert down the rutted track, uncertain of his balance, wondering at his giddiness. Robert stumbled, and his weight dragged on Will's elbow. "Here's the road," Will said. "The going will be smoother now." Robert stopped, turned his head as if searching for a familiar landmark. Will noticed for the first time that he was taller than Robert. Only an inch, but his shoulders were broader, too.

"Will, please, understand my position" Robert whispered, desperation clouding his words. "Six years since Eulalie died, leaving me with no family, not a single child. I planned to marry a fine widow lady in Pittsburgh, but Father objected. You know how he feels about second marriages. 'You must devote your life to Eulalie's memory.'"

Robert had always been a fine mimic, had kept the office in stitches imitating their most irritating customers. But this was the first time Will had heard him mock their father's sonorous tones.

"By God! Will, I wasn't designed to be a monk!"

"So Mrs. Brown isn't the first?" Will asked. Robert snarled. "Does that mean no? Let's walk along slowly. The moon will rise soon. Can you see well enough to walk?"

"Yes." The pebbles of the road crunched beneath their boots. "I can't remember their names," Robert whispered, "which woman came a year ago, two years ago. They get mixed up in my mind." He moaned, a pitiful sound that rose up the scale until it became a squeak. An owl swooped before them, and Will heard the cry of its victim, echoing Robert's cry. Robert a snared rodent. Who was the owl? Mrs. Brown? No! No wonder he felt giddy. He himself, the hunter! The tables had been turned, and his talons clasped Robert.

"I'm not lying, Will. I don't remember Mrs. Brown, or whatever her name is. Natchez women in the bloom of youth are irresistible, but much alike. I don't recall, however…ever thinking someone that plump attractive."

"You don't keep some record—"

"Don't put on that prissy, shocked air, Will! I dare say you've found pleasure with the women of St. Joe, even if you did tell Father the truth last year, when you denied humping the girl on the Clarion." Will gasped. No man in his family, that he knew of, had ever used such vulgar language.

"Anyway, I don't recall, and I like my women more akin to willows."

"She's had a child. That could pad her figure."

"I suppose. I've not had the experience, Eulalie and I being childless."

"And your mistresses?"

"It's not happened that I know of. Sometimes I fear our childlessness was my fault, not Eulalie's. I remember how I blamed her, and am now uneasy. If we should meet in a better world, where all is revealed…"

Will laughed openly. A self-confessed libertine, meeting sainted Eulalie in heaven?

"But, on immediate matters—" Robert interrupted his contemplation of the afterlife "—do you think that child could be mine?"

"What did you call yourself in Natchez?"

"Mr. Brown," Robert said miserably. "But maybe the lady welcomed other men. What's her reputation here?"

He could tell Robert of his adventure with Mrs. Brown, and relieve his mind. But did he want to relieve Robert?

"I don't know the lady's reputation," Will said, side-stepping the question. "But she's looking for a husband, not a paramour, which speaks well of her morals. She's quite knowledgeable about the legalities of marriage, and won't be fooled again."

Robert kicked at a rock. "How much will you tell Father?"

"Why, I can't see that Father need know anything of this! After all, Mrs. Brown intends to marry here on the frontier, and she may be bound to the far West."

"Every person standing around that fire knows the truth," Robert said. "They'll start gossip about a Shakespeare—"

"All are bound for California, except the Englishmen, and why should they gossip about a man they find ridiculous?"

"Me? Ridiculous?" he asked, affronted.

"Of course. Privately, they make fun of everything American. Didn't you hear Anders's remark about your name? In London he'll dine out for a year on the story of the German emigrant who changed his name to Shakespeare. Hilarious to Londoners. But not here. Not on the river, where the name has some level of *honor*."

"Honor," Robert repeated. "So, what do you want?"

"Freedom. You accept that I'm leading my own life. No more threats of arrest for taking my own rifle. No more pleading letters. No piles of banknotes to bribe me. No more letters of credit. You tempted me, Robert!"

"How do I explain to Father? I keep telling him you'll outgrow these childish fancies. He wanted to send the law after you the day you left, but I persuaded him that bribery would be better in the long run. I assured him that regular remittances of cash would trap you in dependence, that you'd see the error of your ways."

"Tell him the truth, that I'm making my own living and in a year, perhaps two, he'll see my name on a book."

"He burned it."

Will shrugged. "I wrote one. I can write another."

"Why do you torture him this way?" Robert cried. "He's an old man!"

"Torture him! From the first time I put pen to paper, he scolded. Nothing but a ledger sheet pleases him. After mother died he blamed me, that she had died heartbroken because I'd gone off to the mountains. Guilt brought me home, I promised to stay, and then I found out she'd died at a dressmaker's in New York. When he threw the manuscript on the fire he gave me no choice. Always before I *had* been childish, running away, at the same time expecting his support. But when those pages burned I knew that if I asked for independence, I also asked for responsibility. Completely."

"Don't exaggerate, Will. Father says that's your problem. You exaggerate everything. He'll welcome you. Your room's still as it was."

"My books?"

"Well, I don't suppose all of them."

"I hate that house, and I'll never step into the front hall again except as a free man. From my first memory I thought the house haunted."

"Haunted! Father's right. You exaggerate. Your mind's filled with silly stories from the vulgar books you read. That house bulges with joy, the evenings of singing, the morning devotions, the whole family gathered round—"

"For you. Did you, or our sisters, or Mother or Father ever think of me? You and Father away on business. Mother with the girls in New York or Philadelphia."

"But...don't be silly, Will, you are ever so much younger than the rest of us, so travel wasn't suitable."

"My only recollection of that house is silence. In the nursery, with Madame Petitpont, and then even she was sent away, and the parson in the mornings for my lessons."

"Father had no choice with Madame," Robert said stiffly. "You were too young to...to...understand."

"Madame Petitpont?" Will cried, incredulous. "You found that skinny old Frenchwoman attractive?"

"Shut up!" Robert snarled. "She was not old. You were quite young. An innocent."

Still an innocent, Will thought. One attempt at sex with Rachel Godfroy, so badly managed she would not try again.

"This is the final break, Robert. You let me go my own way, or I'll tell Father about the mistresses on the river."

"How do I explain to Father! He's certain you'll return. He can't believe his son would have no greater ambition than to be a vulgar writer."

"Robert, any Pennsylvania man who can pass himself off in Natchez as a slave broker can certainly concoct a story to explain his brother's absence."

"I'll make you the agent in St. Louis," Robert said, grasping the fringes of Will's coat in lieu of lapels. "Father need never meet...the squaw."

The word stabbed, like a dagger in his belly. "No. You saw Rachel. How can you use *that* word!"

Robert dropped his hands. "How much do you want to keep quiet?"

Hadn't Robert heard a thing? "Nothing. If we can't establish a brotherly correspondence, forget I'm alive."

"Will, I have barely enough cash to pay off Mrs. Brown, and only if she'll settle for less than a hundred dollars. I can't give you money to support a journey."

"I'm not asking for money. In fact—" he pulled the packet from under his coat "—here's what you sent. I don't need it. I'm going with the wagon train, fifty dollars for acting as their hunter, plenty to bring me east with the book about the trail to California. And after that I'll set out on another adventure. Perhaps to India.''

Robert plodded stodgily past the courthouse, down the main street. He halted in confusion when six yoke of oxen blocked the street in front of the hotel.

"These emigrants made my journey miserable," he said in a low voice. "Most are bound for Oregon, to claim farms. Why have these Hoosiers determined on California?"

"Godfroy and Sampson, they've been to California, and describe it as the earthly paradise. They convinced all their friends and relatives."

"Fools. And if you go with them you're a greater fool. You have a fortune waiting, if only you'd tame your spirit a bit. Come home with me! I'll not tell Father of your fling with the squaw." Will ground his teeth, but said nothing. "You can certainly find a willing mistress in Pittsburgh. We'll be partners, true brothers."

"Brothers bound by the deepest of secrets," Will said, loading the words with irony.

"Yes," Robert said seriously, and Will realized his sarcasm, like everything he said, was wasted on Robert. "And not just in Pittsburgh. If you're willing to use your real name, the prettiest women flirt with a Shakespeare. But the danger...I've found it best to use another name...women in the major ports, even a beauty in New Orleans...race is of no consequence. Why were you taken with the breed girl?"

Will thought back to the morning on the steamboat, when he considered that a squaw man would be banned from home. His face warmed in shame. "Rachel is beautiful—"

"Will, tell me the truth. Do you think that little girl could be mine? Do you see a family resemblance?"

"The light hair is certainly suggestive. You are as fair as Father. And the child seems intelligent."

"Really? I could, tomorrow morning, press my suit, actually marry the bi—woman." He rambled desperately, stumbling over his words. "I could stow her in Cincinnati. Father never need know. You'd keep that secret as well as the present one? As you say, the child has promise, although what good that is in a girl..."

"Strange, that's what I find most attractive about Rachel. Imaginative and resourceful."

"You intend to keep her?" Robert asked in amazement.

"If she'll have me."

Robert laughed with a confidence that mocked. "You complain that we left you alone as a child, but you'll do the same thing. Dash off to some corner of the world that promises a new creature to slaughter, while your wife and children struggle alone. Should I marry the Natchez girl?"

"I don't recommend women." Will laughed, but uneasily. "Only a fool advises on marriage, for if the wife turns out to be a shrew, you've lost a friend."

"Too true," Robert said mournfully. "But you heard what she asks—permanent support. There'll be no end to her demands. Now that she knows my family, blackmail—"

"Possible."

"I'll offer tomorrow," he said. "In the long run marriage will be cheaper. Would you vouch for me? Assure her I was faithful to Eulalie?"

"Were you?" Will asked just as the oxen moved on and they were able to dash across the street. "Were you?" Robert kicked the riser of the stair leading to the hotel veranda. "I see. No, you'll win the woman by your own efforts. Goodbye." He held out his hand, but Robert did not take it.

"Robert, I've grown up. It had to come sometime, that you could no longer force me home with threats and paddlings." Robert turned his back and climbed the stairs.

The fire was abandoned except for the heap of a buffalo robe. "Godfroy," Will whispered. The robe moved. Will steeled himself against Godfroy's recriminations.

"Is it true? You and Rachel aren't legally married because you're not of age?" Will had expected to be accused of lying, of concealing his name and family. This question caught him off balance, just as he squatted on his heels. He caught himself with a palm on the ground.

"Not just my age. Kraft wasn't a real preacher. He masquerades as Dr. Kraft now. He didn't write a certificate for us to sign, and there were no witnesses, except you. And the county requires marriage licenses."

"My mind's hazy. Did you take Rachel to bed?"

"Once."

"You've said the words and lain together. I expect that means you're married."

"Rachel doesn't think so."

"Well, after we're over the river Sampson's brother-in-law can marry you and write out a paper."

"Rachel doesn't want another wedding. She says she's had enough of marriage."

"I'll speak to her. I want you to be my son-in-law."

"I'll not force Rachel. That's no kind of marriage. Maybe in time..." The sweat on his forehead turned icy, and Robert's words rolled through his mind. He would treat his wife and children exactly as he had been treated.

"I'll mention it to her friends. They'll bring Rachel to her senses." Godfroy reared up suddenly. "You don't intend to go with your brother, do you? I'm forgetting, you can ride the top deck on the steamboats and wear fancy duds.''

"No. Never have wanted it. Never will. I'm sorry I didn't tell you the truth about who I was. Avoiding the truth's as bad as lying.''

"I suspected," Godfroy said. "Rachel mentioned the name in your Bible. I've been on too many steamboats, sleeping against crates marked Shakespeare and Company, not to suspect.''

"You didn't say anything."

"What's to say? A man has a right to be who he wants to be. What do you mean to do? I can't see a man raised a Shakespeare being a hunter forever.''

"Godfroy, you've read Frémont's report, I suppose.'' The buffalo robe shifted.

"No, reading and writing's something I never learned.''

Will poked with his boots at the blackened coals. How did he explain his ambition to an illiterate? His father and brother could not understand his compulsion to put words on paper. But Godfroy had asked him a direct question; he must answer truthfully and bear the ridicule.

"I read Frémont's report of his explorations, but he's an explorer, not interested in staying on trails. In *Knicker-bocker Magazine* a man from New England wrote of the plains, but he sneered at the emigrants and wouldn't speak to them. His work is of no use to a man considering a move. I'll write a careful account of the trail to California.''

Will steeled himself against Godfroy's laugh.

"The men who travel with you, they'll be honored if you succeed," Godfroy said slowly. "Tell me what you need to know, what you want to write down, and I'll help you all I can.'' A blow from behind could not have stunned him more.

"My father, my brother, they don't think writing's an honorable vocation."

"I've always envied the trappers who could write," Godfroy said. "What I've got in my head, the pattern of the Rockies, I can tell one man at a time, or a dozen men about a campfire. But to write facts on paper tells the whole world. Just you be sure you write the truth, not like some bastards who spread lies and lead people to their deaths. You write it down, so Easterners understand the trip's not impossible," Godfroy said. "Every man here will—"

"No, no! That's exactly what I *don't* want. If they know I'm keeping a diary, and planning a book, they'll act differently. Would Burdette and Ludlow be so honest with each other, rage about chickens and milk cows, if they knew?"

Godfroy laughed. "You want every man with his bark on?"

"Yes. No one on best behavior."

"Good. I'll keep the secret, but you let me know if I can help. And I'll figure ways for you and Rachel to be alone together for courting. You sharing our wagon helps."

"Thank you," Will choked.

Godfroy stretched out on his stomach and straightened the robe beneath him. "The big problem's with Burdette and Marshall. Why do men figure they build themselves up by tearing other men down? If they keep on they'll split the party before we reach the Platte. And here I am, stove up like a crate dropped off a wagon. You'll take my place."

"But you hired me to hunt. And I haven't the slightest notion of the route, or water, or grass."

"Sampson'll tell you. And we'll turn the hunting chores over to Anders and Reid, and that'll keep them away from the wagons during the day, so they'll only have the evenings to make trouble. At least no one hired Mrs. Brown."

"Mrs. Brown!" He'd forgotten Mrs. Brown. He looked at the white wagon covers shining in the moonlight, wondering which sheltered her. "Where is she?"

"The Englishmen escorted her back to town."

"On Mr. Brant-Reid's suggestion, I presume."

"Anders wasn't pleased, but a gentleman couldn't refuse."

"She's after Anders to marry her. She'll try to get a place in the wagon train to stay near him."

"No one will hire her. The women fear she'll tempt their husbands. Fathers with grown boys, they remember what can happen in the bushes, because most did it themselves. I'd better get some sleep."

"Come inside. Use my bed."

"No, I'll get well faster sleeping by the fire, on the ground, where I'm accustomed. You're a good man," Godfroy said. Will very nearly contradicted him, but that would only lead to more conversation, and Godfroy should be asleep.

# *Chapter Twelve*

Will had to respect Godfroy's commonsense attitude toward marriage. He and Rachel had said the words, and for a brief moment they had been man and wife, of one flesh. A gentleman could not casually put that aside. He knocked on her door, a warning, before he lifted the latch.

"No!" she said the moment his foot lifted over the threshold. She pulled the blankets over her head. "No!"

"We need to talk, Rachel."

"Stay away from me."

He walked blindly into the room, keeping his distance from her, and ran into the quilting frame. She sat up.

"Don't knock the quilt over!"

"Rachel, I guess we aren't really married."

"That's fine with me," she snapped. "I don't want to be married. Ever!"

"I took your virginity. As a gentleman, I must ask you to be my wife."

"No. Go away."

"Your father thinks we're truly married. He doesn't think licenses and ordained preachers are necessary. We said the words, and I bedded you—"

"He knows?" He saw her white nightdress. She was sitting up, her legs dangling over the edge of the bed.

"He asked me directly. I couldn't lie."

"Dear Lord in heaven! He'll parade us to Reverend Ludlow in front of his rifle."

"No. He's enlisting your friends to persuade you. He'll figure ways to get us alone together."

"I don't care what he does, or my friends!" she said.

"I didn't suppose so. Would you marry me if you felt a grand passion?"

"I don't know what grand passion is. Do you love me?" she asked.

"Don't ask impossible questions, Rachel. I'm not sure I know what love is. I respect you. You're a fine woman. But you want grand passion—"

"Not anymore! I've had enough passion to last a lifetime."

"Then I'll not court you. But we're stuck sharing a wagon for four or five months, Rachel. Can we be friends? Brother and sister?"

The white disappeared as she arranged a blanket over her legs. "Sit down here, beside me. You can tell me the truth now. About who you are." What did she expect to hear? He decided to give the bare essentials.

"I was born in Philadelphia. My grandfather and father owned a wholesale shop. Father moved the family to Pittsburgh when I was two years old."

"And your name's William Shakespeare?"

"No, that's the name given me at birth. I changed it. William Hunter."

"I suppose being William Shakespeare *would* be difficult. Boys can be terribly cruel. But now you're grown up."

"It's impossible."

"Why?"

"I've told Godfroy my secret. Now I'll tell you, for you're my sister, and I trust you." He took her hand. "I cannot remain at home, because I want to be a writer. My father considers it a low occupation. I can't be William Shakespeare! What would a publisher think, getting a manuscript from William Shakespeare?"

"That would be difficult," she agreed. A tendril of dark hair had escaped her night braid and smudged her cheek.

"Don't mention this to a soul. I'm keeping a diary of the trip, and I'll write a book about the trail to California. It must be a secret, for if people know they'll not treat me like a hunter."

Rachel's hand tightened on his. She leaned slightly in his direction and laughed. "Burdette would be terribly shocked, seeing the things he said written down."

"Exactly. You'll not tell anyone? Even your friends?" She pulled her hand from his, slapped it over her mouth. "Good night, then."

"Wait, I've got more questions. You went through the marriage ceremony for the same reason I did? Because you thought Father was dying?"

"That, and you're very beautiful."

"And you wanted me in your bed?" she asked shyly.

"That, too."

"You still do?"

"Only if you want me there, Rachel."

"But you feel…the way men feel toward women?"

"Yes."

"Your brother, he's a…"

She hesitated, so he said, "Libertine," the kindest word he could think of.

"This is hard for a woman to ask, but do you have similar…desires? For other women?"

"I came to you pure!" he exclaimed, a bit hurt by her

accusation, but also bitterly recalling his arousal under Louisa Brown's hand.

"I'm sorry. But under the circumstances, we must be practical. If you feel the urge to seduce women...well, I can't think of a single woman traveling with us who would be a partner in such a... There are...fallen women in St. Joe, if you need, if the feeling is irresistible...before we leave..." Her voice died away.

He rose, stood so close his leg touched her knee. "I am not my brother, Rachel."

"I'm sorry I said anything."

"No, I asked you to be open with me. That's the only way we'll get through this thing."

"We must never be alone together."

"Not much to worry about. There's precious little privacy in a wagon on the plains."

"If my father or friends try to get us together..."

"We'll find some excuse to be apart. We'll have fun, Rachel, brother and sister in cahoots, sabotaging the adults' tricks. I never had a sister or brother near my own age, one to play this sort of game with."

"I never had a sister or brother at all," she said. She brushed the hair off her cheek with a gesture of confidence, but the slope of her shoulders said she had doubts.

Rachel knotted and cut her thread, and walked around the frame to continue the line of stitches beyond Tildy's tulips. Tildy had come at first light to finish the center.

"Do we have a wedding this evening?" she whispered.

"No."

"I should think the sooner the better."

"Last night Will and I decided we won't get married."

Tildy leaned across the quilt so their heads nearly touched. "But Rachel! What if you're in a family way?"

"I'm not."

"You mean, you and Will…took precautions? I'm glad. Matt insists, not wanting me burdened on the trail, although we'd be in California before a baby came."

Rachel scanned the door and window for eavesdroppers. "We did it only once, and it hurt so much, I wouldn't let him finish. It doesn't count."

Tildy withdrew her left hand from under the quilt, rested it on her hip and stared at the rafters thoughtfully. "I think it counts, no matter what happens. If he hurt you, you're no longer a virgin."

"It doesn't count," Rachel said sternly. "We're not getting—"

Meggie walked through the door. "Where's Faith?" she asked. She bit a length of thread off the spool and struggled to insert the ragged end in the eye of her needle. Her stabbing reminded Rachel of the night with Will.

"Cleaning up from breakfast, I suppose. She has no one to help her," Tildy said. "You should cut the thread with your scissors. We're lucky, Meggie. You have your mother, and Granny does most of the cooking for me and Matt."

"Mmm," said Meggie, pointing the thread on her tongue. Did women do that to men? The idea made Rachel gag.

"Here she is! Hurry, Faith. The feathers are lagging behind, like Ludlow's mules." Faith stopped in the door, swayed a little, caught herself on the doorpost. Pale, as if she had just witnessed some horrible sight.

"Faith!" Tildy cried. "What's wrong? You're white as a sheet."

Faith slumped on a bench. She bowed her head almost to her knees. "Pa," she whispered.

"An accident? Your father's taken sick?" Rachel asked in alarm, dropping her needle. "I'll go—"

"No, he and the boys set out for St. Joe."

"Why should that—" Meggie began, but Faith silenced her with a wave of her hand.

"Mrs. Brown," Faith said flatly.

"Mrs. Brown?" all three said.

"Pa says the little girl reminds him of me when I was a baby, all that light hair, and talking so young, and he fretted half the night, pacing around the wagon, what was to become of her and her mother? He admires Mrs. Brown's spunk, refusing to marry that awful man who seduced her. He says a weak woman would have jumped at the chance."

"Why, she's younger than you!" Meggie said. "Don't talk nonsense!"

"It's not nonsense. He took the boys to meet her. He says he'll make sure she can cook and sew and tend a house. He won't saddle me with a worthless stepmother."

"Then you'll have help," Tildy suggested brightly. "Not have all the cooking and cleaning on your shoulders."

Faith shook her head. "He won't need me," she whispered.

"Of course he needs you," Tildy cried. "Whatever makes you think he'll—"

"I had my life all planned. I'd stay home after the boys left and take care of Pa, and never marry. But if he remarries, he has no need of me! A woman young as Mrs. Brown won't want an old maid daughter around. She'll be sweet about it, I don't doubt, but she'll hint it's time I looked for a husband, and invite single men to supper."

"Being married has its good points," Tildy said, and blushed a trifle.

"There's little difference between a wife and a slave," Faith said. She lifted her head, showed a tight face, holding back the tears. "You're lucky, Tildy. Since you and Matt married you've lived with your family. Wait until you set up housekeeping, and a baby comes, and you'll find out what being a wife's truly like." She stared at Rachel. "Look at Rachel, quilting her fingers raw, and expected to do all the work in this house."

"That's not true!" Rachel exclaimed. "Will helps me all he can, but with Father sick—"

"Exactly!" Faith cried. "Your father gets sick, and who stays up half the night tending him? You! The extra work's always laid at the woman's feet. And then comes sundown, the man starts hinting, so a woman can't get her rest."

Rachel turned back to the quilt so she had a reason to hide her face. Nursing, cooking, cleaning, quilting. How long would she hurt from those few moments with Will?

"What am I to do?" Faith wailed.

"Stop whining and get to work on this quilt," Rachel snapped. "Or we won't have vinegar to carry along."

"I'm sorry," Faith said after a moment of shocked silence. Rachel felt every eye upon her, condemning her want of sympathy.

"There's work to be done," Faith said. She sighed. "Maybe I'm just borrowing trouble. Perhaps Pa won't ask that woman to marry him. I hope she hates boys."

"Just hope your pa has sense enough to be cautious," Rachel said as Faith searched for the spot where she had left off last night. "Mrs. Brown will say yes to anything that wears pants."

Faith sniffed. "Life's hard for a woman alone, I know, but if she marries Pa, *I'm* the woman alone!"

"No, you're not!" Rachel said firmly. "There's two of us. I won't have a husband, either."

"Rachel, don't say that!" Tildy protested, but Rachel silenced her with a glance. She wished she had not confided in Tildy about the sex.

"Once we get to California, Faith, you and I'll find a

way to make our living," Rachel said happily. "Just think of what I did here in St. Joe, getting hay and vinegar by quilting."

"There won't be many women looking for quilting or dressmaking in California," Meggie said, deflating her optimism. "Granny says times are always hard for the first years in a new country."

"What else might a respectable woman do?" Tildy mused. "Perhaps you should spend the summer with Granny, write down everything she says and set yourselves up as midwives."

"Women expect midwives to have birthed babies of their own," Faith observed.

"Pshaw!" Meggie exclaimed. "In the cities women hire male midwives, and you can't say they've had babies."

"It's different. They're doctors."

"I don't see it's different," Meggie insisted. "Schoolmarms aren't married and don't have children, but they're expected to manage a whole roomful."

"Schoolmarm!" Rachel said. "Why, Faith, with two of us we could open a school!"

Faith stopped sewing. "I've had experience, raising four brothers. I taught them all their letters."

"Of course you did. And we've got school certificates from Pikeston. I hope you packed yours, because we'll display them to show we're qualified."

"It takes money to start a school."

"Last night the men voted me ten dollars for quilting the hay," Rachel said, opposing Faith's depression and giving herself hope at the same time.

"That's not enough," Faith said.

"Ask Will," Meggie said. "His family's got scads of money. Shouldn't he pay you something for keeping house and marrying you without the right?"

Rachel ducked her head and concentrated on stitching all the way to the edge of the quilt.

"Take money from a man!" Faith said. "Women who take money from men set gossips talking, and if Mr. Hunter's like his brother, he'd take advantage of Rachel again, thinking she'd keep his terrible secret, for money."

"Oh, Will would never—" Rachel shut her mouth so quickly her teeth clicked. She knew him by the rhythm of his footsteps.

"Pardon me," Will said. Were his cheeks a little red? How long had he been outside? "The men wonder how soon you could have the quilt done?"

Tildy cocked her head as she counted the rows left to do. "Tomorrow afternoon, if you find someone to fix dinner and supper for Faith's family, and for you and Mr. Godfroy."

"I'll shift for myself and Godfroy, and I'll ask around for someone to feed the Toles."

"Why the hurry?" Meggie asked.

"Sampson's found two teamsters who will drive along with us the first week, carrying hay and grain. The grass on the plains isn't high enough for pasture, but by carrying feed we can set out now."

"We'll be finished!" Meggie cried. "I'll work all night! Hooray for California! I can't wait!"

"Rachel." Will sidled toward her and winked. "Your father says, as soon as the quilt's done, I'm to take you to the Perrys' to haul the vinegar here."

Rachel returned his wink. "I don't think that's practical," she said. Will was right. This was going to be fun. "The wagon's partly loaded, and taking it to the Perrys' would jostle the load. The four of us—" she waved a hand to include Meggie, Faith and Tildy "—will walk to the Perrys' with the quilt. We want to see Mrs. Perry's reaction.

Faith's brothers can go with us and haul the vinegar on the Perrys' handcart. Not far for them, hardly a mile, and you'd not be bothered when you're so busy.''

Will smiled. ''Sounds like a good plan.''

''We'll be done sooner than tomorrow afternoon if Mr. Tole's new wife can quilt,'' Meggie said. She pointed out the window, and Rachel looked just in time to see Mr. Tole, a tiny lacy bonnet resting on his shoulder. An elaborate black hat kept pace between his shoulder and Kit's.

''Tole's new wife!'' Will said. His jaw dropped. He turned so quickly his heels made deep marks in the floor. Meggie giggled. Faith sighed.

''Faith, once you wished you had a little sister,'' Tildy said. ''Rather than four brothers.''

''So I did,'' Faith said. ''Take care what you pray for. It might come true.''

''We *will* have a school,'' Rachel said to give Faith courage. ''Perhaps we should walk to St. Joe this evening, look for books to take along? I'm not sure in California—''

''Mr. Sampson says take money, not things,'' Meggie reminded her. ''The oxen would have to pull those books.''

''Of course I know how to quilt,'' Mrs. Brown said just beyond the door, ''but this time of day I should be fixing your dinner.''

''You don't cook today. Not on your wedding day,'' Tole said. He shoved Mrs. Brown ahead of him.

''Faith, Mrs. Brown and I have reached an agreement. I thought perhaps she might sit with you and your friends, get acquainted while I go to the courthouse for the license.''

Mrs. Brown stared at the floor. She took Merri from Tole's arms, stood the baby in front of her like a shield. Merri had her thumb in her mouth. Rachel found a crust of bread and handed it to the little girl.

''Than oo,'' Merri said.

Faith rose from the stool slowly, eyes wide, the back of her hand against her mouth, and Rachel was uncertain whether she would laugh or cry. Somehow she overcame both emotions. "She talks? But she's so tiny!"

"She's an amazing child," Rachel said.

"Please be kind to her," Mrs. Brown whispered. "You know the truth, from last night. She's a...bastard. But Mr. Tole says he'll give her his name."

"Oh, don't think a thing about it!" Tildy said airily, waving her needle. "My husband's a bastard, but they elected him captain." Mrs. Brown's chin quivered.

"Do sit down," Rachel said, pointing to the spot Faith had vacated. "I'm sorry, but the quilt must be done tomorrow, so I can't stop to make tea."

"Call me Louisa, please. Give me a needle and show me what to do. I can help until Kit fetches my trunk from town. Then I must alter my dresses. Mr. Tole disapproves of a married lady showing so much...throat." Louisa looked at every face around the quilt and smiled a painful, uncertain smile. "Mr. Tole is wonderful. He's buying calico, so I won't be in black all summer, which he says is inappropriate." She turned to Faith. "You know what styles Mr. Tole likes. Would you help me cut out my dresses?"

Faith stammered, tongue-tied, so Rachel filled the gap. "We'll all help, once the quilt's done."

"And please tell me what are Mr. Tole's favorite dishes," she whispered. "I mentioned perhaps we could carry tinned oysters to make an oyster pie as a change from salt pork. But Mr. Tole said he dislikes oysters."

"The boys hate them," Faith said.

"You must tell me. I shouldn't want to upset Mr. Tole in the slightest. Not when he's so good to me."

Rachel smiled at Faith, gestured for her to sit on the

bench beside her. "We'll not turn *ourselves* into such crawling slaves," she whispered.

The chill of early morning held the mosquitoes at bay. Will paced a wide circle around the wagons so he did not run into one in the dark. Canvas tops would have reflected the starlight, made them more visible, but Hull had ordered all the wagon covers removed for the drive to the ferry. Too many low-hanging branches in the thickets of the bottomland. And the tops would catch the wind like sails once the wagons were on the boat.

Will stood at the dark landing, twisting his hands behind his back. *Parrott's is a mistake, and I'm to blame.* The ferry in St. Joe carried placid oxen across, but Parrott insisted that the stock swim the river. A quarter mile of fast-moving water! If any mules or oxen drowned, their owners would accuse him of poor judgment.

A definite lighter tone in the eastern sky. A glowing spark caught his eye. Rachel squatted beside a rusty sheet-iron stove that had been abandoned last year.

"Up early," he said. She blew on the coals, encouraging the flame, and did not answer. He pulled his rifle from beside his bedroll. The wagon moved above him as Rachel opened the provision box. She put a tin cup on the stove. Godfroy's medicine, morning and evening.

Will checked the rifle load, dug in his pocket for a cap and walked to the river. A light haze obscured the far bank. He fired into the fog, the shot echoing as a flat clap in the dampness. Godfroy rolled out from under the wagon and pulled himself upright by hanging on to the wheel.

"How are you doing?" Sampson asked, emerging from a finger of haze that drifted through the camp.

"Fine," Will lied. He had slept very little, worrying about the cattle.

"Anders is arguing with Parrott again, and Parrott's given in so far as horses. He'll let the horses aboard if we blindfold them and each has a man hanging on the bridle. But not mules and oxen. Says he's seen too many accidents caused by stock aboard a ferry."

"This is the best place to swim them?" Will asked, repeating a question he had asked last night.

"Absolutely. I want you and Godfroy over first, for you have the most horses. The boys go along to hold them, and they'll be on the shore to meet the oxen." Will nodded. "Soon as possible. We want the animals in the water before sunup. Reflections on the water drive them crazy."

Rachel handed him a cold biscuit warmed with a thick slice of bacon hot from the stove. She had not bothered with a skillet. He forced it down, waved away a cup of coffee.

"Get stuff in the wagon. We've got to start," he said.

Rachel winked, diverting him from the problem at hand. "I'll cross with Faith," she said. "She and Louisa have promised to help me cut out my feathered star."

"Your what?"

"The pieces for my feathered star patchwork." She might as well be talking Greek, but he did not have time to quiz her, because Parrott's slaves herded the horses to the landing. Will caught his three, Godfroy's two and Rachel's spotted mare. Had Sampson remembered to tell the boys they'd be crossing with him? In answer to his thought, Tole's three eldest and the three MacIntyre boys walked out of the haze. Kit Tole and Josh MacIntyre were both seventeen, almost men, Josh skinny and gangly, Kit already showing the broad shoulders of a blacksmith.

"Howdy," Kit said. The others laughed uneasily, and like boys everywhere poked and tussled to cover their nervousness.

"Enough of that," Will said sternly. "As soon as God-froy's settled in the wagon we shove it aboard." Godfroy had not climbed into the wagon, but stood rooted, staring at Rachel. With a thoughtful look on his face, he gave a slight nod and hoisted himself over the tailgate.

"Kit, you lift the tongue," Will ordered. The boys would settle down if he put their twitching muscles to work.

Godfroy clung to the side of the wagon box, leaned over and coughed. He grasped the front of his hunting shirt, looked pitifully at Will and coughed, again and again.

"Father?" Rachel asked. "Are you sure you feel like doing this?"

Cough, cough. "Spoonful…honey," Godfroy gasped.

"Essence of lemon," Rachel cried. "Whoa!" Before the boys stopped she lowered the tailgate and lifted the planks to uncover a storage compartment.

Cough, cough, cough. Rachel poured the mixture of honey and lemon into a spoon, put it into her father's mouth at the first gap in his spasms.

"Now a drink of water, slowly. Lie down." She climbed into the wagon. She'd hemmed her dress three or four inches above the ground, what the women called a wash dress. The older boys stared at her ankles, and the hint of calf exposed when she went over the tailgate. The sight reminded Will of her hips and thighs. She knelt beside God-froy.

"Good girl," Godfroy whispered.

"I'd better stay with you," she said. "Mr. Sampson, would you tell Faith and Mrs. Tole that I must stay with Father?" She held Godfroy's head in her lap while the boys shoved the wagon onto the ferry, the wheels rolling easily into the grooves on the deck. Rachel leaned over the side of the wagon to watch the operation. Will observed God-froy. No more coughing, and a rather smug expression on his face. The big faker! For as long as it took the ferry to bring over the second wagon, he and Rachel were together.

"Tie your bandannas over the horses' eyes," Will said to the boys. "Then lead them on board, one at a time. Keep two hands on the bridle until we're across."

"Go!" yelled Parrott when the horses were aboard. He shoved with a pole and the flatboat floated in the shallows. A tall black man scampered to the bow, his eyes on the complicated arrangement of ropes. The ferry ran on a cable stretched from shore to shore, with no power except the river itself. Under the force of the spring flood the boat soon bounded over the swells. An eighth of a mile, halfway across. Will kept a watchful eye on the six horses.

"I feel like I'm at sea," Rachel said.

"Wait until we cross the Platte," Godfroy said. "I've seen it more than two miles wide. But not this deep."

"You sound better, Father," Rachel said, stroking his forehead. Will felt a soft touch, like a spider's web, on his own forehead, realized he was looking at Rachel, not the horses and the boys. Another reason he and Rachel must resist being thrown together. The next time he caught Rachel's eye he winked, and nodded at Godfroy. Her eyes flew open, she glared at her father, dumped his head off her lap and scrambled to the tailgate.

"You got over your coughing spell awfully fast."

"It's that good medicine Granny MacIntyre helped you fix," Godfroy said. "Can't use that again," he muttered in Will's direction.

# Chapter Thirteen

The ferry slowed under the timbered bluffs of the western shore. The ferryman snagged a fixed rope, heaved and the boat grounded in the shallows. Will leaped to the sand.

"Take the horses to the foot of the bluff," he said. The boys began chattering, their nervous silence ended the moment they stepped onto solid ground. "You two—" he pointed to the smallest "—you stay with the horses. The rest come back here to roll the wagon off."

The opposite bank of the river crawled with activity, rather like a beehive. The yells of the men, punctuated with the crack of whips, carried across the silent morning water. Another wagon had been rolled into position.

"Heave off," the ferryman said. Will tossed the rope and shoved the boat into the depths, wetting his boots as he did so. By squinting his eyes against the morning brightness he could see cattle wading into the water, sinking from sight, then dark, horned heads pockmarking the golden sheen of the river. The horses must be got out of the way. Will yelled at his crew, only to find that Kit had anticipated him, and the horses were already trotting up the road.

"Ho!" Godfroy yelled. He was standing in the wagon, pointing across the river. He ducked under the bows and

dropped off the tailgate, still pointing. The ferry bucked the
midstream waves almost broadside. The bow lifted so Will
saw the full length of the deck. He ran to the water's edge,
and from this new vantage saw, beyond the boat, a huge
snag tangled in the cable.

"No more wagons across until they clear that," Godfroy
said.

Will had no time to watch the plight of the ferry. The
strongest steers stood in the shallows, their shoulders
streaming brown water, and the bulk of the oxen had passed
the main channel of the river.

"Drive them up," he called to the boys, who waded into
the shallows with willow switches. Six mules clustered on
a sandbar.

"Where's Anders's mules?" Godfroy asked. "Those belong to Ludlow."

"Maybe his mule skinners will swim them in a string,"
Will suggested, but Godfroy shook his head.

"Damn party's falling apart before we even cross the
river," Godfroy said. He slumped onto the damp sand.
"God! but I wish this weakness would pass. I should be in
the saddle, up there. Who's watching the horses?"

"I'll go," Will said. "I'll have the boys round up two
yoke of oxen to pull this wagon to the top. You can sit in
it and keep an eye on the herd, and order the boys about."
He waited for Godfroy's objection, but he agreed by slowly
hoisting himself into the wagon.

From the top of the bluff Will saw a skiff setting out
from the other side. Using his pocket telescope, he could
see three men in the rowboat. Will didn't envy them their
job, cutting the snag away from the cable. Dangerous business. But not his business. He had enough to do here, man-
aging horses, oxen and mules. He found a south-facing
slope, where the sun had encouraged the grass. Only a

small patch—the stock would crop it down in a few hours and start wandering, looking for more. But then, that's why the feed wagons... *The feed's on the other side!*

Until Parrott had cleared the snag, he and the boys must circle the herd, so the oxen did not wander away from the river. Until noon, he figured. Kit stood before him, twisting his hat in his hands.

"The cable's parted."

"Parted? The rope strung from shore to shore?"

"Yes." Time reared before him, a barrier, an enemy. Replacing the cable would take hours! Perhaps days. Kit understood the problem, for his whole face frowned.

"I think—" if he twisted his hat more the braided straw would rip apart "—I think one of the fellows chopping at the roots went downriver with the snag." He shook his head, either denying what he had seen or commenting on the possibility of the man's survival.

"You're sure?" Will asked "My God! The chances of living on a tumbling snag...not good. Are you sure?"

"No," Kit said. "But I think...he yelled when it went." Kit pressed his hand against his mouth so tightly his fingers made white streaks on the brown of his cheeks. He moved it just enough to talk. "But that's the sort of thing they'd send Pa out to do!" he cried.

"No," Will said. "No. Parrott would send one of his men." Not a man with a wife and six children. "They'd send one of the ferrymen," Will said firmly, to convince himself as much as Kit. "Someone who knows the channels of the river, how to get out in case of accident."

"It's something Pa would do," Kit muttered.

Get his mind on his job. "Are those mules rested enough to climb up the bluff?"

"They're just coming," Kit said miserably. "Only six made it across. We looked downstream, but didn't see the other four. Musta gone down in the middle. Ludlow'll be mad as hell.''

"Preachers don't get mad as hell," Will said.

Kit twitched a half smile. "You don't know him. It was when we waded out to get the mules that Josh saw what happened in the river, and I looked up...."

"Get the younger boys riding around the stock, to keep them from spreading out for miles. We don't have saddles, except for mine and Godfroy's."

"No matter. We're all accustomed to bareback rides out in the pastures."

Another fleeting smile. Will imagined the fury of Pikeston farmers when they found their horses, put to pasture for a day of rest, as winded as if they had worked.

"If it's Pa—"

"Stop looking for trouble," Will snapped. "You don't know who was on that snag."

Kit nodded, but Will heard the boy's teeth chatter. Will hiked back down to the river. The ragged end of the ferry cable heaved at his feet. What to do?

*First thing you do when you finally decide you're lost, you sit down and think.* Zack, the caretaker at the country house, had so advised him. Will sat down on a flood-bent sapling and stared across the river. The ferryboat had drifted to the opposite bank, a quarter mile downstream from the landing. Already men clambered over it, and judging from their movements, they were stretching ropes and pushing with poles. Would they be performing such normal tasks if a member of the party had drowned?

If the stock were on the other side, they could pull to the St. Joe ferry. Should he swim the animals back across the river? No. Oxen who had twice breasted the Missouri would be in no condition to bear yokes. He would wait until Sampson or Hull rowed across in the skiff and gave him orders. Or until Parrott had the ferry in operation.

Six boys, Rachel and a man recovering from fever. Six horses, six mules and more than a hundred oxen. Where the hell were Anders's mules?

*Stop asking questions you can't answer. You're as bad as Kit, jumping to conclusions.*

His job was to protect the stock and keep them near the river. That meant setting up watches through the night. The two older boys could be trusted with weapons. Food. He would speak to Rachel about dinner. The boys must be ravenous after the sketchy breakfast they had snatched at dawn. Plenty of food in the wagon.

Send a boy—no, they must go everywhere in pairs—to scout out a spring or creek with clear water, so Rachel could make a decent pot of coffee. Take no chances, for white renegades lurked here, beyond the jurisdiction of the Missouri sheriffs. Indians this close to the border posed no threat unless a wandering band of Pawnees... The news of a lightly guarded herd would travel fast up and down the river. Godfroy would know better about the Indians. Will trudged up the road.

Rachel had lowered the tailgate of the wagon as a flat workplace. The sun reflected from the meat cleaver. Godfroy lay beneath the wagon to escape the midday heat.

"Where are the boys?" Will asked Rachel.

"Kit found a little stream of good water and he sent one of his brothers off with the water buckets."

"Fine," he said, "but two should go. As soon as they come back I'll have them put up the wagon cover. Godfroy needs a comfortable, shady place."

"We'll do it now," she said, dropping the cleaver.

"But you're starting dinner."

"I can't boil the ham without water. And I don't need to make bread. I baked four dozen biscuits yesterday."

The pristine canvas lay at the front of the wagon box, fan folded, ready to pull over the bows. Rachel climbed up the spokes of the front wheel and stretched her arms.

"I'm not tall enough," she said.

"We'll have to get inside." Rachel pushed the ham aside and scrambled into the wagon.

"You pull and I'll lift from underneath," she said. The canvas, stiff with oil and paint, slid six inches.

"We've got to lift and pull at the same time," Will said. "I'll count to three. One, two, three." He tugged, the cover unfolded in a rush, and he fell backward, slamming his neck into the bow behind him. The canvas thrashed about and Rachel's head poked out.

"Are you all right?" He rubbed the back of his neck and nodded, grasped the edge of the cover.

"Again, one, two—"

"Wait until I get myself set," Rachel said. The top rustled as she lifted the sagging fabric. "Now."

"One, two, three!" He controlled his strength better this time, and the cover slid easily across two bows. Rachel backed toward him, came into view—not her head, but her rump. Since she was bent over, her skirt fell forward, exposing the shape of her hips.

"Count," she ordered. "It's hot under here."

"One, two, three," he muttered. Amazingly, the canvas unfolded another three feet, although his arms seemed to have no strength at all. He stepped back, putting space between them, but he had only a few seconds of respite. She backed from under the cover.

"One, two, three," she said, and he obeyed her command. One more heave and she could get out of the wagon, and he would finish by himself. Over the blaze of white he spotted a boy, staggering along with two overflowing buckets.

Rachel backed from under the canvas, her feet searching for secure footing on the loose planks of the false floor. Her full weight came down on the very end of a plank, it tilted and she toppled backward. Will tried to dodge, but she carried him down, her hips securely molded against him. Against his firm arousal. She twisted off his legs. He saw her face, very red and angry. She clutched at the side of the wagon bed and hauled herself past him, to the tailgate and safety.

"No! Never!" she whispered.

"Of course not! Why should you even—" One of her flailing boots had slammed against his tender flesh. He took two deep breaths, and resisted grabbing his crotch.

"The water's coming. We'd better finish this job," he said through clenched teeth.

"You get underneath," she said. Will crawled under the cover, glad to be out of sight of the boy.

"One, two, three," she said, without the slightest quaver in her voice. She did not pull with his strength.

"Rachel, I got the water here," the boy said.

"We'll be done in a minute or two," Will said from beneath the canvas. "One, two—"

"I could do that, and Rachel could get back to cooking."

"That's a fine idea," Rachel said. She abandoned him with his arms high. Will peeked out, saw her settle her skirt, brush her hair back with her hands. The boy climbed into the wagon. Beads of sweat ran down his face, digging furrows through the dirt. Will crawled out from under the wagon cover. Give the lad a moment's rest.

"Indians!" the boy screamed. He flung himself under the canvas. "They got one of the mules!"

Rachel calmly stepped in front of her father.

"Get my rifle," Godfroy ordered, rolling out from under the wagon. Rachel shielded him with her skirts.

The mule staggered for an instant as it made the final leap to the top of the bluff. The man—Will saw only one, but a whole band might be lurking in the timber—clung to the animal's mane. Both mule and man were russet colored.

"He's no Indian," Will said. "He's wearing shirt and trousers."

"Indians can get regular clothes" came a muffled protest from under the canvas.

The man staggered toward the wagon. He lifted an arm weakly, an appeal for help, fell to his knees and from the movement of his shoulders, Will guessed he was retching. "No, Rachel!" Godfroy yelled. She hoisted her skirts and took off running, right toward the man. A trap! Will threw himself out of the wagon. A white renegade distracting them from a raid on the stock. Or, terrifying thought, looking for a woman or child to hold for ransom. Rachel had her arm about the man, helping him to his feet.

"It's Mr. Brant-Reid," she called.

The mud that covered the mule and Brant-Reid now dyed Rachel's dress. Will got his hand beneath Brant-Reid's arm, and with Rachel on the other side, they staggered to the fire. Brant-Reid sank to the ground, retching again.

"Salt water," Godfroy said. "Strong salt water to bring up the river filth."

"You were on the snag?" Will asked. Brant-Reid nodded.

"Not Pa?" cried the boy. He crawled from beneath the sagging wagon cover. "Not Pa!" He jumped down, his feet churning the moment they hit the ground. "I'll go tell Kit." He grinned through the tracery on his face, some now caused by tears. "Not Pa!"

Will watched the boy bound over the tangled hillocks,

all exhaustion gone. He envied him. Once Miss Petitpont had taken him aside and explained his father had been on board a steamboat that had exploded. He had dutifully prayed, but felt nothing. Until a day later, when they found out his father had been on another boat. To this day Will flushed with shame, remembering his glum feelings when he learned his father had survived.

What would it be like to be one of Tole's kids, to gallop across the prairie shrieking, "Not Pa!"?

Brant-Reid stripped and sat down in a meander of the creek. He dipped his head under, splashed about, and a dirty plume spread downstream. "I'd just climbed onto the snag when the whole thing gave way."

"You're lucky to be alive," Will said.

"Wouldn't be, except an eddy caught the snag about a mile downstream and sent it toward the shore. I took off my boots and jumped clear. Bespoken boots, at the bottom of the Missouri," he growled. "Shouldn't complain, though. That bedraggled mule was waiting on the gravel bar."

"Why were you on the snag? Why not one of the ferrymen?"

"Parrott doesn't own the men who work for him. He hires them, and if one died, he'd have to pay the owner his value." Brant-Reid crawled out of the creek. He waved away the breeches and shirt Will held out to him. "Just give me a blanket until Sir Anders arrives."

"Sir Anders? But he'll not be here until the ferry—"

"After you left, Sir Anders and Mr. Parrott exchanged angry words about mules on the ferry. Sir Anders left, quite furious, taking our men and mules to St. Joe for passage on *that* ferry. He'll join us here."

"So that's why none of your mules came with the stock?"

"Precisely."

"But why didn't you go with Anders?"

"It seemed ungracious, after we had agreed not to abandon the wagons. Sir Anders gave me permission to remain, that I might help load the wagons on the ferry."

Will held out the clothes. "Put them on. Sir Anders has four or five miles to St. Joe. Wagons will be lined up at the ferry, and he'll have to wait his turn."

"Sir Anders will pay a premium for immediate service."

"You don't understand," Will began, then decided this was not the time to explain that a line-cutter, no matter how aristocratic, might be shot. "He'll have to ride west to avoid the gullies along the river, altogether as much as fifteen or twenty miles."

Brant-Reid accepted the cheap cotton shirt and the baggy trousers without comment. Strange, Will thought, that a man with gumption enough to climb out on a snag should team up with Anders and bow to his orders.

"Why are you traveling with Anders?"

Brant-Reid did not look up from buttoning the breeches. "Sir Anders is very wealthy. My father died three years ago, in straitened circumstances. My older brother, who inherited the title, married an heiress of moderate fortune. I am engaged to Sir Anders's sister."

And a moderate dowry, Will thought to himself, sneering at a man who married for money. Then he recalled that he had considered marrying Rachel for her heritage. Freedom either way.

By the time they got back to the wagon and dinner, Rachel's cache of biscuits had disappeared and she was making flapjacks to fill the youthful stomachs. Only shreds of meat hung from the ham bone.

"I managed to save you a bit of ham in the wagon," she said, glancing at the boys with disbelief. "How does Faith do it?"

Rachel spread a blanket under the trees that fringed the creek, unpacked the calico scraps she had chosen for her feathered star. She brushed damp curls from the back of her neck, took off her hat and wished for a cooling breeze. No, a breeze would play havoc with the scraps she laid out. A feathered star, she saw now, was not a good choice for patchwork while traveling. So many tiny triangles to cut and keep track of. She sorted the cardboard patterns she had made on the St. Louis steamer. Meggie had warned her to make something simple. But she had committed herself.

First cut out the elongated arrowheads that formed the central star burst. Her throat contracted and her fingers numbed as she lifted the template. She laid the cardboard on the fabric, carefully centering the rose and blue flowers. A horrid shape, reminding her too vividly of a night she wanted to forget.

*They are simply diamonds,* she told herself, *with one extended point.* Sharp and wounding. Will had wounded her, and today was her first day free of pain. Despite his protests, despite saying they would live together as brother and sister, he wanted to do it again. When she fell against him, sat on him, his sex moved. Through the barriers of skirt and petticoats he bulged against her, and something deep in her had responded. Faint throbs of pain. She hurt just *thinking* what he wanted to do.

She shoved the stiff template under the pile of fabric so she would not see it, and picked up a small triangle. Start with that, since she needed nearly a hundred. Too bad she was not with Faith and Louisa, and Meggie and Tildy, who would help her. She shot an irritated look in her father's direction, remembering the faked cough. But what if she hadn't come? Will was so busy with the stock, he would not remember her father's medicine. And the boys would have torn the wagon apart looking for something to eat.

Rachel traced around the cardboard with a pencil, then cut out the triangle, leaving enough fabric for a seam. She laid the tiny piece in front of her. A beginning. Perhaps she would have half the triangles cut before she must stop to fix supper. The rustle of leaves stopped her pencil halfway.

"May I sit with you, Rachel?"

"Yes." She couldn't tell him to go away. Mr. Brant-Reid and her father napped beneath the wagon, and the boys were out of sight, watching the cattle. She shoved the fabric aside to make room on the blanket, exposed the threatening arrowhead, snatched it up and thrust it deeper in the pile.

"I'm sorry, Rachel," he said. He sat down, cross-legged, facing her. Only her work separated them, a fragile defense. She picked up her scissors.

"For what?" He must make a better apology than that. Just because they shared a wagon and she cooked his meals did not mean she would tolerate crude behavior.

"I'm sorry how things turned out, that we're alone here...you're alone, without your friends."

"It's not your fault the cable broke. You don't need to apologize for *that!*"

"I'm sorry I upset you." Better, but not the details she expected. "A man who respects a woman should have greater control over himself," he finally said.

She bent to her work. "You insulted me, Mr. Hunter. Is that how you respect women?"

"Assaulted you?" he asked. "I was standing quite still, and *you* launched yourself—"

"I did not launch myself! How dare you?" The pencil skittered off course. "I said *insult*. You in-sult-ed me."

"Your foot slipped. It was an unfortunate accident."

"So it's my fault," she said. She held the template firmly against her knee and started the pencil line again.

"What do you want me to say?" he asked helplessly.

"You should apologize to me, for letting carnal desire rule your better nature. Assure me it won't happen again."

"In plain English?"

"What better—" The mischief in his eyes startled her, she was so accustomed to his caution. Had the change come all at once, or had she ignored a gradual alteration?

"I can't guarantee I won't grow hot and swollen for you later today, next week, on the Platte, crossing the Rockies. Whenever it happens, if I think you've noticed, I'll apologize. I'm sorry. If over the fire tonight I hand you a tin cup, and our fingers meet—"

"Shut up!" She picked up the calico and the pattern, searched for the pencil.

"The pencil rolled beneath your...skirt," he said, and the way he said "skirt" she knew he meant "leg," and the idea that his fingers had been there, had touched her more intimately... She almost cried with mortification. She would not give him the satisfaction. She bit her tongue, hard.

"Where have you been?" she asked sharply.

"I walked to the top of the hill to look for Anders. I don't want him riding past the camp."

"He can't miss us. He'll cross this road."

"Perhaps I'm insulting a gentleman," he said apologetically, "but Sir Anders might ride across a track as wide as the National Road, and ignore it because it did not resemble the Great North Road out of London."

Rachel giggled, and the pencil line jogged to the edge of the calico.

"Here, let me do that," Will said. "It'll go faster with two of us. I'll draw the lines, and you cut out the pieces." She shifted the template and pencil so he could take them without any danger of their fingers touching.

"The little triangles, I need forty-eight of the flowered calico and forty-eight of muslin. No, don't draw them so close together. Leave room for a seam." He slid the template across the calico, his fingers exerting just the pressure necessary for the precise movement. "There! That much." The insides of her thighs quivered with the memory of his touch, and the throbbing pain began.

"What are you making?" he asked.

"A feathered star. A woman on the St. Louis steamboat had the pattern and she helped me copy it."

He marked half a dozen triangles in silence. "I hope Anders and his men get here before dark. The boys shouldn't be out all night, guarding the stock."

A muscle twitched nervously on his jaw. She should have sympathy for Will, left in charge of all the stock, with only six boys to help. Caring for a sick man, and another who held his stomach in agony after two bites of ham.

"Do you have more of this?" he asked, holding out the scrap of flowered calico, covered with penciled triangles. She thrust her hand in the pile; her fingers froze when they touched the threatening bit of cardboard. Not at all like his organ, soft and hard at the same time, and warmly moist.

"What's wrong, Rachel? Has a snake crawled in there?"

"It's all right," she said hastily. "I just remembered, I'd best start the bread for dinner." He grabbed her wrist.

"Truce, Rachel?"

She nodded. "Truce."

"We're to be brother and sister. That means we'll be honest with one another," he said.

"Will, does a man, after he's been with a woman, want to do it again, even when it was so horrible—"

"He wants to do it again."

"Faith and I have pledged, when we get to California we're starting a school for the children of emigrants. We'll both stay single. Maiden ladies." *Maiden. Faith, perhaps, but not me.*

## Chapter Fourteen

The beans were not quite done, but the boys wolfed them down without complaint. Mr. Brant-Reid nibbled a crust, his pale face turned slightly green and he gave up the effort. Will slanted his hat to shade his eyes against the rays of the sinking sun. The long shadows emphasized the lines of fatigue on his face. Rachel lined up tin cups.

"Coffee, Mr. Brant-Reid?" she asked.

"Call me Reid," he said as he took the cup. "My name sounds silly out here."

"Not so silly as *Sir* Anders," she said.

"How about Lord Brittlebane?" he asked.

Rachel laughed. "It sounds like brown sugar candy." He smiled. "You're teasing me," she protested.

"Not at all. That's my brother's title."

"I'm sorry I laughed," she said.

"I'd not thought of it before, but it does sound like brown sugar candy. Fortunately, my brother has a son, so there's no danger I'll become Lord Brown-Sugar Candy."

He got to his feet without help. By morning he would have his strength back, Rachel decided. He joined Will and the boys. "Give me my orders," he said.

"Nothing. Good grief, Brant-Reid! You nearly drowned."

"I did not 'nearly drown.' I simply swallowed a gallon or two of the Missouri. And call me Reid. Brant was my mother's maiden name, and my father thought if he added it to his own, he'd receive a larger inheritance. In vain. The old man left everything to found an orphan's home."

Will stared to the west. "You can keep the fire going all night, so Anders—"

"That's my job," her father said. "I can't collect the wood. Send the boys for a heap before it's dark."

"I insist upon doing my part," Reid said.

"Then trot down to the river and see how the repair work's going." Reid left, his feet dragging a trifle. Upon first meeting, Rachel had labeled him a milksop. Now she found herself admiring his determination.

"Get the wood," Will said to the boys. "Then circle out a mile and start the cattle heading in this direction. Not too fast. Let them snatch every blade of grass they can. But by dark I want them near the river. We'll take turns sleeping." They scattered into the timber.

Rachel dried the dishes and put them away. She walked away from the fire to shake out the flour sack that served as her dish towel. A man—a white man, she saw instantly, for he was totally naked—walked along the ridge. She backed to the wagon, crying out in alarm, wanting to turn her head, but unable to take her eyes off him.

"Good evening, Miss Godfroy." He ducked his head in what might be considered a bow, if he'd had clothes on.

"Anders!" her father yelled. He shrugged out of his coat and threw it at the man. "Cover yourself!"

Anders crossed his hands to conceal himself, approached the coat sideways and knotted the sleeves behind his back, like an apron. He straightened up, head erect.

"Indians," he said. "And the cowards I hired to accompany me ran off, leaving me to defend my belongings."

"Not very well, I see," her father said.

"They held me down, and…and the squaws stripped me. I'll kill the old hag who egged them on. One of the young ones was not half-bad looking, but with my mules being herded away, I had no beads or trinkets to tempt her."

"Sir Anders!" Wood clattered from Reid's arms. "What are you…in this state?"

"What does it look like?" Anders snapped. He repeated his complaints against mule skinners and Indians. "They came at us like cowards, begging, but I saw through their ruse. They intended to take us prisoners and torture—"

"Indians don't usually ride out to fight with their women along," her father said.

Sir Anders sneered. "Fortunately, I had my rifle at the ready, across my saddle, and drew a bead—"

"They didn't show you papers?"

Sir Anders's hauteur dropped for an instant. "Perhaps," he snapped. "One or two of the savages may have offered dirty papers, but they soon pulled back when the young one toppled off his scrawny horse."

"Toppled off?" Rachel asked. If he had killed an Indian… Had they followed him? The boys! The cattle!

"With my ball in his shoulder. It would have been lodged in his heart, but that cowardly Hooper tugged at my arm. And then took to his heels with the bloody mule drivers."

"Rachel, go find Will and the boys. Get them up here," her father said. "Reid, you washed those rags of yours. Give them to Anders so I can have my coat back."

Rachel ran into the trees, still holding the dish towel. "Will!" she called as she passed into the twilight. "Will, Kit, Josh!" She nearly ran into a boy leaning against a tree, supporting a heap of wood almost as big as himself. "Where's Will?" He jerked a thumb over his shoulder.

She plunged toward a stream glowing with a reflection of the sky. A man leaped across. "Will! Anders is here, with nothing, not even his clothes, because Indians took everything. Father's upset. They had some kind of papers, and Anders shot one of them."

"Papers?" He paused, a long stick halfway to the pile in his arms. The way he spoke sent shivers down her spine.

"What does it mean?"

"It means the band he met, Sac and Fox, or Iowa, or Pottawatomi, had a note from the government agent, asking travelers to give them money. To pay for the wood and grass we use while we pass through their country."

"Father said all the boys should come to camp."

"Can you carry this wood?" he asked. She nodded, and he piled the sticks onto her outstretched arms. "Get to camp," he ordered. "I'll round up the boys."

Anders, clad in mud-stained breeches and shirt, slumped near the fire, not saying a word. Her father must have lectured him on his muddleheaded behavior. Reid was scouring the dirty bean pot with a leafy branch and sand. Three boys had already reached the fire, and Rachel heard the footsteps of another right behind her. Two more to come. And Will. If anything happened to Will because of Anders's bravado, she would kill the braggart. The Indian women had stripped off his clothes. She'd take off his skin!

She scanned the line of timber, saw him step from the cover of the trees. He gestured for her to follow him to the wagon. He thrust a cold pistol into her hands.

"Remember what I told you? You have a single shot. Threaten. Never let them taunt you into firing." She nodded. "Put it through your apron strings, at the back," Will said. He turned. "Godfroy, tell us what to do."

"Reid, what's going on over the river?" her father asked.

"I cannot see that a crisis should throw good manners into abeyance," Sir Anders said. A glare from every eye shut him up.

"They've hitched oxen to the ferry and are hauling it back to the landing. I didn't see anything that suggested they're restringing the cable. No men in the skiff."

"How far downriver did you meet these Indians?" Anders shook his head, still staring at the ground.

"You don't know?" her father asked more insistently.

"I walked miles and miles," he whined. He lifted his legs to show his feet, bloody and bruised.

"How far off are the cattle?" Will asked.

"A mile. A few maybe a mile and a half," Kit said.

"Go out together," her father said. "Don't separate. Get the biggest, closest bunch of steers and drive them this way. The rest will tag along when they see others moving."

"I'll go," Reid said.

"No, Rachel and Godfroy shouldn't be left alone," Will said. "I'll leave my rifle, and Godfroy has his—"

"I'll take care of the woman," Anders said, wincing as he pulled himself to his feet. "Mr. Brant-Reid—" he stressed the two syllables of the name "—can help with the cattle." He reached for the rifle, but Will snatched it away.

*"You'll take care of the woman?"* Will mocked. "If he so much as steps in your direction, Rachel, shoot him." He shoved Anders to the ground. "If those Indians turn up you'll hide behind her skirts. Rachel's got more gumption in a finger than you've got in your whole flabby body."

"You're just like the savages!" Anders cried as Will left. "They would not listen! I tried to tell them who I was, but they…would…not…listen!"

Rachel experimented drawing the pistol from her apron strings, making sure Sir Anders saw her practice. She poured the cold dishwater into the bean pot and set herself to scouring, for want of something better to do. And she had to do something or she would pace back and forth, and her father would know she was frightened. She should put more beans to soak, and dried apples, as well. She had complained about cooking for Will and her father! If she had known that the first day over the river she'd have ten men to feed, she might have stayed at home.

"They can't be coming with the stock already," her father said, squinting into the growing darkness. A pair of horns loomed in the twilight, and behind them another. And a gale of boyish laughter, and Will's voice booming with relief.

"We forgot the milk cows came over with the steers," he yelled. "We ran into the whole herd, not a quarter mile out. The cows were hell-bent for the wagon because they're frantic to be milked, and the oxen are trailing behind!"

Milk cows! The men would expect her to milk! A woman's job, like cooking and laundry. Faith had spoken truly—any work men didn't want to do, they laid at the women's feet.

Kit swung off his hat. "Your cows, ma'am!" She put her hands on her hips.

"I've never milked a cow in my life! Simply because I wear skirts—"

"She was raised a lady," her father said. "Mrs. Ridley, Rachel's aunt, bought her milk and butter."

"Rachel does not milk cows," Will said flatly. "Who knows how?"

"That's woman's work," Kit said, his mouth drooping almost to his chin. "Faith took care of the cow."

"Not me!" Josh exploded.

"How many?" Reid asked wearily.

"Six, I believe," Will said. "You know how to milk?"

"My grandfather on my mother's side, he made his fortune with a dairy. Happiest days of my life—" he gazed at the sky and shook his head "—helping the sweet milkmaids. Do you have a bucket?"

Sweet milkmaids! *Helping them what?* Rachel leaned into the wagon for the bucket. Hay-filled lofts, short-skirted girls, the young master, women who dared not refuse him!

"I wish, Brant-Reid, you would not mention subjects of that vulgar nature," Sir Anders said. Rachel handed Reid the bucket, wondering when Sir Anders had started being concerned with vulgarity. "References to one's ancestors," he continued, "who were forced to work for a living detract from a gentleman's stature."

Will touched her shoulder. "American gentlemen," he whispered, "are not ashamed to work, but are too prone to load work on their wives."

"Thank you," she whispered.

Will handed pistols to Josh and Kit. "Don't shoot at anything! Fire in the air if you're sure someone's sneaking up on the stock, and Reid and I'll come running."

"What if the Indians surround us?" Josh asked.

"Call for help. Shooting a man's what started this."

"They threatened me," Anders said petulantly, but Will did not even look at him.

"Do you have a churn?" Reid held out a bucket.

"No. We didn't bring a cow, so I thought a churn useless weight." But she did have a covered can. "Shinny up a tree in the gully, and hang the milk out of reach of skunks and mice," she said, handing him the can.

Breakfast! Thicken the milk with flour and one or two of the eggs she had buried in the cornmeal. Add the stewed apples. No one would dare complain if she served apple pudding and flapjacks for breakfast!

"Rachel," Will asked, hat in hand, "how many blankets do we have?"

"I appreciate that deeply," Anders said. "The savages—"

"For the boys. They have no bedding and they'll get chilly away from the fire."

"Your bedroll, my bedroll, Father's bedroll."

"Nothing extra?"

"The weight, remember. There are a few gunnysacks. If I had my quilts along…but I left them in Faith's wagon."

He nodded. She watched from the corner of her eye as he separated the blankets of his bed. "You'll have to imitate puppies," he said. "Pile up to keep warm."

"I have my buffalo robe," her father said. "Anders and Reid can share my blanket."

"You need your blanket," Rachel objected, walking into the firelight. "If you get chilled, the fever might come back. They can have one of mine."

"No," Will said firmly. "You're the most important person in this party. Without a woman's influence, we'd start bickering and fists would fly. Then the cattle would wander off. Men alone are pitiful creatures. You keep all your blankets. I'll pitch the tent for Reid and Anders, so they can sleep out of the dew."

"What about you?"

He waved away the question. "I'm the night watch."

The boys clustered about the fire, toasting themselves on all sides before leaving. Will hauled the tent from the wagon and lifted the center pole from the brackets on the side of the box.

"Not too close to the fire," her father reminded him. "We don't want sparks setting it afire the first night."

"And not over a hill of creeping poppy," Josh muttered. He glanced at his friends around the fire.

"Creeping poppy?" Reid asked.

"Why, creeping poppy's just about the worst plant in America, trapping men who sleep too close," Kit said.

"Back in Indiana, met a man without a foot," Josh said darkly. "Camped on the river and the creeping poppy came round his legs and he cut off his own foot to escape."

"I've never heard of this plant," Anders said, "and I consulted all the botanical—"

"Don't suppose you have," Kit said. "River people don't like to mention it, for if Easterners and foreigners knew, they wouldn't come west."

Reid grinned suddenly. Josh elbowed him. Reid frowned.

"Hunter, you look close where you pitch that tent," he said.

"I've never—" Anders began.

"At least there's no balloon jimsonweed hereabouts," Kit said. "Grows nearer the Rocky Mountains, I hear."

Rachel tightened her cheek muscles as her father joined in. "Big problem to trappers. Grows along the beaver streams. Step on it, it inflates itself, knocks a man down. Worst is when a horse or man accidentally eats the stuff. It expands inside. Eat too much, they split open and die."

"Good God!" Anders cried. "How do we protect the mules?"

"Look real close where we pasture the animals. You see a jimsonweed with a flower like a pillow, step back."

Wood cracked, the sound of a stick breaking under the weight of a boot. Rachel lifted the wagon cover an inch. Will poked at the fire. He squatted beside the flames and extended his hands, then he dug in his pocket, took off his hat and tied a kerchief around his head, knotting it beneath his chin. He hugged himself.

The damp cold of the river bit her cheeks. She pulled the blanket around her shoulders, glad she had slept in her clothes. No need to chill her arms and legs getting dressed. Will turned about and warmed his back. He'd been up all night. How cold he must be!

She carefully arranged her blankets in their original position to retain the heat, and wrapped herself in a shawl. Will must have heard her feet hit the ground.

"Rachel?" Less than a whisper.

"You're cold," she said. He gestured to the hump of the buffalo robe and joined her at the wagon.

"Only a little cold," he whispered. He pointed east, and she saw the morning star low on the horizon. "And we've made it through the night."

"The hunter's star."

He shivered, hunched his shoulders and chafed his upper arms. "No hunting this morning."

"You're cold. Take off your boots and climb into my bed. The blankets are still warm."

"No need. In an hour or two—"

"You're cold deep down. What if you should take sick? Father and I depend on you. Get in!"

"Then you'll get cold."

"It's only an hour or two to sunup."

He leaned into the wagon and grabbed the ends of her blankets. "We'll sit together at the back of the wagon, under the canvas, out of the damp. We'll both be warm."

"I don't think that's a good idea," she said, stepping away from him.

"Rachel, I've got all my clothes on. In fact, two pairs of breeches. You have all your clothes on. What can happen sitting together?"

Chill already seeped through her shawl. She climbed into the wagon, shifted a bag of crackers and leaned against the provision box. As he tucked one end of the blanket about her, his hand touched her cheek.

"Your fingers are like ice!"

"Sorry." He hoisted himself into the wagon and wriggled about beside her, adjusting the other end of the blankets. Then he kicked off his boots and sat on his feet.

"Give me your hands," she said.

"I'm fine." He hunched his shoulders.

"Give me your hands," she ordered. "A sister would warm a brother's hands." Clasping his hands was like holding a bunch of icicles. She lifted the blanket and blew on them.

"Don't you have sisters?" she asked from the corner of her mouth.

"Four."

"Didn't you warm one another after you played in the snow?"

"My youngest sister's ten years older than I. We never played together."

"And Robert's your only brother?"

"Yes. I wish you could do that to my toes." His fingers flexed in her hands.

"Your toes are cold?"

"The coldest part of me. Maybe creeping poppy's snaked around my ankles and cut off the circulation." Rachel giggled under the blanket. "The Tole and MacIntyre boys are very imaginative in their practical jokes," he said.

"Everyone in town suffered from their antics! Josh and his brothers turned over privies on Hallowe'en, and they had snowball fights in the public square, so you risked a clunk on the head if you walked down the street. Kit once had half the men in town worrying that the Miami Indians had moved back to Indiana, because he made tomahawks at the forge and claimed he'd found them cached at the river. Do you think Sir Anders truly believed those silly stories about creeping poppy and balloon jimsonweed?"

"He looked over the ground pretty carefully before I put up the tent."

"If he's so gullible, the boys will make his life miserable!"

"I've got to move. My leg's going to sleep." Will shifted, his knee jabbed her thigh, and the impact turned to throbbing pain. Would this last all her life?

"I'll ask Granny if she collects balloon jimsonweed," she said, and laughed her breath on his hands again. "It could help someone who has lung trouble."

"Skinny women could drink the tea and look plump," Will said. His shoulder jiggled against hers and the movement slid into her stomach to join the other ache.

"I think I best start breakfast," she said.

"In the dark?"

"It's not dark. There's a bit of gray in the east." She edged out of the wagon so she did not disrupt the blankets, snatched her shawl, found him standing beside her. His hands grasped her waist, and he picked her up and seated her, startled, on the tailgate.

"Too early. Crawl in and rest," he said.

"I can't. The boys will come in chilled, crying for coffee. Did anyone remember to fetch water last night?"

"I doubt it. Too much excitement. I'll get some right now." He balanced on one foot to pull on a boot, leaned against her leg for an instant.

The bucket rattled when he picked it up. "Shh, not so loud," she said. "You'll wake Father." She knelt by the fire, studying the wood supply. The buffalo robe stirred.

"I'm awake," her father said. "You two make as much

noise as a pair of cats in heat.'' He sank back into the confines of the robe, only the back of his head showing.

Wood fell through Rachel's fingers, landed in the midst of the coals and sent sparks flying. She brushed frantically at two glowing on her skirt. Her father thought...he supposed...that she and Will had...!

# Chapter Fifteen

"No band of thieving natives will dissuade me from my summer's hunt," Sir Anders said. Will thought he looked a bit like an Indian himself, wrapped in a blanket. "Brant-Reid." He spoke to Reid's back, for the man curled against the flanks of a cow. "Saddle two of the horses. We will ride to St. Joseph and enlist Mr. Robidoux's help in replacing our outfit. And the two oldest lads, also mounted and armed, in case the savages are out and about—"

"No," Will said. "Parrott's already in his skiff stringing the new cable. By noon he'll have the ferry in operation. Borrow horses from Parrott to ride into town."

"I don't trust Parrott's ferry!" Anders said.

"We can't spare a single horse," Will said, turning away to show Anders the subject was closed. Without the Englishman the morning would be perfect. The sunrise turned the brown river to flame, and the warm breeze thawed every finger and toe. Will was astonished at how good he felt, considering he had not slept. Perhaps a glow from the warming hour with Rachel. More likely her apple pudding.

"You force me to act in my role as officer."

"Shut up, Anders," Godfroy said. "The boys can't be spared. They'll drive the teams to the river as the wagons arrive. There's no room on the flats for sixteen wagons. Horses? Rachel and Will got to ride out and find a new campsite, four or five miles down the trail." Will saw Rachel drop the pot she was washing, straighten up and square her shoulders.

"But I must have horses," Anders protested, "and the saddles. I am not a savage, to ride bareback."

"The cattle can't stay here another night," Will said. "They've eaten the grass to the roots."

"I do not take orders from a boy who constantly harps on the bloody cattle!" Anders cried.

"You do," Godfroy said softly. "Will Hunter's my agent."

"And those worthless lads, out there—" Anders pointed west, down the length of the ridge "—exhausting the horses with pointless riding about."

Horses? Will turned slowly. The boys had taken the horses to the river, in case Parrott needed them to haul the new cable. The weapons... He checked the position of the rifles and pistols.

"Rachel, move behind me," he said calmly, imitating Godfroy's demeanor. He squinted at the ridge. Eight horses, perhaps more, but the morning haze made it impossible to be sure.

Reid abandoned his milking and leaned over the cow. "Are those Indians?" he asked, betraying his excitement by kicking over the bucket of milk without noticing. Anders scrambled around the fire and crawled behind Godfroy, who was sitting cross-legged on his buffalo robe.

"Next they'll fly a white rag! Just like yesterday," Anders said in a tremulous voice. "The traitorous beasts."

"They came to you with a white flag?" Godfroy asked without shifting his eyes.

"Of course, to get near us, gain our trust and then take

our scalps. You can't expect aborigines to understand the honors attendant upon a white flag!''

"You are the dumbest bastard in the world!" Godfroy yelled. He sprang to his feet. Rachel clung to his arm. "Don't hover, girl. I'm getting well. A few nights sleeping on the ground's just what I needed. Now, you get behind Will, like he said."

Godfroy set out across the grass, his steps uneven but his arms firmly stretched to the side to show he carried no weapon. Two figures slid off their horses and walked toward him, one dressed in trousers and a shirt, the other in a shift of dark leather.

"Gray Woman," Rachel said.

Anders's eyes bugged out. "Don't give me to them! I shot the boy, so they'll torture me. For God's sake—"

"Shut up, Anders," Will snapped. Godfroy met the couple and the three approached the fire.

"Goddamn no die," Gray Woman said to Rachel, twisting her mouth in Godfroy's direction. Anders hid behind Reid and Rachel, babbling about old hags, but Gray Woman paid no attention. From this lack of recognition, Will knew Gray Woman's band had not attacked and robbed the Englishman.

"This is Jack Bordeau," Godfroy said, indicating the man who towered over Gray Woman. "Gray Woman's son."

"We've been looking for you," Bordeau said. "Parrott said only your wagon made it across."

"You speak English!" Anders cried.

"I went to school in St. Louis," Bordeau said dryly. "Yesterday morning my mother tried to find you, but you'd left the cabin." Gray Woman pulled a small packet from the front of her dress and handed it to Rachel.

"Bad medicine," she said.

"My mother returns your gift. It brings great unhappiness to our family." Before Rachel had the leather half open, gold cascaded through her fingers. Gray Woman sidled behind her son, her eyes on the fabric.

"Unhappiness?" Rachel asked.

"Each of her sons claimed it should be his, as reward for his bravery." Bordeau included himself by lowering his head in shame. "Her daughters fought with her daughters-in-law." A flush of embarrassment. "Her sister pined away in her lodge, crying because she had no star cloth. The longing will kill her unless the magic is taken away. My mother says it does not harm you."

"It belonged to my grandmother, my mother's mother," Rachel said. Bordeau translated her words. Gray Woman gestured toward the cloth of gold, and spoke at some length.

"My mother says your grandmother must have great skill, to weave the star threads and put such strong curses into a thing so fine. She rejoices to see it in your hands."

"Star threads?"

"Many winters ago, when I was a boy, a star with a tail appeared in the sky. For many nights. My mother says this cloth was woven from hairs pulled from that star's tail."

"I believe she's right," Godfroy said. "I saw the same star on the morning Rachel was born."

"The star cloth must stay with the Star Woman," Bordeau said. Gray Woman turned to leave.

"Wait," Godfroy said. He jerked a thumb at Anders. "Yesterday this man crossed at the St. Joe ferry. He claims Indians robbed him. All his animals, his weapons, even the clothes he wore. Have you heard of it?"

Bordeau's face lengthened. He nodded. "My mother was called at sundown to take care of the boy."

"Boy!" Rachel exclaimed. Gray Woman extended the

fingers of both hands, then only three. "Thirteen! Father, is that what she means? A boy of thirteen?"

Bordeau nodded. "The Iowas asked for payment for the grass and the game. The men talked long last night, why he acted as he did, and decided this white man could not understand the marks on the papers."

"What!" Anders cried.

"When he shot his gun, the boy's grandmother went crazy."

"I understand," Godfroy said. "They had every right to ask and to take revenge. Will the child live?"

"Nothing but a scratch." Bordeau raised a hand to his shoulder to show the location of the wound. "Already this morning he has gone hunting, to find a rabbit."

"So, if the boy's not badly hurt, could you ask this band to return Sir Anders's things? A gun, his trousers and shirts? A coat? The food, of course, they may keep."

Bordeau frowned. "I'll ask, but they're angry."

"One of the men who rode with Sir Anders struck the barrel of the gun so the boy was not killed. That man should be thanked, his clothes returned out of gratitude."

"I'll try."

"If your mother won't keep the gold cloth, we still owe her for helping Father," Rachel said.

"Flour," Godfroy whispered. "This is the hunger time of year. A whole sack. We'll send back to St. Joe for more."

Rachel crawled into the wagon and pushed the heavy sack to the tailgate. Will lifted it, carried it to Bordeau, who balanced it easily on his shoulder.

"I will speak to the Iowas, about the things they took from the English bastard and the one who struck the gun. The Iowas talk of going to the agent," Bordeau said. He gave Anders a sidelong glance.

Will waited, tapping his toe impatiently, until the man and woman had passed out of earshot. "If they go to the agent," he said to Godfroy, "Anders might be arrested."

"And we'll be stranded here waiting for a trial. We're all witnesses," Godfroy said.

Will grabbed Anders's shoulder before the man saw him coming. "Get out of here! Get down to the river and wait there for the ferry. Ask Robidoux to help you with new horses and supplies, fast as possible, before evening."

"I do not take orders—"

"Out of my sight," yelled Godfroy. "Before I order Kit to throw a rope over one of those trees and string you up!"

Anders stumbled on the hummocks of grass, then recovered enough to walk, bent over, the blanket dragging behind him. Godfroy's shoulders sagged and he rubbed his head as if trying to clear his mind. Will guided him to his buffalo robe, where he collapsed more than sat.

"Reid, can you keep Anders out of trouble for an hour or two?" Will asked. "Persuade him to go back on the ferry. He can warn everyone about the Indians, make himself seem a hero instead of a fool."

"He doesn't take orders easily," Reid said.

"Try. Anyway, you should be at the river when the skiff arrives, so they see you lived through your dunking."

"True. I'll go back with Anders and make sure my packs are loaded in a wagon."

"Your packs?"

"Yes." Reid smiled. "You see, my decision to stay with the wagons angered Sir Anders and he threw my packs off the mules. My things are still at Parrott's."

"Honor is rewarded," Will said. "Get down there with Anders, and take care of him."

"After I've milked the last cow."

"Go ahead," Rachel said. "I'll try, if you show me how.

While Will rides out to find a campground," she added. She spoke slowly and looked at Godfroy to be sure he understood.

"I can't do much but sit around, anyway," Godfroy said. "I'll milk the cow." Rachel glared at her father.

"You shouldn't, Father. Becoming tired—"

"Tells me I'm still alive," he snorted. "You carry my pistols, Rachel. I'll keep my rifle, in case of trouble."

"I'll get the horses," Will said.

Will held back his sigh until he dropped over the bluff. Godfroy would take every opportunity to throw them together.

"My new ma's in the skiff," Kit yelled before Will reached the flat. Louisa? Will shaded his eyes against the reflection. Sure enough, he could see a black sunbonnet in the bow, staring to the west, not moving.

"Why?" he asked no one in particular.

"Don't know, but she sits still and doesn't wave, so we judge she's helping the oarsman keep the proper heading."

The rope snaked behind the skiff, Parrott himself playing it out. Not the cable, Will saw, but a smaller rope that would draw the large one across.

"Ready there?" Parrott called.

"Ready," yelled the boys in a chorus. Several hands reached up to grab the rope. A few seconds and it tightened around the peeled log of the windlass.

"Wait until I'm there before you haul," Parrott said.

Kit helped his "new ma" over the pointed bow. "All those sacks come," she said, nodding her head toward the boat. "Good morning, Mr. Hunter. Mr. Tole's fretted all night about the boys. Nothing I could do would settle him. He must stay with the wagons, being the strongest man—" she lifted her head proudly "—who can't be spared when it comes to pushing them on the ferry. I'm to make sure the boys eat. And the women sent food along, so Rachel and I can spread dinner as the wagons arrive. We all agreed it wasn't fair to put the burden on Rachel alone. And of course Mr. Parrott needed an experienced person—"

"Experienced?"

She giggled. "Well, I never said before, for my having a child out of wedlock shamed my family. That's why they gave me the money to come west to find a husband. But now that we're crossing the Missouri, I suppose it'll do no harm for you to know my father's Mr. Merrill, who owns the ferry in Natchez, and I've made many a trip across the Mississippi."

"Where's Merri?" Will asked. He had never seen the baby more than a few feet from her mother's skirts.

"Oh, she's taken to her big sister something fierce, and hardly leaves Faith's side. She waved bye-bye to Mama so prettily. Now, I need help carrying this truck."

She turned away from the skiff, straightened in surprise. "Why, Mr. Brant-Reid! You *are* alive!"

Reid bowed. "Moderately so, madam."

"Mr. Parrott said you'd either crawl out on your own or drown, that it did no good to search. Reverend Ludlow held a short prayer meeting."

"I shall thank him."

"Sir Anders! I didn't recognize you! Perhaps you and Mr. Brant-Reid—"

"They're heading back in the skiff," Will said. "Anders had a bit of trouble and needs to get to St. Joe. Kit, send two of the boys to carry dinner to the wagon." He picked up a gunnysack, threw it over his shoulder, grabbed the bridle of his best horse and trudged up the bluff smiling. Rachel had to stay in camp. They had been rescued from a morning on horseback because Tole had fretted all night that his sons might be hungry.

\* \* \*

The supper fires burned low outside the circle of wagons. Will squatted on his heels beside Godfroy and Sampson, wishing he could get his diary. The difficulty was, Rachel and her friends clustered around the tailgate, covered with a colorful blizzard of scraps.

"You did fine today," Sampson said. "Good thing you rode out early and put our claim on this spot, since the Oregon wagons crossed this morning on the St. Joe ferry."

"Oregon wagons?" Will asked.

"Don't know what they expect their stock to live on, with no feed wagons along," Godfroy said.

"That's no skin off our nose," Captain Hull said, looking over his shoulder because he stood with his back to the men, warming his hind end. "I spoke to their captain. They thought, because we'd pulled out, that the grass was ready."

Godfroy grunted, as if to say that was their bad luck.

"Burdette's already on me about elections," Hull said. "He'd be over here right now if Anders had caught up. He told me Anders is a colonel, and accustomed to command."

"Tell Burdette and Marshall we have elections at the Big Blue River," Sampson said. "That's tradition. A hundred miles—it gives us a chance to test a man's mettle."

"I'll talk to him," Hull said, dropping his coattails.

"I'll mosey along," Sampson said.

"Sorry you and Rachel didn't get your ride this morning," Godfroy said once he and Will were alone.

"Rachel is content without my company," Will said.

"What? I thought from the squealing and wagon-box rocking this morning, the two of you'd made up your differences."

"Nothing happened, except I warmed my bones."

"Hmm." Godfroy frowned.

"She and Faith Tole plan to open a school in California."

"Old maid schoolmarms," Godfroy hissed. "And where's my grandchildren then? I'll figure a way to get her with you."

"I'd rather not, truly. Forcing Rachel's not the way—"

"Tomorrow morning I'll get up before dawn and ride—"

"You will not! You won't last half a day in the saddle."

"She'd fix breakfast for you, all alone."

"Later. When you're feeling better."

"Another night on the ground and I'll be fit to ride down a buffalo."

"Two days in the wagon, and we'll see how you feel."

"I don't take orders from no boy," Godfroy said, but he laughed afterward, probably because he had managed a hint of an English accent.

"Will." Kit squatted at the fire and pulled off his hat. "There's horses on the road, back toward the river."

"Maybe it's Anders and Reid."

"They'd have a string of mules, don't you think? And bring the servants with them? Shall we herd the cattle nearer the wagons?"

"Yes," Godfroy said, taking the decision out of Will's hands. "Always do the safest thing. When we're four hundred miles out there's no place to get new teams. Might as well pretend that's the case now, so no one gets bad habits. Go tell Sampson and Hull, Kit. Will, get on a horse and if it's Jack Bordeau's band, ride out a ways and parley. It's too late in the evening for company."

Will didn't bother with a saddle, simply flung his leg over his horse and rode away from the camp. One of the women standing at the wagon stared after him. He rode to the high point above the spring that furnished their water.

A mixture of clothing, a small woman with long gray hair in their midst. Will relaxed. Jack Bordeau separated from the group and rode toward him, leading a pack mule.

"The Iowas say the goddamn can have these things, because he's crazy and needs his spirit bundle." He handed the mule's rope to Will.

"Thank you. I hope the boy's mending." Bordeau nodded. "The Englishman, with his friends, are riding from St. Joe to join us. This time they'll give money for the trespass."

"Hope so," Bordeau said, grinning. He wheeled his horse, headed back to his family, now invisible against the dark eastern sky. Will waited until the soft thump of hooves faded, then tugged on the rope and rode to camp, a glittering circle of campfires. His route led him past the heaps of calico, now transferred to a blanket on the ground. The women looked up as he passed, but one head turned, two dark eyes followed his movements. A band around his chest, light and strong as spider...star thread! He could try to separate from her, but the thread had wound about him the first time they had been alone. It tied them together.

*There's no such thing as star thread!* He flung himself off the horse. *You're as gullible as Anders.* But the radiance burned into his skin.

Sampson helped him unpack the mule. "White buckskins," he said, amused. "Shotgun. Not useful to the Indians, for they'd have no shells. Portable writing desk, books."

Will slanted an unfamiliar flat metal box toward the fire. "Oysters! Tinned oysters!"

"We'll remember that," Sampson said. "Oyster stew. Godfroy's hoping we have something to celebrate soon," he said in a low voice. "You and Rachel."

"Rachel doesn't want me," Will said.

"But you want Rachel?"

How was he to answer truthfully, when the star thread still warmed him? "The wedding was a mistake," he mumbled, "done for Godfroy's sake. How do I explain to Godfroy?"

Sampson chuckled. "I got in that fix once, with a chief of the Gros Ventres. Gave him a horse that he admired, and next morning his daughter was sitting in front of my tent, all dressed up in her best doeskin."

"What happened? How did you get him to take her back?"

"Didn't. She's my wife. I'm meeting her and the babies at Fort Bridger."

"How long since you've seen her?"

"Last summer. On our way back from California. This year I take her with me."

Years gone, children left as lonely as he had been in the nursery in Pittsburgh. Not fair to any child....

The trail meandered along the ridge in a sweeping S-curve. Matt spurred his horse through a damp slough, up an adjoining ridge so he could see the line of wagons. Two stood out, white topped, looking a bit like small sailing ships on a green sea. The wind threatened to lift his hat. Matt pulled it off, folded it and thrust it in his belt. A fine spring day, except for the west wind that caught the wagon covers and pulled against the teams. He had suggested that all the covers be removed, but Mrs. Ludlow would not hear of it, certain her two-year-old twins would take sick if exposed to the sun. And Tole, who should know better, was so obsessed with his young wife and baby daughter, he had let Ludlow convince him that a sunburn could be fatal.

Two dogs trotted companionably in the shade of Tole's wagon, a black-and-white mongrel that belonged to Kit, and a golden-coated stray that had joined the party in St. Joe. No family claimed it, but the boys slipped it biscuits enough to survive.

Matt could just make out the string of mules, the animals handled by three mule skinners Anders had hired in St. Joe. Anders and Reid had cut off the road to hunt, leaving the servants, Hooper and Tibbels, in charge. Actually, they simply rode along, since they knew no more of pack animals and prairie camping than little Merri.

Jim Mac's four wagons had the lead today. Even from this distance Matt could see Meggie's tabby cat stretching and yawning on top of the provision box. If he had known about the cat when they left Pikeston he would have told her to leave it at home. But they had been in Illinois when the mewling of newborn kittens had betrayed her presence. Strange how the animals adjusted to the routine of travel. Matt had been sure the cat would be left behind some morning, but the moment the oxen came to the wagons, the cat would slip from a nearby thicket, usually with a new, wriggling victim.

Matt frowned at the sight of Tildy walking beside the oxen of the third wagon. His wife should not be driving the teams. But the young men in St. Joe had wanted to join parties heading for Oregon, not California. His wagon—Granny's, rather—looked like an unroofed herb shop. Bouquets of flowers and weeds dangled from the bows. A journey to California did not stop an herb woman from gathering plants. Granny walked at the same speed as the oxen, but several yards off the trail, her eyes on the ground. She had looped her apron over her left arm, and it bulged with the fragrant bundles she would hang to dry this evening.

The youngest Tole boy plodded beside Godfroy's oxen. Matt could see nothing of Godfroy, but assumed he dozed

in the nest of blankets Rachel had made for him. Thank
heavens for Will Hunter! Until Godfroy could last a day in
the saddle Will was indispensable. Few men who signed
on as hunters would be willing to pitch in and help drive
the loose stock. But there Will rode, edging the mules,
steers and milk cows onto the trail, away from the boggy
holes that forced the road onto a crooked track.

Matt sometimes felt sorry for Will, a stranger dumped
into a crowd of friends and relatives. But he laughed at the
boys' jokes, even when they played a prank on him, fetched
water for the women in the evenings and took his turn at
night watches. From what Rachel had confessed to Tildy,
and Tildy had whispered across the pillow in the dark of
their tent, Matt knew the marriage had been consummated.
Why did Rachel jump at a flimsy excuse to end it? Sex
was more important than a legal paper or an ordained min-
ister. From the day he and Tildy had met by the river, and
one thing led to another, they had been married. And Godfroy was damned miserable, wanting Will and Rachel back
together again.

Two wagons lagged behind, so far back they would soon
tangle with the stock. The preacher? No, his wagon was in
its proper spot, behind Ira MacIntyre's three wagons.

Burdette! Matt spurred his horse through the bog, keeping to the driest path. He suspected Burdette was half-
dozing, that he had only to wake him up. But the moment
Burdette saw him he called, "Whoa!" Behind him twelve-
year-old John cried, "Whoa!" and both wagons rolled to
a stop.

"This road's crooked as a county judge," Burdette
yelled. "You should take us through the way you just
came."

"No road for a wagon. Barely one for a horse."

Burdette scratched his head, and John imitated the gesture. "We're heading south, not west. Going this way, we drive twice the distance getting to the Platte River."

"We've got to follow the ridges," Matt said as evenly as possible. Sampson had explained this simple fact at noon.

"Must be a better way," Burdette insisted. "Why hire scouts, when they just lead us on the same old track?"

"The track's old for good reason," Matt snapped. "Might be because it's best. Catch up and stay closer."

"Almost asleep on my feet, what with watching the cattle last night. I want new elections."

"Like Sampson said, wait until the Big Blue. That's customary. Now, say 'Giddyap,' or the loose stock will pass you and I won't tell them to keep back."

He slapped his horse's rump and it sprang away, leaving Burdette's protests behind. He would welcome elections. Let someone else take over this thankless job. Then he could walk beside the oxen, have time to talk to his wife, give Tildy a chance to ride in the wagon and rest after the hours of work in the morning, at noon and at nightfall.

Three riders crossed the road about half a mile away. Rachel, the only woman who owned a sidesaddle. Meggie, easy to spot because her skirts flapped behind her. In St. Joe she had traded with an Indian woman for a pair of doeskin leggings, so at least her legs were covered. He was not sure of the third horseman until he turned in profile. A flat English saddle. Reid.

Pointing and gestures. Meggie took off at a gallop, passing the pack train. She must be heading for Sampson, who rode ahead to the camping place. Rachel turned toward the wagons and Reid headed south, cross-country. Some problem, and since Anders was not in sight, it probably involved him. Matt sighed and rode to meet Rachel.

"There's a stray horse," she called. "Sir Anders thought

he'd cornered a panther. But then the horse walked out of the brush, came quite near them.''

Domestic horses often joined wild herds, until the memory of grain overpowered the appeal of freedom. This was a stroke of luck, for Ira MacIntyre, Marshall and Burdette had brought no riding horses.

''Tell Reid to bring it in.''

''He and Sir Anders can't catch it. It's wearing a bridle, and a saddle turned beneath its belly. Mr. Reid says its hind legs are raw where the saddle hits. But when he or Sir Anders get close the horse snorts and kicks.''

Tole and Kit, Matt thought, both accustomed to handling fractious horses. But who would replace Kit bossing the boys behind the loose stock?

''The poor creature,'' Rachel said, subtly pushing him to make a decision. Why not do Godfroy a favor?

''Rachel, do you have any sugar lumps in your wagon?''

''Of course.''

''Get a handful. I'll tell Will to join you. I want the two of you out with Reid.''

''I'm sure with Will's help, Mr. Reid could—''

''Look Rachel, I know you don't want to be around Will, but if that horse ran off from a family it's accustomed to women. Horses learn women are more likely to have an apple or a carrot behind their skirt. You just hold out your hand and speak tender words. He may walk right up to you and nuzzle that sugar while Will cuts the girth.'' She objected by frowning. More than a frown; she made an ugly face.

Will also frowned when he heard the plan. But he nodded and trotted off, as Matt knew he would. Will detoured by the feed wagon, filled his hat with grain, folded it and stuck it under his thigh. A man who knew how to catch a horse, Matt thought with approval.

Rachel kept her distance from her erstwhile husband while they rode to the adjoining ridge. Rachel had determination enough to hold off the whole world of men. Matt smoothed his beard. Tildy was right, it was getting too long. He would ask her to trim it tonight. And maybe he would repeat some of their pillow talk to Granny. She was the best matchmaker around.

## Chapter Sixteen

The horse dodged when Anders galloped toward it. The saddle bumped against its hind legs, and Rachel saw pain and terror in the frantic toss of its head.

"Tell him to stop hassling," Will said to Reid. Reid shouted, Anders hesitated, Reid waved a second time. This time Anders gave up and joined them. He carried a knife.

"Nearly got it once," he said.

"You're trying to kill it?" Rachel asked, appalled at the length of the blade.

"No, cut the saddle girths."

"I'd dodge, too, if a man came at me with a knife." She turned to Will, appealing for his support. He paid no attention to her, or Anders or Reid, for that matter, but leaned on his saddle horn, staring at the horse.

"What we must do is surround it," Anders said. "Ten or fifteen men. One of my herders is an expert with a rope, and could snag it if he got within eight or ten yards."

Anders's proposal was ridiculous, because there were only twenty men in the whole party, and not all had horses. Rachel looked to see Will's reaction. He watched the horse, a hunter observing his prey. The horse took a step in their direction, ready to shy if attacked.

"What do you think?" Anders demanded impatiently. Will sat up, a faint smile twitching one corner of his mouth.

*He's been waiting for Anders to ask for advice!* If Anders *asked* for Will's opinion, he could not sneer, "I don't take orders from a boy." She put her hand to her mouth and pretended to cough.

"Let the horse think we've given up," Will said. "But you and Reid circle around, far off, so it doesn't notice." Anders nodded. "If I raise my hand like this—" Will stuck his arm in the air "—you hold back, and if I put it to the side, come on as fast as you can."

"Surround, just like I said!" Anders exclaimed. "Come, Brant-Reid." He jerked on the reins with one hand, the other hand, holding the knife, resting on his thigh.

"And don't carry a naked blade while you ride," Will yelled at Anders's back. "A tumble could drive it right in your belly, and that's usually fatal." Anders stopped long enough to sheath the knife.

"What do we do?" Rachel asked.

"Sit still for the moment." Will pulled his telescope from his pocket and focused on the horse. He laughed.

"What's funny?" Rachel asked.

"Hull suggested you be bait. Won't work." He handed the glass to her. It swayed heavily in her hand, giving views of prairie and sky before she focused on the horse. The stray edged toward them, presenting a side view. On the hip was a large brand: US.

"An army horse!"

"Probably escaped from Leavenworth. If we cut the saddle we're destroying government property, and if we put it in the herd, we're appropriating government property."

"We can't leave the poor thing like that!"

"No. If we meet soldiers we'll turn it over to them." His eyes, narrowed against the sun, gave nothing away. But then, they never did, icy, cautious, except... "Would you be afraid to go near him on foot?" Will asked.

"No." Except that to remount, she had to depend on Will.

"We'll approach him like stable hands. Here." He held out his hat, bunched up into a sack.

"But what about Sir Anders?"

"They're out of the way. Englishmen dash right in, like they're fighting a battle. That's how they conquered an empire. Take this barley. We'll walk up to him together, and while he eats, I unbuckle the saddle."

They loosened the reins so their horses could graze, and unwound the trail ropes to drag behind. The army horse waited about thirty yards away.

"Keep close to me and act very confident."

"Pretend you're brave and you will be?" she said.

"Exactly. We're stable hands, coming out to get the animals after a long day. We don't brook any nonsense."

"My skirt might spook him."

"Not too different from a blacksmith's apron, since you've left off wearing a mass of petticoats."

"How do you know about my petticoats?" The farther they traveled, the fewer she put on, until this morning she had tied just one about her waist.

"Obvious. Your skirt doesn't stick out so far."

The horse lifted its head and neighed. "Poor thing, poor frightened thing," she crooned. It walked toward her. The horse nickered twice before burying its nose in the barley.

"You've got to carry your saddle," Will said. "It's a heavy one." She heard him grunt as he lifted the saddle onto the horse's back. The horse turned his head, his hide twitching. He stared at Will for a few seconds, then returned to the barley.

"I'll lead him. You get our horses," Will said.

"Here's your hat." Half a mile back to the wagons. No, the wagons had moved while they caught the horse. Half an hour to walk beside him, to bear the throbbing pain that had started while Will leaned on the saddle and gazed with distant eyes.

"You were right to send Sir Anders away," she said to distract herself. "He behaves like a bull, running straight at anyone who opposes him. Shooting the Iowa boy—"

"Assaulting you!" Will exclaimed. "I had a dream the other night, Anders holding you, and woke up ready to strangle him. If I'd stayed away two minutes longer—" Not the direction she wanted.

"But Mr. Reid's not like Sir Anders. At first I judged him a coward, but he went onto that snag. I don't understand why he lets Sir Anders—"

"Anders bought him. Reid's family is poor, Anders pays him to be a friend, and will pay him to marry his sister."

"Oh! But that's very evil!"

"Evil? No, not evil. Just a choice. I could do the same, go home, join Shakespeare and Company, and be very rich."

"It's not the same at all, Will! It's your family's business, your father's money."

"But not the life I want, so I'd be bought all the same. Might not be a bad life," he mused.

Will, giving up! She leaned around the horses to stare at him, saw a smile that brightened his eyes. "Lovely home, beautiful wife. Like Robert, a woman in every river town."

"You wouldn't do that!" she said.

"I wouldn't?" Eyes teasing. Thank heavens the wagons came into view and she had an excuse to look away.

"You're too good to be immoral in Robert's fashion," she protested. "Look! The wagons are circling." Her father crawled from the wagon, stretched, looked about, and she knew he was searching for her. "I'm not there to build a fire and fix Father's medicine!"

"Captain Hull will tell him about the horse, and that you're with me, which will please him. Hull's part of the conspiracy to bring us together, I believe."

"Yes," she said.

The Tole boys gathered at their wagons, and their hands reached to help Louisa down. Kit swung Merri off the tailgate and the boys scampered ring-around-the-rosy, the little girl in the center, laughing, until Mr. Tole broke through and snatched her onto his shoulders. He galloped about like a horse, Merri shrieking with delight.

Her cries were drowned out by pounding hooves. The army horse neighed, bucked and pulled at Will's tight grip, eyes wild. Rachel wedged herself between Josefa and Will's horse for protection as Anders and Reid galloped into camp.

"You were gone when we got to that southern ridge!" Anders yelled, flushed with anger.

"Quiet! Quiet!" Will mouthed, waving a hand for caution. "Back! You're frightening him!" Anders wheeled away. "It was amazing, he simply walked up to us!" Men gathered a safe distance from the army horse's heels, Mr. Tole among them, still carrying Merri on his shoulders.

"Horsey," Merri said, pointing.

Rachel handed the reins of the horses to Josh MacIntyre and ran to her father. "I'm sorry," she gasped, "Captain Hull told me to ride...." Why had she gone? She might have declined Captain Hull's order, said she was tired, that the sidesaddle caused a cramp in her right leg.

"I heard. Anders and Reid found a stray horse. Looks like Anders isn't too happy."

She pulled wood from the canvas sling under the wagon. The next patch of trees she must gather more. Bending compressed her stomach, and the pain got worse. She drew the shovel from the wagon but had to wait until she caught her breath before she dug the fire trench. Will's fault that she hurt like this. He must be nearby. But he stood far away, watching the antics of the Tole family.

While she blew the tinder to flame she told her father how Will had forced Anders to ask for his advice, how he had sent Anders and Reid away on a wild-goose chase, and how she had tamed the horse with barley.

"Always knew he was a good man," he said, clasping the cup of medicinal tea. "Ready in an emergency. How long do you plan on feeding me this foul stuff?"

"Until you manage to stay in the saddle all day."

"Tomorrow," he said. "You had a good time, out on the prairie. Put some color in your cheeks."

She ground her teeth. "As you say, Will's a good man. A good *friend*," she said. "It seems sometimes that he's the brother I never had."

Her father's eyelids drooped and he pursed his lips.

Granny sat on the step of her wagon, twisting bits of string about the plants she had gathered during the day. "Hello, Rachel," she said without looking up, as if she had been expecting her.

"Granny, Father's complaining about his medicine, but I can't believe he should go without. He's still weak."

Granny detached a few dead leaves from a stem. "Willow bark tea *is* bitter," she said. "And men, when they start to feel better, think the cure's done."

"Is there something else?"

"Why, blackberry tea, perhaps, or mint. A gentle stimulation. Does he complain of pain in his legs?"

"Only when he does too much. He'll moan tonight, because he rode his horse this morning."

"But when he stays in the wagon?"

"He says the jostling bruises him all over, but he exaggerates. I made him a bed of blankets."

"Not sassafras, then. You look a bit flushed, Rachel. Not chills or fever, I hope."

"I rode too long. The sun was going down and shone right on my face."

Granny climbed the steps leading to her wagon's side door. Anders had made fun of it, calling it "a palace of the plains, fit for Her Majesty, the apothecary." But Granny had laughed right back.

"Sarsaparilla," she said. "Come help me hang the herbs I picked and then I'll find where I stowed the sarsaparilla." Rachel stooped under the lintel and stood amid the thicket of drying plants. Granny produced a tin box filled with long, dark roots, spread a bit of muslin and rasped one of the roots across a grater until a tablespoonful of powder lay heaped on the cloth. She pulled the edges together, tied them into a little bag with a piece of string she took from her apron pocket.

"Use this to make your father a cup of tea. And drink a cup yourself. Do you have any onions?"

"A few."

"Wrap one in mud and bury it in the ashes of your supper fire. Break it out in the morning, and feed it to Godfroy for breakfast, with a little honey if you have it." She stacked boxes and bags in one end of the wagon, uncovering a narrow cot. "Sit down." Rachel obeyed. "Now, what's this I hear—Will is your husband, but you won't be his wife."

"He's not my husband. He's not of age."

"Balderdash! Jimmy MacIntyre was nineteen when we got married, and no one ever said we weren't husband and wife."

"But there's supposed to be a license and a certificate."

"A license is nothing but a way for the county to put a tax on marriage. Jimmy and I had no license. But you're right, the preacher wrote out a paper for us, although now that I think about it, I never saw the paper after that winter the cabin flooded. Reverend Ludlow can write out a certificate for you."

"I don't want to be married," Rachel muttered. This was none of Granny's business. She should *never* have told Tildy about being in bed with Will.

"Will's near sick with wanting you."

"He is not sick! He's quite spry. You should have seen how happy he was today. Will doesn't want to be married any more than I do." Change the subject. "Today he outwitted Anders and Reid, and brought in a horse that escaped from the army. Did you hear?"

"Yes, and Godfroy told me the Englishman threw you over his horse and would have carried you off but for Will."

"Yes." Rachel picked fragments of grass off her skirt.

"And Matt says Will did very well on the day the ferry broke down, that he's equal to any man, no matter that he's only twenty. And you fed the boys, proving you're a woman, if only eighteen. I've seen the Tole boys eat, and feeding them's no mean feat."

Rachel smiled unwillingly, recalling the speed with which hotcakes vanished.

"What did you cook, that they're still raving about your breakfast?" Granny asked.

"Mr. Reid milked the cows, so I had a bucket of milk, and I had buried two dozen eggs in the cornmeal. I made pudding with stewed apples. I'm glad they liked it. The only person who mentioned it was..." Rachel turned away to toss a handful of grass stems out of the wagon.

"Who?" Granny asked, laying a hand on her knee.

"Will."

"A husband who thanks his wife for a meal—"

"Will's not my husband!"

"Who thanks his wife, he's a treasure indeed."

"Did Mr. MacIntyre thank you?"

"No. But sometimes he said he loved me. And I always knew he did, even when he didn't say."

"How? Did he bring you presents, or pick flowers?"

"No. Some nights, after the boys were asleep and I'd already crawled into bed, he'd blow out the candle, and I'd hear him laughing while he took his clothes off. That meant he wasn't putting on his nightshirt."

Rachel's hands hurt. She found she was wringing them in the folds of her skirt.

"Did you mind it horribly?" she whispered.

"Mind it?" Granny let the words out on a long breath. "Is that the trouble between you and Will?" Rachel tightened her eyes to bury the memory. "Oh, dear! Oh, deary! But you and Will can work it out."

"No. I'll never let a man near me again!" Rachel stood. "We *have* worked it out. We're not married."

Marshall and Burdette stood shoulder-to-shoulder at the evening campfire, their fixed jaws preparing Will for inevitable complaints.

"I don't like these night watches," Marshall began.

"Needless trouble," Burdette said.

"Makes a man tired through the next day, and wakes the children when we're coming and going."

"What do you propose?" Sampson asked. "That we let the oxen wander?"

"Why not? At home I don't set out with my cattle," Burdette said.

"At home you have a fenced pasture," Godfroy reminded him. "Before long we'll be in Pawnee country and they'll pick off any mule or ox they find roaming free. And the first thunderstorm, you'll learn how an ox can run."

Burdette grunted. "Other thing, we neither one brought a saddle horse—" Burdette jerked a thumb in Marshall's direction "—but we put in money for the feed. Don't seem fair, that grain goes to horses we don't get to ride."

"You put money in for each animal," Sampson said. He seldom showed any emotion, but Will heard his exasperation.

"He didn't put in no money," Burdette said, pointing a triumphant fist in Will's direction.

"We agreed to pay the hunter fifty dollars and board him. I supposed that extended to his horses."

"He gave that stray horse feed this evening, and we didn't make no bargain about that. And where's all this fresh meat he's to bring in?"

"*I* would have shot an antelope today," Anders interrupted, pushing two men aside to stand beside Burdette, "except the rifle I bought in St. Joe, to replace the one stolen by the savages, casts to the left." Reid, in the shadows, turned his head aside.

"Hunter's doing his job," Godfroy said from his seat on an upturned bucket. "Until I'm full strength, he's filling in for me. Won't be long. Granny MacIntyre gave me new medicine this evening, and I already feel better."

"Fairground quackery!" Anders snorted.

"Hunter'll bring in game in due time," Godfroy said.

"Yeah! Army horses," Marshall sneered. "I think we should send Hunter back to St. Joe for all he's worth, and save our money. Let him tag along with some other wagon train." Burdette tilted his head toward Marshall and nodded his agreement. Will considered a variety of replies, decided nothing he could say would alter their opinions.

"We'd save money," Burdette was saying. "Sort of make up for the fifty cents I paid out yesterday to get rid of two red-blanketed Indians. They have no right—"

"They have every right," Will said, deciding he could honorably speak in the Indians' defense, if not his own. "We take their wood—"

"Whoever heard of paying for wood gathered in the wilds?"

"Burdette, for once use your eyes!" Sampson, who had been warming his rear, swung to face the complainers, anger lowering his voice. "There's no trees here except along the streams. This isn't Indiana, where trees spring up so fast you gotta jump back when an acorn falls. Think, man!"

"I am thinking!" Burdette yelled. "I'm thinking I'm gonna be poor as a church mouse by the time we get to California, besides being wore out, getting no sleep. You didn't tell us we'd be dropping quarters and dollars on every mangy rascal who holds out his hand."

"Must be one of Granny's curses," Godfroy said, amused.

Heads turned, eyes half fearful, in the direction of Granny's wagon. Sampson used the moment of silence to stretch his arms, indicating the subject was closed. "Now, about tomorrow, we'll cross the Nemaha River, but it should be of no consequence."

Reverend Ludlow cleared his throat. "Mr. Sampson, tomorrow is the Sabbath. We should not travel on the Sabbath."

"Reverend, there's twenty-four wagons one day's drive behind us. They have a great herd of cattle and they're hauling no feed. Right now our stock has the pick of fresh grass. If the Oregonians pass us, with their near starving oxen, the grass'll be skinned clean near the trail. Now, as I was saying, the Nemaha's a pretty little river, no problem at all to roll right across. If we leave early, we might noon there and have time for a service of thanks, Reverend.''

"Beg God's mercy for ignoring his commandments," Reverend Ludlow said sourly.

"That's something else we need to talk about," Burdette said. "The reverend's mules eat more grain than my oxen, yet he put the same money—"

"We'll make him say a prayer for us every morning and evening, and not pass the collection plate," Godfroy said. "That should even things up." He left for his own fire.

"But we haven't talked about elections!" Burdette cried.

"No," Sampson said. He fell in behind Godfroy. Will trailed them, sick at heart. Marshall and Burdette had planted a seed of doubt. The next toll levied, the cost of the ferry on the North Platte, as their hoarded coins disappeared, the men would consider ways to save their money. Get rid of the hunter.

*I'll leave in the morning, at the rise of the hunting star,* he resolved, *and bring in* something. But Rachel needed his help striking the tent and loading the wagon. Until Godfroy had regained his full strength, he dared not leave her with all the work.

"Will? Could you give us a hand?"

Meggie held a hammer and a thick rope. Behind her stood Tildy and Rachel. "You see, the kittens, they want to scramble over the tailgate, but their little claws don't get a purchase on the varnished wood. So I thought I'd fasten on a rope for them to climb?" Her voice rose on the last word and solicited his advice. "Here, hold this." She thrust the end of the rope into his hand.

"I don't understand what you mean, Meggie," Rachel said.

"Tildy, ask Mr. Tole if he has nails." Tildy obediently trotted off, dodging around the horses fenced by the circle of wagons. "Now, Mr. Hunter, you hold that rope right here." Meggie guided the rope to the edge of the tailgate. "Rachel, stretch it tight, real tight across the top, so when they get their little claws—"

"Meggie, don't you think it's dangerous to encourage the kittens?" Will asked. "They might tumble out."

"Cats have better balance than that," Meggie said. She adjusted Rachel's hand at the opposite side of the tailgate. "There! Where did Tildy go? There she is, talking to Louisa instead of asking about nails. Makes no difference, since I forgot to bring the knife to cut the rope."

"I've got a knife right here," Will said. He shifted the rope to his left hand, pulled the knife from the scabbard, but Meggie had already vanished beyond the horses.

"Do you have any idea what she means to do?" he asked Rachel. She shook her head and looked after Meggie. A rustling in the wagon, then the tabby appeared.

"She must have been feeding her kittens," Rachel said. The cat sat between him and Rachel, washing herself. She licked a paw and smeared it over her head and face.

"Be a lot easier keeping clean if we washed like a cat," Will said.

"Ugh." Rachel made a face. "My hand's getting tired. Do you suppose I'll mess up Meggie's cat ladder if I let loose of the rope?"

"I wouldn't think so." Will dropped his end.

Rachel patted the cat on the head. The cat gave her a disgusted look and moved out of reach.

"She heard that nasty sound you made," Will said. "About the way she takes a bath."

"Cats are so dreadfully independent," Rachel said.

"They have no earthly use, except to catch rats. Unlike dogs."

"Cats take responsibility for themselves, unlike dogs," he retorted. "You don't find this cat hanging around the campfire, begging biscuits. She's down in the thickets, catching her own meal."

"The cat doesn't help herd the cattle," she said.

"Neither do the dogs when the sun's hot and they'd rather trot along in the shade of a wagon."

"You like cats because they're as untamed as you," she said. "Hunters, who kill for the sake—"

"Rachel, would you look at Tole's wagon?"

"Why should I want to spy on—"

"Because I saw a laughing face and a head of auburn hair peek around their wagon. I think we've been abandoned."

"Abandoned!" Rachel spun around.

"Is a kitten ladder a sensible project?" he asked.

"No. It's the silliest thing I ever heard... They did this to get us alone together!" she cried. She grabbed the rope, twirled it so the end thudded on the side of the wagon. The cat snarled and leaped into the jumble of pots, pans, bedding and food bags.

Will leaned on the tailgate and laughed. "They plotted to bring us together, and all they accomplished was to start an argument about cats."

Rachel's eyes opened wide, but then she smiled. "We *have* been arguing," she said. "We don't argue very often."

"Hardly ever."

"You didn't come straight to the wagon for supper this evening. You watched the Toles before you took care of the army horse. Do you find Louisa beautiful?"

"Louisa?" he gasped. Was Rachel jealous? "Rather attractive," he said calmly, "but she's another man's wife. I watched because…" Why had he? "It's fine to see a family like the Toles, like families are supposed to be."

"Did you learn anything?" she asked archly.

"Yes. I've learned it's no good for a father to be gone year after year, then expect his children to follow in his footsteps. No child is happy left alone. And if I marry, that's how it will be. I'll not make the same mistake my father and mother did, Rachel."

# Chapter Seventeen

"I believe I should exercise the army horse this morning," Will said. "See how he behaves before the boys climb on."

A fine idea, Rachel thought. She would not see him until noon on the Nemaha. Her father's eyes flickered, and she prepared herself for some excuse to send her off with Will.

"Somewhere between here and Leavenworth he pitched off his rider," her father said. "Rachel, you go out with Will. He shouldn't ride an uncertain horse alone."

"Meggie will be there, on her pony," Rachel said. Her hand tightened on her fork until it cut her palm.

"Her pony's too frisky," her father said, "Will needs a partner mounted on a calm horse."

"You said *you* would ride this morning," she reminded him. "You go with Will."

"I'm a bit stiff." He shrugged one shoulder. "I'll walk beside the oxen as far as the river."

Rachel searched for a logical excuse. Dinner? No, she had made noodles last night and baked extra bread, boiled eggs this morning and chopped the leftover ham.

"Faith and Louisa asked me to ride with them," she lied.

"Since the road's so hard and level, we'll sew while we're traveling."

"On the Sabbath?" her father asked. Rachel gasped. She had forgotten what day it was. Of course they would not sew on the Sabbath.

"We'll move only as far as the Nemaha," her father said. "Four or five miles. The reverend will preach after we've crossed the river. If there's grass enough, we might spend the night. You two ride ahead and meet us there."

Will reached around her to put down his tin cup. "Four or five miles," he muttered. "No more than an hour, and you'll please him." He jerked his head in her father's direction. "Take your sewing, Meggie will meet you, and the two of you can sit and talk at the river."

"About kitten ladders!" she said.

"Meet you at the river," Sir Anders cried as the string of mules trotted by. Meggie rode a few lengths behind.

"Ride along with *them*," Rachel said.

"I would, but if the horse misbehaves he might spook the mules," Will said. "They'd toss packs all over the prairie and Sir Anders itches to lift my hair as it is. Sorry."

"I'll ride with you if we stay in sight of the wagons," Rachel said. "I must be near if Father should get tired."

"Catch up!" Captain Hull yelled. The boys were driving the oxen to the wagons. Will helped with the yokes and chains. Burdette's wagons rolled out of the circle, the rear wagons of yesterday automatically the leaders of today. Will saddled the horses. The army horse showed no discontent. Rachel steadied the toe of her boot in the cradle of Will's fingers, accepting his boost into the saddle.

"Stay back," he said. "Sometimes army horses spring out the moment they feel weight in the saddle." But the horse stood still. Will clicked his tongue and touched his spurs to its side. The horse laid its ears back.

"Not a good sign," Rachel said. The horse shifted its hindquarters and gave a halfhearted buck.

"If that's the best it can do, I'm safe," Will said. The horse switched its tail violently, as if it could brush the rider off. It threw up its head, leaped forward and trotted a zigzag down the trail.

"Stay behind," Will yelled over his shoulder.

The horse made a twisting leap, but Will stayed on. It stopped, feet splayed and head down. Will whacked it on the rump. It took off, passed Burdette's wagons at a gallop, and Rachel had to spur Josefa to keep up. Far on the horizon Rachel saw Anders and Reid, their servants and hired hands. The trail curved, and the string of horses and mules made a glittering arc as the rays of the sun reached them and reflected from the polished chains.

The trail followed the top of a prominent ridge. Rachel found the green swells of the prairie, all the way to the horizon, at her feet. The army horse must be growing tired, because she and Josefa had closed the gap.

"Come on up," Will called. "He's settling down. Not happy, but obedient." Rachel rode even with him, separated by the width of the road. She looked back to see the distance they had covered.

"We're much too far ahead of the wagons," she said.

"Stop for a minute," he said. "I'll find out if this horse will stand still while we let the wagons catch up."

On her right grass and weeds grew thick among early stalks of cattails. "Look! There's the broad-stemmed grass Granny gathered yesterday." Cattails meant a bog, but the slope looked dry enough, and the grass grew right on the edge. She turned Josefa's head.

"Watch out! There may be water there."

"I am watching. Whoa." Rachel leaned over Josefa's mane to see the depth of the hoofprints. Nothing dangerous.

And the grass grew taller near the cattails. She shook her foot from the stirrup and slid off. A cloud of insects flared the moment her boots hit the ground, buzzing around her head, dodging at her eyes.

"Rachel, take care!" The population of buzzing insects doubled as Will jumped down. He took off his hat and beat the air. "This is exactly where a snake—"

She swung her hat around her head. If she leaned over to pull the grass, the bugs would find easy pickings on the back of her neck.

"What the hell's Burdette doing?"

Rachel stopped swatting long enough to look down the trail, but no wagons were in sight.

"He should swing left, to circle this bog," Will said. Rachel put her hat on her head and waved her hand in front of her face. A team of oxen, instead of turning left, headed straight toward her, as if to cross the swamp. The wagon rolled down the slope, so steep she could see the entire length of the white cover.

"The fool!" Will waded into the bog, ignoring the mud now halfway up his boots. "Go back! You'll get mired!" Will pulled one boot free. It made a hollow sucking sound. "Rachel, throw me the trail rope on my saddle, so I don't leave these boots behind."

The foot he stood on sank until the mud ran over the top. Rachel jerked at Josefa's reins. "Keep talking, Will, so I know I'm heading toward you. I've got to keep my eyes on the ground so I don't get in too deep."

"You stay back," he ordered.

"You cannot order me about, Will Hunter!" The mud closed over the instep of her boot. She stopped. Close enough, if he leaned in her direction.

"I'll toss the trail rope. Josefa can pull you out." Her first toss fell short.

"Tie something on the end, to give it weight," he suggested. Nothing in her saddlebag but calico and thread. Her scissors, heavy enough, but too precious to risk.

"I should have guessed we'd find quicksand," he said casually.

*Quicksand!* The horror of the plains! But didn't quicksand have a distinctive character? This looked like...well, mud! She looped the rope through the scissors.

"Be careful how you catch, or they'll poke you." She twirled the rope and heaved, breathed when she heard the impact on his leather glove. She wished she had taught Josefa the trick of walking backward, like Meggie's pony. She tugged on the bridle with both hands, making the horse turn in a short curve so she stayed out of the muck. Josefa objected to the weight hanging from her trail rope, shook the bridle from Rachel's hands, leaped onto solid ground.

"Thank you," Will said as he stepped beside her. "You have great presence of mind. Godfroy will say 'I told you so.' He's right. I did need a capable partner."

"Kit Tole or Josh MacIntyre would have done just as well. Better, in fact, for they'd not have gone down in a swamp to pick grass for Granny, and Burdette wouldn't have been tempted to get off the road. Has he turned around?" She shaded her eyes to see what was happening beyond the bog. Burdette's wagon no longer hung at the steep angle, but it did not move. "What is that noise?" she asked.

"Oxen, bellowing in helpless rage," Will said, quite disgusted. "They're mired. Three yoke up to their bellies, and the front wheels to the hubs." He had his glass to his eye. "Good, Tole's unhitched. He understands...no, it's Godfroy, he's got men in the bog, unyoking the teams."

"I should be with Father. He'll exhaust himself. Help me up." He cupped his hands to receive her boot, and as she settled in the saddle, he placed an unnecessary steadying hand against the small of her back. She tried to ignore the pain as Josefa trotted beside the army horse.

The first thing Will noticed was Captain Hull, wallowing in the mud, staggering under the heavy yokes. Other men, hip-deep in the mire, strung ropes and chains to the struggling animals. Reverend Ludlow fluttered on the edge of the bog, dodging the men, periodically holding his hands over his ears. Will could imagine the blasphemies filling the air.

"He caused it," Burdette cried the moment Will slid off the army horse. Burdette swung his fist into thin air, snarling as if he regretted that it did not land on a jaw. "He waved at me, told me to come straight across. He yelled there was no need to go clear round the loop."

"From a quarter mile away, I told you that?" Will yelled back, then remembered Sampson's patience in dealing with Burdette, and counted to five slowly.

"You have no right to give directions about the trail," Burdette said. "That's Sampson's job."

"Then why didn't you follow Sampson?" Rachel asked icily. He had not been aware that she stood at his elbow.

"Because Sampson's way out ahead, not doing his job, and here's Will Hunter, standing a few yards down the trail, waving his hands about—"

"Mosquitoes," Will said.

"What?"

"I waved my arms because the bog's full of mosquitoes."

"So you admit, you signaled me to come straight across."

"He did not!" Rachel cried.

"And three horses ain't enough, you take out the stray, while men with no horses pay for the grain and hay!"

"You want the army horse, Burdette, you got it." Will thrust the reins into Burdette's hands.

Burdette studied the tattered leather. "Mighty ragged, these reins. You figure they're good enough for the likes of me, I suppose?" He tilted his head, daring an answer.

"Drag me about on the ground for two or three days," Will said as lightly as he could, "and I suppose I'd be tattered, too. Perhaps even a bit muddy." He looked pointedly at the men in the bog, ran his eyes up and down Burdette's dry pants and shirt. Burdette pulled back a fist so tight his fingers seemed to have disappeared.

"Stop it!" Somehow Granny had sidled in between them. "Mr. Burdette, go help dig your oxen out of the mud before they're too exhausted to pull the wagon. Will, tell the boys what to do with the loose stock. Should they hold them on the trail, or go ahead to find grass?"

Burdette's face flushed dark, then darker. "Yeah, boy. Get to your work."

Will ignored Burdette, met Granny's eyes. Her humor cleared his mind and relaxed his hands. He had very nearly allowed Burdette to taunt him into a fight.

"Thank you, Mrs. MacIntyre," he said. He turned his back on Burdette, took two steps, then looked over his shoulder. "Your horse should be rubbed down, Burdette. He came round that two-mile loop at a gallop. And he's fractious on first mounting." For a long moment Burdette stared, undecided, then tied the horse to his second wagon.

Will found the loose stock milling about, the boys dashing here and there to keep them out of the bog.

"How long will they be?" Kit asked Will. "It's the very devil to keep them from miring themselves."

"Drive on. The road detours around this swamp about

two miles, then you'll see a line of trees marking the river, a mile or two beyond that. Sampson will show you where to ford and the best grass.'' He stayed with Kit, walking in the dust of the herd until they were safely past the wagons.

"Keep them on the trail,'' he said as he turned back. "That mud's like quicksand, and we've got more stuck steers than we need right now.'' Kit looked a little hurt that anyone thought it necessary to tell him his job.

Will tipped his hat back and studied the wagons. If the women were willing to drive, most could follow the stock. But three wagons could not move because their teams had been unhitched to rescue Burdette's animals and wagon.

*I shouldn't have sent the spare oxen ahead!*

Rachel! Josefa idly swished at the bugs roused by the activity in the swamp. Rachel's rump stuck out the back of the wagon. She emerged, holding a Dutch oven.

"Rachel, I made a mistake. Ride up the trail, catch Kit and tell him to cut out every spare steer, drive them back. I wasn't thinking straight.''

"Take the noodles to Faith,'' she said, thrusting the pot at his chest. "She and Louisa are putting together a dinner.'' He looked for a way to get rid of the pot so he could help her into the saddle, but Rachel climbed on the spokes of the wheel and settled herself in the saddle.

Louisa and Faith were frying bacon. Will put the Dutch oven next to the fire. The women, without consulting scout or captain, had decided the wagons would not move until after dinner. He had sent Rachel on a needless goose chase, and Burdette would howl if he mounted the army horse to go after her. Will felt like sitting down and putting his head on his knees. Instead he went back to the mired wagon.

Five oxen had been rescued, and the sixth bellowed as he was dragged through the morass. Men shifted chains to the wagon. Reverend Ludlow barely missed being tripped up when one unexpectedly tightened.

"I think we should stand back," Will said.

"This would not have happened if we had rested on the Sabbath," Ludlow said, shaking his head sadly.

"No, it would have happened when we came by this place tomorrow," Will muttered. A mile to the east, the unmistakable arc of a wagon cover. The Oregon party. He watched helplessly as twenty-four wagons closed the gap, caught up. The thin oxen plodded by without looking to right or left, and as the last wagon rolled by, the dust of hooves and wheels obscured the road. Out of the dust came a sudden crowd of animals, and he heard a feminine voice urging them on. Rachel swung a short whip.

"Good thinking," said a very muddy Captain Hull. "Burdette's animals are in no condition to work. If the wagon comes out of that hole in one piece, we'll count this as our nooning, and pass the Oregonians at the river."

The chains tightened, the wagon rose slowly, the top shivering, the running gear creaking under the strain of the ropes. Men supported the tongue, slipping and falling as they followed it out of the muck.

"Ho!" a dozen voices called, a whip cracked, the oxen gave a great heave, and the wagon rolled onto the road.

"Looks fine," Captain Hull said with relief. With a crescendo of crackling wood, the left front wheel collapsed.

Burdette's crippled wagon pulled in at sundown. Rachel left her supper fire long enough to admire the brace the men had rigged so the front axle cleared the ground by a few inches. A strange, discolored man walked behind, left the procession to squat by her own fire.

"What's this?" asked Will's voice. He pointed to the stew pot. His clothes were stiff with mud.

"Prairie chicken, Sir Anders calls it. He brought in a whole flock, and gave us one. I saved half for you."

He gobbled the food she handed him, not seeming to notice that the meat was cold, the dried apples not quite soft, the bread a little burned.

"Is there any cheese left?" he asked as his fork rasped on the tin plate. When she returned to the fire, she found him prying the burned crust from the Dutch oven.

"Didn't get any dinner," he said, looking a bit guilty that she had discovered him. "Where's Godfroy?"

"I gave him supper and put him to bed on my mattress in the wagon, because the ground's damp here by the river. He's asleep. The MacIntyre boys helped me pitch the tent. How did you get muddy?"

"A chain tangled around a stump, and someone had to wade in to free it. The men took one look at my spotless condition and elected me."

"I haven't been to the river, but Father said there's a good bathing spot a bit upstream. Past that big sycamore."

"I'd better wash before dark." He snatched one more mouthful of cheese and crackers, swallowed all the coffee in the pot without bothering to pour it into a cup. "I'll get some clean clothes."

"Wait" she called, running after him so he did not climb into the wagon. "Don't touch a thing! I'll get your clean clothes. Go undress and get in the water. I'll leave the clean things on the bank for you."

"Better give a hail first," he said. "Make sure I'm alone down there."

"Yes. Of course."

Rachel found her father curled on his side, sound asleep. She climbed on the provision box, crawled forward until her hands found Will's bag. She distinguished trousers and shirts by the texture of the cloth. Then she counted to three hundred while she scoured the Dutch oven. That should give Will plenty of time. A few clouds reflected the last sunlight and illuminated the path. The sound of splashing brought her up short.

"Will," she called. "Are you alone?"

"Blissfully wet and all alone." His head was a dark spot on the shining water. "Put them in the crotch of that little tree, just to your right." His dirty clothes hung from the branch. She jammed the shirt and trousers in the tight angle. "Put the coffeepot on," he called.

A few feet down the path a plume waved in the grass. Meggie's cat, Rachel thought. But the sharp-nosed creature who stepped out was black, with a white stripe down its back. Rachel clutched at the trunk of a tree. The skunk turned in her direction, hesitated, looked back. Another nose poked from the grass, small and black, then another.

A mother skunk with babies! Rachel pivoted slowly on her toe, putting the tree between her and the family. Walk to the river backward, she told herself. She retreated to another tree, this one so narrow it gave no real protection. She jumped when something brushed her shoulder. Will's muddy clothes. She felt with her foot, and her toe dropped over the edge of the bluff.

"Will," she called softly, trying to project her voice over her shoulder while watching the path.

"What are you doing here?" He crouched just below her.

"Skunk. With babies," she whispered. "They're coming this way."

She heard the faint splash as he slid into the water. "Take off your shoes and get down here," he whispered.

She pulled off her camp moccasins, draped them on the branch that held Will's clothes, sat down and dangled her legs over the bank. Her toes touched the water.

"It's only six inches deep," he said. She lifted her skirt and petticoat and slid off the bank. The procession came into view, mama and four babies, the twilight reflecting on their stripes, their tails like proud flags.

"They're heading for that low spot," she muttered, nodding to a place ten feet away where the bank had caved in. The slightest movement could startle the mother. Will's hand closed on hers, and he pulled her away from the bank. Water lapped at her calves and wet cloth slapped against her legs.

"No," she said.

"Quiet! Those clothes in the tree are my last clean things!" he whispered. The bed of the stream fell away quickly now, the water rising to her hips, almost to her waist. Her skirt and petticoat floated behind her.

"Look," he whispered. The mother skunk herded her babies through the tumbled clods and roots, to the edge of a still pool. Four little faces dipped in unison. One snorted and sneezed, but the mother paid no attention. The mother examined the bank and the river as if she scented danger.

"Down," Will whispered. The cold water touched her breasts. "I'm squatting. Sit on my knees."

She had to cling to his shoulders, for her buoyant skirt threatened to drag her into the current, away from him. The mother skunk, satisfied that her family was safe, drank herself. She nosed the babies away from the water, and under her urging they climbed halfway up the collapsed bank, into a little cave created by a tree root.

"How do we get out of here?" Rachel asked.

"We'll float downstream, around the bend. Can you swim?"

"No."

"Then hang on."

The stream deepened at the bend, and Will turned on his

back. Nothing to do but stretch out on top of him and hold on. Her fingers identified the separate muscles of his shoulders, the bulge lifting to his upper arm, the cords rising to his neck.

"Good, there's a tree. We'll climb up the roots."

Her saturated skirt now threatened to pull her down. She hoisted it, freeing her toes to search out footholds in the tangle of roots.

"Stop," Will said. "Let me climb out and I'll pull you up." His legs and torso shone white, a lithe creature more at home in water than on land. She closed her eyes.

"Your hand," he said. She had to look to catch it. From this angle he seemed enormously tall. "Now the other one." He pulled until she knelt on the edge of the bank. "Steady?"

"Yes."

"On your feet." His final pull lifted her clear. Supper fires sparkled not fifty feet away. Will naked, she soaked to the skin. Six wagons between her and shelter.

"I'll sneak back and get my clothes," he said.

"My moccasins, please."

"Tell everyone that you washed yourself and your clothes, all at the same time," Will suggested wryly. She shivered. "Dry yourself off," he said.

She tried to run, but her skirts weighed a ton. Thank heavens she had reduced her petticoats to one. The grass hid a thousand prickly weeds that stung her bare feet. *I'm not cold.* Her shivers had nothing to do with temperature, everything to do with Will.

She wrung out the bottom of her skirt, started to climb into the wagon, then remembered that all her spare clothes were under her father. When she packed the wagon it had seemed very handy to put her drawers and petticoats in a compartment at the front, right beneath her pillow. Very unhandy now. She put beans and apples to soak. Mrs. MacIntyre had given her a pint of milk, which she must hang safe from prowlers. She'd **make** milk flapjacks for breakfast. The clouds in the west faded from coral to dark gray, and a few spread to the crown of the sky. Rain? She spread her wet skirts before the fire.

"I told you to change your clothes." Will held a mass of dripping garments. "I rinsed the worst of the mud out. I'll use them if I have to thrash about in another swamp." He flung the shirt and trousers over the wagon wheels.

"My clothes are under Father. I don't want to wake him, he was so tired. I'll sleep in the tent." Will stared at her, but in the dusk she could not see his expression.

"What's to be done?" he asked.

"I think we should lift the tailgate and tie the puckering strings, because it might rain."

He tilted his head and examined the sky. "You go in the tent, take your clothes off and crawl in your blankets," he said. "You shouldn't be out in this wind all wet." She had not noticed that the breeze had increased to a wind.

Rachel crawled naked into her father's bedroll, under the buffalo robe. She chafed her hands together to warm them. She should have asked Will how long the wagon repairs would take. She might have time to set up the reflecting oven and make a cake.

*Scritch!* She sat up in alarm. The skunk was at the tent! "Will," she whispered.

"I'm digging a trench to carry away the water. It's already sprinkling. Be with you in a minute." Be with her? She had forgotten that he slept in the tent in wet weather.

He thrust the flap aside, canvas rustling as he spread his blankets on the other side of the tent pole. The muffled bump of his boots, a faint patter of drizzle, an occasional plop from a larger drop. He was in the center of the tent, the only place high enough for him to stand erect.

A hum, tuneless, the murmur of a man deep in thought. *I'd hear him laughing while he took his clothes off. That meant he wasn't putting on his nightshirt.*

"No pillow tonight. My coat's wet. Rachel."

"Yes."

"It's a little tiring, these everlasting tricks to get us together."

"Yes," she said forcefully. "Father, and Tildy and Meggie, and Granny, too."

"Granny?"

"Yes."

"I thought of a way to stop it."

She raised herself on her elbow to look at him, although in the dark she could see nothing. "How?"

"We get married."

"What!"

"We get married. Once we're married, no one will expect us to spend every hour together. I've been watching what happens in the evenings. The wagons stop, the men take care of the animals and the women cook supper. Then the men loaf around one fire, and the women gather to sew and knit. It's only single people who are expected to mix."

Very true, she thought. Only one problem. "I don't want to be married."

"Neither do I. Like I told you, I realize now that if I have a family, I'd end up treating them exactly the way I was treated, off doing my business, leaving them alone. So we get married. Granny and Godfroy, your friends, they all think they've won, but we go on as we've been, friends, brother and sister, and once in California you and Faith set up your school, and I go my own way."

"That wouldn't be honest, Will. When you get married, you make promises."

She lay awake until she heard his steady, sleeping breath. Marry him again? Out of the question.

## Chapter Eighteen

**W**ill hiked downriver, the hunter's star hanging in the eastern sky. No antelope or deer leaped at his approach. Anders had brought in prairie chickens, establishing his reputation as a hunter. Will raised his rifle when a rabbit erupted from the underbrush, lowered it. Carrying a rabbit to a camp of forty people would cause more ridicule than returning empty-handed. He must put up with their gibes until they found buffalo. If they kept him on so long.

From across the river came the clank of chains and the cries of "Catch up." The Oregon party. No chance of passing them today, for Burdette's wheel must be repaired.

He turned back when a crescent of sun pushed over the horizon. No man remarked upon his return, for they all clustered about Pete MacIntyre, who shaped the replacement spokes. Will's stomach growled, and he remembered he'd had no breakfast.

At every wagon a tin washtub sat on the fire. Rachel already bent over her tub, rhythmically lifting and dropping a petticoat. The coffeepot simmered near the fire. He found a plate of bacon and biscuits, long since grown cold, on the tailgate.

"I couldn't wait if I was to do the washing," she said.

"I didn't expect you to." He sat down cross-legged, far enough from the washtub to avoid the splashes.

"No game," he said.

"Father said there wouldn't be." Her toneless words warned him she was upset. Upset that he had mentioned marriage. She was right, of course. The wedding vows were sacred and permanent. To mock them must be a great sin, although he could not recall a Bible verse that specifically forbade marriages of convenience. Nor had he ever heard a sermon blasting men and women who got married but did not live as husband and wife. He scraped the plate, mopped up the congealed bacon grease with the bread.

"I'll see what I can do about repairing the bridle for Burdette," he said to account for deserting her. She said nothing.

He carried the tack where he could be alone, away from the crowd around Burdette's wagon. He whistled as he trimmed the new leather, cut out the ragged spots from the old and sewed solid joints. He recalled the day Robert had found him working under the tutelage of an old harness maker. Robert had thrashed him twice. One for running off, and again for doing servants' work.

The women tied blankets around the trees near the swimming hole. Will was half aware of a steady parade of women and girls to the river. He studied the saddle, undecided if he should try to repair the frayed girth.

"Will." Kit, Josh, all their brothers stood around him. "We wanna show you something."

Something wrong with one of his horses? A problem beyond the wagon wheel? He scrambled to his feet. "What's wrong?"

"You'll see." He stripped the leather protector from the palm of his left hand and dropped it with the awl and needle.

"Be real quiet," warned Kit. They had found the lair of the skunk? Kit's mouth twisted up on one side, an unwilling twitch of smile. They had figured a way to spy on the women at their baths!

"Kit, it's hardly proper—" But Kit circled the wagons instead of going toward the river, past the wash lines strung from wheel to wheel. Something funny, for two of the younger boys could not control their giggles.

The two youngest MacIntyre boys ran ahead of the pack and jerked two stakes from the side of his own tent. They had helped Rachel put it up. Did they want to show him a cunning way of taking it down? Kit's muscular arm clamped round his neck, a hand over his mouth. Will twisted and swung his elbows, too late. Other arms pinned his wrists. He kicked at the hands about his ankles, but only landed them in a firmer trap. His feet left the ground.

"In you go!" cried Josh. Will hit the ground so hard his breath exploded in a great "wagh." He rolled across the grass, under the wall of the tent, his yell of panic cut off by a mouthful of dirt.

Rachel was screaming. Screaming and snatching at a petticoat. She wore nothing but a very short chemise. Her slender, muscular legs reared above his eyes like white columns, supporting the spread of her hips. He wiped his face on his sleeve, his tongue, too, to get rid of the sand. She wriggled the petticoat over her head, the firm twist of her rounded rear end charming beyond belief.

"How dare you!" she cried the moment her head cleared the petticoat. He scarcely heard her over the great howl of victory outside the tent. Will grabbed at the canvas, but the weight of two or three boys held it down. He got to his hands and knees, wiping his tongue again, spitting grass. He looked for the exit, wondering how the hell he could explain this to Rachel. The petticoat hung from her shoulders, one arm free. She lifted her hairbrush.

The howling rose, and he imagined the boys dancing in a circle like triumphant Indians. Her hair hung in wet tangles, a medusa demon, the hairbrush drawn back. He dropped to the ground, his arms clasped over his head, waiting for the blow. "Please, Rachel!"

"We did it, Meggie!" a boy screamed.

"They...they made you?" she gasped.

"Made me!" He lifted his head. Her arm had relaxed a bit, only half drawn back. Get her sympathy. "I think Kit twisted my left arm out of the socket." He groaned. "Now I know how you felt when Anders..." He tried to move his left arm and this time groaned in earnest.

"The beasts!" she said, and snarled, a mother defending her young. She sprang toward the tent flap, the hairbrush lifted once more. "I'll beat them within an inch—" He managed to grab the petticoat with his right hand.

"No, Rachel." She dropped to her knees beside him, hand over her face. "Laugh," he whispered. She peeked through her fingers with a look that condemned him as crazy.

"What a pretty dress," he said loudly, pointing to the garment hanging from the tent pole.

"Oh," she whispered. "Ha-ha-ha." Her laugh sounded artificial. She grabbed the skirt.

"Ha-ha-ha. Let me help you brush your hair," he said loudly.

"My corset," she whispered from under the dark skirt. "Hand me my corset. Ha-ha-ha."

"Leave it off. Get dressed," he hissed. "There for a minute I thought you'd brain me with the hairbrush," he added. "Ha-ha-ha." Her head emerged from the skirt.

"Well, what did you expect? Coming into a woman's tent."

"I didn't come in. They threw me!"

"What a childish trick!" she shouted in the direction of the howling, which fell off a trifle. The tail of her bodice covered the top of her skirt. He helped with the buttons.

"I landed on my shoulder," he said. "Could you rub my left shoulder? I think it's bruised."

"What's going on here?" Godfroy. Murmurs of denial.

"Really, your shoulder hurts?" Rachel whispered.

"Really." She massaged and he took over the buttons. Something in his upper arm inside eased back into place.

"Good," he murmured.

"Why?" she asked, a vehement whisper.

"Boys love to play embarrassing tricks. They thought you'd be naked. Give me the hairbrush."

"I was!" she hissed. "Well, almost." She giggled, so he laughed loudly to cover the sound before he lowered his mouth to her ear.

"No, you had your dress on, remember. You were brushing your hair. Give me the hairbrush."

"Will! Don't pull so hard!" she said to the canvas as she handed him the brush.

"You're learning," he whispered. Her dark hair twisted in curls. He stretched each tress to its full length, but when he removed the tension the hair sprang back into waves.

"Did your mother have curly hair?" he asked.

"I don't know. She must have, for Father certainly doesn't, and I have a dreadful time keeping my hair up. It sneaks out of combs and pins."

"It's lovely." He worked his way around her. Wet, her hair looked black.

"No one's brushed my hair since I was a little girl." She

giggled, so he gave a great laugh again, in case anyone still waited outside.

"Will, what you said last night, it's very wrong, you know," she said in a low voice.

"Very wrong, I suppose," he whispered.

"But if it would stop this sort of thing—"

"We'll cross our fingers when we say 'I do.' That cancels the promise, I understand."

"And you promise with all your heart, truly and faithfully, that we'll be brother and sister?"

"I promise."

"But what if someday you meet a woman, and want to get married?" she asked. "This time Reverend Ludlow will write out a certificate, and I'll be your wife, legally."

He brushed her hair back from her forehead. "A lot of years, thousands of miles in the future. Probably never. I'll cross that bridge if I ever get to it. Now, I just heard some cheering from the direction of Burdette's wagon, so I expect the wheel's finished. We're going to step out laughing, and say what a great joke they played on us, and we're thinking maybe we should get married. Ha-ha-ha!"

Rachel swatted at the mosquitoes. The slightest movement set the lace sleeves of Tildy's wedding dress swaying, and they touched the bites she already had and made them itch.

"I wish we'd got beyond this buggy swamp before we camped," Faith said from the vicinity of her waist. "Hold still, Rachel, or I'll poke you with the needle."

"Hmm," agreed Louisa, her mouth full of pins.

"Too bad you girls aren't more of a size," said Granny from the floor, where she hurriedly folded a pleat in the flounce so it did not drag on the ground.

"Don't rush," Rachel said. "The men aren't done unloading the grain from the feed wagons."

"They just finished," Tildy said. "Josh says they're dressing Will so he looks respectable."

"We didn't mean to cause all this trouble," Rachel said. "Your silk wedding dress will be filthy, Tildy. It'll have grass stains on the skirt."

"You can't be married in calico," Tildy replied.

"Turn about," Granny said. Rachel made a slow quarter turn, and heaved a deep sigh. All this bother!

"Don't breathe," said Faith. "I want the bodice to fit snug as possible."

"I'm afraid the men are celebrating ahead of time," Tildy said. "The teamsters brought whiskey along, and Josh said they're sharing it, since they'll turn back tomorrow."

"There!" Faith said. "Snug as a—"

"Don't you dare say bug, Faith Tole!" Rachel snapped, shaking her head in a futile attempt to dislodge the mosquitoes feasting on her neck.

Meggie leaned around the corner of the wagon. "Will wants to know, where's the ring?"

"Under the boards of the false floor, on the left side, with my petticoats," Rachel said. "It's wrapped in my grandmother's cloth of gold."

"Bring the gold cloth, too," Tildy said.

"Turn," Louisa muttered through her barrier of pins.

"I have a fine gingham dress that fits without all this trouble," Rachel muttered, but no one paid the least bit of attention. She tried to swat mosquitoes without moving her arms above the elbow.

"Stay still," Granny said.

"Here," Meggie said. From the corner of her eye Rachel saw Tildy's hands overflowing with gold.

"Turn," said Granny. Rachel could not see what Tildy did with the gold cloth, but the pins were drawn from her bun and fabric brushed her neck. Or perhaps a very large mosquito?

"Hold still, Rachel," said Tildy.

"I can't. I'm being eaten up." Why all this fuss? Will had quietly asked Reverend Ludlow if he could write out a marriage certificate, since they had already gone through the ceremony. And suddenly the whole camp went crazy. Now the men were decking Will out, while they got him drunk, probably, and Mrs. MacIntyre had unpacked her reflector oven and she and Mrs. Burdette were wasting precious cinnamon and dried fruit making a cake.

"There!" exclaimed Granny. She and Louisa bent close to bite off the threads. "Tildy, go see if the men are ready. No, wait! Who do you want to stand beside you, Rachel?"

Who? Which friend to sign the mockery of a marriage certificate? Faith leaned against the wagon, disapproval plain on her face.

"Faith."

"Me!"

"She wants you," Granny said. She shoved Faith away from the wagon. "Walk with her."

Rachel took Faith's hand as they rounded the wagon. "We'll still have our school. Don't worry."

"You're getting married," Faith said morosely. "I knew they'd talk you into it."

Will stood beside her father, dressed in a claw-hammer coat that was too small for him. All the men ranged behind him. Firelight gleamed on an earthenware jug as Mr. Marshall swung it behind his back. Kit and Josh smirked, proud of their responsibility in the decision.

Reverend Ludlow began the ceremony the moment Will took her hand. Rachel noticed that Kraft had left out certain parts. Or perhaps she had not heard them, what with listening for her father's death rattle. "If any man knows cause why these two should not be joined in wedlock, let him speak now or forever hold his peace." She waited, half hoping, certain someone had guessed they were not serious. Silence.

She vowed to love, honor and obey, with the fingers of her left hand crossed in the fullness of the silk skirt. Will promised to love, cherish and care for her, so earnestly that she lowered her eyes. He had forgotten!

The ring slipped on her finger. She waited for the final words, braced herself for Will's kiss, but Reverend Ludlow turned to his wife, who handed him a Bible.

"Let us find the future the Lord has in store for this young couple," he said. He closed his eyes, opened the book at random, ran his finger down the page, opened his eyes and tilted the Bible toward the firelight. He gasped, and his mouth dropped open. He stammered a word or two, composed himself. "'She gave the king an hundred and twenty talents of gold, and of spices great abundance, and precious stones: neither was there any such spice as the Queen of Sheba gave King Solomon.'"

He read the words slowly, as if he did not believe them. "The Lord blesses you with great abundance," he said in awe. "I now pronounce you man and wife."

Did he truly believe this prophecy? Rachel giggled, which spoiled the chaste kiss, for her mouth was open when Will put his lips to hers. Faith signed the certificate with a sour face. Tildy looked so pleased, and Meggie so mischievously happy, that Rachel asked them to sign, too. Mr. Tole signed as groomsman, even though her father had stood beside Will, and she felt a wave of gratitude that Will had eased over the problem of the signature, not exposing her father's lack of education.

"How much is a talent?" Rachel asked Reverend Ludlow as he added his signature. "Since I'm bringing Will one hundred and twenty, how much in American money?"

"A talent, as I recall, is weight, not cash. At least a thousand pounds," he said.

"Sixty tons of gold?" Burdette said, awed.

"Seems Mrs. Hunter's overloaded her wagon, Captain Hull," Marshall said.

"Sixty tons of gold!" Anders dismissed the prophecy with a wave of his hand. "The only place in the world with that amount of gold is Her Majesty's treasury."

Rachel removed the pins holding the cloth of gold to her hair, balled up the almost weightless fabric and laid it in Will's hand. "Here. This doesn't weigh nearly sixty tons, but it's a beginning."

"Now the dancing!" Tildy cried. She held her banjo. "And the cake!"

"Before any celebration, I have an announcement," Reverend Ludlow said, raising his hand. "My wife and I, after prayerful consideration, have decided. We shall return to St. Joseph with the feed wagons."

"What?" everyone cried.

"Already this journey weighs us down. The sun, the wind, frightening rain without proper shelter, and three of my mules drowned. Brother Sampson says we've not faced a tenth of the burdens. Tomorrow morning we turn our faces east. I beg of you, come with us, before all are lost."

"Go back?" Granny asked, unbelieving. "But we're only a few days on our way. And just now you said Rachel and Will have a future of plenty. That doesn't foretell disaster."

"Their prosperous future lies in the East, not in California," Reverend Ludlow said primly. "As I understand, great wealth *would* shower upon Mr. Shakespeare if only he restrained his youthful temper and returned to his father's house and governance."

"The verse said *she*—Rachel—would bring him wealth," Granny said.

"Let us ask again." Reverend Ludlow sighed as he closed his eyes and repeated the process of divination. "'And the glory of the Lord went up from the midst of the city, and stood upon the mountain which is on the east side of the city.'"

"That's plain," Kit said. "Head for the mountains."

"The quick, unthinking voice of youth," Reverend Ludlow said. "The verse speaks of a mountain to the east of the city, and you're traveling west."

"Perhaps," Sir Anders said, winking very obviously in Mr. Reid's direction, "this foretells a great city in the wilds of California, complete with sixty tons of gold. In that case the mountain *would* be to the east."

If he had meant to make fun of Ludlow, he failed, for Kit jumped on the interpretation. "That's what it means for sure," he yelled. "Ho for California!" The rest of the boys joined in the shouting.

"Ho! Ho! Ho!" Merri screamed.

"The cake and the dancing," Tildy said, holding up her banjo.

"Cake," Captain Hull said sharply. "Then to bed. Because we pull out at daybreak to pass the Oregonians while they noon." He leveled a stern look at the boys. "And no shivaree for the newlyweds, no wagon rolling or tent poles that disappear. First watch out to the cattle, second watch to your blankets, because the night passes fast."

Will felt silly pacing in front of his own tent, waiting for the women to arrange his bedroll beside Rachel's. They would have to thrash about in the dark, pulling them apart.

He tugged on the too-short sleeves for the hundredth time. What had possessed him to wear Ludlow's ridiculous coat?

"Ready," Tildy said as she ducked out the tent flap, her yellow silk dress dangling from her arm. "She's not at all afraid, so be easy this time," she whispered.

The tent was as dark as the inside of a bear. "Where are you?" he whispered.

"Here. On your right." He knelt, groped about for his blankets, dragged them to their accustomed place.

"Will, I hope you don't believe that silly prophecy of Reverend Ludlow's."

"Of course I don't. There's not that much gold in all the United States and territories. Including California."

"Good."

"But the jewels and spices, that might come true. You'll bring me good luck, Rachel."

"I hope so. All I want is peace and quiet."

"That, too. Good night."

"Good night." Her blankets rustled as she settled into a comfortable position.

Good luck? Rachel would bring him the best of luck. He was married. No matter what woman tempted him in the future, he was married, and would never father children he'd be tempted to neglect. Something buzzed under the blanket! He slapped at it, threw the blanket back and waved his hands.

"Awake?" Rachel asked.

"A blasted mosquito!"

"If I had sixty tons of gold, would you keep your blankets next to mine, and make me be your wife? So you could have the gold?"

"What the hell would I do with sixty tons of gold? Sit on it? I can't think of a more worthless dowry."

\* \* \*

Rachel prodded the near ox. "Come up," she yelled as loudly as she could. The chains tightened as the oxen stepped out, following the wagon before them. She kept pace, pretending to be in charge, knowing all the while that the oxen would do very well on their own.

Her father rode far ahead with Sir Anders. Will had vanished early, leaving the tent so quietly she had not awakened. His lack of success in hunting bothered him, and today was his last chance before reaching the Big Blue River. She hoped he killed something. Burdette had set out on the army horse, determined to show his own prowess as a hunter. And demonstrate they need not pay a professional.

"Hello," Louisa said.

"Low," Merri said, peeking around the shawl that supported her on her mother's hip.

Louisa grinned. "I think marriage agrees with you," she said.

"It does." Very much, Rachel thought wryly. Yesterday she and Will had been apart the entire day, and not one person had made up a trivial excuse to bring them together. Last night she sat with her friends, and Will lounged with the men, and no one wanted to make kitten ladders....

"I never thanked you, for bringing Mr. Tole to me," Louisa said.

"Me? I did nothing—"

"You let me be your friend. You guessed, I'm certain, that I wasn't a widow, but you kept it to yourself. I never would have dared follow Sir Anders that evening, except I could pretend to be calling on you."

"I'm glad I helped."

"And what a wonderful husband! Mr. Tole tells me exactly what I'm to do, so I *know* I'm pleasing him. Not like some men, who think a woman can mind read. Mr.

Brown...Robert did that. Never said a word, then pouted when I didn't do as he thought proper."

"That would be difficult." Rachel pretended the lead team needed her attention.

"And—" Louisa's voice dropped to a whisper "—he's jolly at night."

"I'm so glad."

"Much more attentive than Robert ever was."

"How delightful." Rachel wished she had cut the brims of her sunbonnets two inches wider.

"I thought...perhaps Mr. Hunter's like his brother, not...skilled, shall we say. He could speak to Mr. Tole, get some pointers."

Rachel tugged on her sunbonnet and heard the snap as stitches broke.

"Or maybe you don't know. A woman can have a rollicking good time in the blankets." She stepped in front of Rachel and peered beneath the brim. "Mr. Hunter's been short and sharp, hasn't he?"

Rachel lifted the goad. "Gee," she said to the lead team. Oh, bother, she meant to say "Haw." It made no difference—the oxen followed the wagon ahead.

"You tell Mr. Hunter, before you'll let him in your bed again, he's to talk to Mr. Tole." She stepped so close, Merri touched Rachel's hip. Louisa giggled. "Mr. Tole's taken to wearing moccasins in bed, because his toes rubbed raw, we been going at it so heavy."

"Horsey," said Merri, pointing to the oxen.

"No, dear, those are oxen. That is a horse. Good day, Mr. Hunter. Any luck today?"

"No. Rachel, ride out with me to the river thickets. I might have a chance if we're the first ones there."

"I didn't ask Tony Tole to drive the oxen today. He

charges ten cents a day, and by the time we reach California, that will add up to ten or fifteen dollars."

He waved the cost aside. "I'll fetch Tony and saddle Josefa."

"I believe," Louisa said after Will had gone, "that he's more considerate than his brother. You tell him to speak to my husband. Everyone noticed, the morning after your wedding, that you were a trifle serious."

"And talked about me?" Rachel asked in horror. Marriage had not put a stop to the busybody interference.

"Of course. And the women decided I should speak to you, since Mr. Tole's in a position to help."

She must ride out with Will, Rachel decided. She would put on a broad-brimmed hat, so everyone saw her smile. She would be the ecstatic bride they expected to see.

Will noticed that Rachel's spirits improved as they rode away from the wagons. She must ride more often. "See the dust," he said, pointing behind them. "The Oregon party. They're driving hard to keep up."

"They should rest a day and let their poor oxen feed."

"Tomorrow we join the road from Independence," Will said. "They'll find another party. I never told you, you were beautiful in your wedding dress."

"It's Tildy's. Her mother hired a seamstress to make it when Tildy married Matt Hull."

"How do you enjoy being a married lady?" he asked, making sure his grin was conspiratorial.

"Yesterday I thought we'd put everyone off. But Louisa. She's…they're…" Her words trailed away and she looked straight ahead. A spot of red touched her cheek.

"What's bothering Mrs. Tole?" he asked.

She opened her mouth, closed it. The spot of red ex-

panded. "She thinks you should speak to Mr. Tole. She
said he'll give you pointers on pleasing a woman."

"I thought I *was* pleasing you," he said.

"Of course you are," she said. "You stay on your side
of the tent pole and I stay on mine."

Will straightened up, pushed back his hat to see if the
timber along the Big Blue might be in sight. "No sense
arriving at the ford too early. Let's ride south. I think the
river flows at the bottom of this ridge. We're more likely
to find game off the road." She nodded, and pulled her hat
down on the left to shield her face against the sun. The
ridge dropped to the river in a long gradual slope.

"Flowers!" Rachel cried. As far as he could see, the
prairie was pink, verging into lavender. "Flowers, flowers
everywhere!" She slid off Josefa, so he dismounted,
stepped on a carpet so crowded with blossoms his foot
trampled a multitude wherever he put it down. Rachel was
already picking a nosegay.

"I'm so glad you asked me to come." She pulled on the
lacing of his hunting shirt, enlarged one of the holes and
inserted the bouquet. She stepped back, tilted her head. "It
needs something more, a white blossom, perhaps. Yellow!"
she cried. She tore at the tough stem, leaving a ragged end.
She tugged at the hole, but the flowers already stretched it
wide. She thrust again and again until the thick stem slid
in and the yellow flower shone in the midst of the pink.
Thrusting, as he had done...wanted to do. The lightning
flashed through his loins without warning. She smiled, innocent of the potent symbolism. He turned away, staring
with hunter's eyes at the landscape.

# Chapter Nineteen

"I believe something's moving below us." His blood pulsed so strongly, Will found it difficult to focus the telescope. A small limestone outcrop capped the river bluff. It changed shape.

"Will, something's in the grass." He turned in time to see a light streak heading for the rock.

"A wolf," he said. It hesitated for an instant on the flat rock, then dropped over the edge.

"Slowly," he whispered. He held out his hand and she hooked a finger over his. The breeze blew in their faces. The wolf would not catch their scent.

"Drop Josefa's trail rope," he said quietly. "They'll graze here."

Upstream from the wolf's den another rock had eroded, not flat, but a protuberance, like a snag in a river, like his desire for her. He tugged at his hunting shirt to make sure he was covered. Ferns grew in profusion at the base of the rock. Amid the leafy stems, coils of new growth thrust upward, sensual, suggestive of reaching male power.

"Down," he whispered. The wolf was resting, barely visible against the gray rock. Two pups cavorted in the crevices, coming in and out of sight. Will pushed the glass into Rachel's hand, and their gloved fingers touched. A shock, even through the leather. He knew the moment when she focused on the wolves. A long inward breath of wonder.

"Will, they're just like puppies. Look at them tumble! Two adorable babies!"

"Who next year will be full-grown wolves," he reminded her. "I left my rifle—"

"Don't shoot her, Will! Please! Don't kill her babies!"

"I left my rifle on the horse," he said.

Her pleading eyes led him into a foolish, feminine sentimentality, into the emotions that made women poor hunters. He tried to smile, but knew it had not been successful. "Who wants wolf meat? And there's no time to dry pelts...."

She lowered her head. "I'm sorry, Will. I'm not a very good wife, am I? Not like Louisa, who would walk through fire if Mr. Tole ordered her to."

He considered catching her chin with a finger, lifting her head so he might see the apology as well as hear it. But if he touched her ever so slightly he might do more. Do all he dreamed of, lift her skirts, plunge into her, thrusting again and again, ignoring her cries of fright and pain as he attained the ultimate fury of sex.

"You're a fine wife."

"No, I gave you orders. I'm the one who vowed to obey."

"But you had your fingers crossed, so you can order me about all you want. Let's ride on down the river."

"You forgot to cross your fingers," she said, flashing a smile that cascaded through his loins. "I looked when you said the vows."

"I was afraid I'd get the ring tangled up, and wouldn't have it ready to put on your finger," he said.

He helped her mount, the touch of her boot lodging the weight of a brick in his gut. He thought of Robert, the walk to St. Joe, how superior he felt. Not superior after all, only retarded. At twenty, for the first time, experiencing the yeasty, foaming expectations, which would grow to insatiable hunger, until he, too, seduced women wherever he went. He must be discreet in his affairs, so he did not shame Rachel. Or disappoint Godfroy.

Three buzzards dozed on the skeletal limb of a dead sycamore tree. He and Robert, buzzards preying on women. He spurred ahead, recalled his duty to search for game and slowed near the river. Rachel caught up, stopped beside him, their legs almost touching, and threw her arms around his neck.

"Thank you for not killing the wolves." Flames licked his legs, enveloped his torso, a precursor to the torments of hell. He thrust her away.

"Don't touch me! We're brother and sister, remember?"

"But sisters hug their brothers!" Her eyes were hurt. "Particularly when they do a favor."

He closed his eyes and slumped in the saddle. "I'm a man, and a man can bear only so much," he said thickly. "There on the ridge, it came into my mind—"

"You promised!" she whispered.

"My mind promised. Not...not..."

"Your body?" She was remarkably calm, not like him, dismembered, being fed piece by piece into the fire.

"I won't bother you, Rachel. Just keep your hands off me." He must explain. "I'm glad we're married. You understand my nature and won't condemn me. I'll be very careful that no scandal touches you. No one guessed that Robert was unfaithful to his wife. I'll be as cautious."

"Will, no woman here would even consider—"

"Tomorrow we join the Independence road. Among that

crowd there'll be sporting women. And farther west...I promise, nothing will reflect upon you.''

''I see,'' she said. She flicked the reins easily and Josefa walked away.

''You do not see!'' he shouted at her back. Why didn't she object? Why didn't she say, ''You're not your brother?'' Because he and Robert *were* brothers, both caught up in the chase to satisfy their lusts. He should have known, long ago, that his primal nature would one day emerge.

Will helped the boys herd the cattle across the Big Blue and drive them a quarter mile off trail, to an expanse of lush pasture. Tiny pink flowers lifted their heads through the mat of vegetation, flowers matching the blossoms wilting in his hunting shirt. Back at the ford he found the wagons had divided into two groups: Burdette and Marshall stood with Anders, the servants and the mule skinners. The rest of the men clustered about Matt Hull. Will headed toward the captain. and at the same time Anders sauntered in that direction.

''I believe this is the Big Blue River,'' Anders said. ''I count nine men behind me, and Captain Hull but seven.''

''It's all yours,'' Hull said, sweeping his arm to embrace every wagon, animal, man, woman and child.

''We shall lay by for the rest of today,'' Anders said proudly. He turned to Kit. ''Have you found a suitable pasture?'' Kit nodded. The boy was so pained at being denied a vote when the English servants had one that he stamped his feet, trampling pink flowers into the ground. ''No need to watch the stock, if the grass is good, but look close there's none of that jimsonweed. But I suppose we're not that far west yet. Godfroy, Sampson, you'll stay with me and explain the exigencies of the trail to the Platte.''

"I'm off hunting," Burdette said. "We'll have fresh meat tonight." The army horse pawed the ground, bucked, but finally settled down. Will got back in the saddle. *I'll stay out until I find game.*

He searched every thicket along the river. The tall rock loomed over his head. He left the horse to graze by the stream and climbed the bluff, carrying his rifle. The wolf lazed in a shady nook of the rock. No pups romped, so they must be napping, too. Will settled down to wait. This was the life he was meant for. Open country, no ties, no feminine sympathy, no traps of guilty love. Tonight Anders would rig a vote to dismiss him. No job, no fifty dollars. Perhaps a party from Independence would hire him. He should ride out now, to reach the junction by nightfall.

He could stay with Godfroy, Will reminded himself, for Godfroy was his father-in-law. Poor man, he knew nothing of the deception he and Rachel played. If he left he shamed Rachel, and Godfroy would learn the truth and think badly of him. He didn't want Godfroy to think badly of him. Trapped! As firmly as if he'd been married in the biggest church in Pittsburgh. He could not simply ride away.

The wolf raised her head. Another wolf scrambled up the bluff from the river. A whole family! He examined them over the sights of the rifle, waiting until one presented a perfect target. Both broadside to him at the same time. Which one? They touched noses, licked muzzles, their tongues sensually intertwined while they uttered little cries of welcome. Or love? The sights wavered. A pup climbed, in a puppy's awkward way, onto the rock, pulling at his mother to claim her attention.

Will dropped the rifle, grabbed his crotch to eliminate by main force the swelling his trousers could hardly contain. He curled in the bracken, moaning from the pain that swathed his loins. The pain of wanting her. A fern encircled his neck, the touch like Rachel's.

How long since an arm had gone around him, lips touched his cheek? Almost two years, in the mountains of Pennsylvania, when he heard of his mother's death, when he told Zack and Alma he would give his father at least a year. Alma had tried to throw her arm across his shoulders, had laughed, remembering the first time he walked into their clearing, his head below her shoulder. Even Zack, after a masculine handshake, had embraced him, wished him good luck.

Then home to the mansion in Pittsburgh, where everyone kept a proper distance. Except for the servants. The butler had hugged him in the pantry, the cook stained the back of his new coat with her flour-covered fingers. Fifteen years ago, on the first expedition from the nursery, he had gone to their cottage behind the house.

"I didn't run to them for open spaces, or for hunting," he said aloud, for this amazing thought required a public airing. Hugs and kisses had been the magnet. He had given his flight manly blessing by saying he wanted to learn woodcraft, to handle a gun, to ride a horse and yoke oxen. Yet, thinking back, in every house of refuge there had been a buxom mother. Sometimes a tangle of half-wild children. The shy joy on first encountering them, older boys holding him down, beating on him, or tickling him until he screamed. Tolerating their strange ways until he held his own in roughhousing, then a grudging place as foster brother, accepting their affection.

Will sank lower among the ferns. Horses and rifles, ax and saddle. All excuses. He ran away from the empty nursery, the echoing house to feel an arm across his shoulders and experience a good-night kiss.

"Rachel," he whispered. He trailed a stem of fern across

his mouth, as he might kiss a tress of her hair. He must go to Rachel and confess that things had changed. That he loved her. Loved her father. Wanted them to love him, too.

The thickets cut off his view of the ford, but he heard men's voices, then the splashing of horses. Several of the men must have gone out hunting and had immediate success.

A scream. A panther? A woman! Renegades or Pawnees. Rachel shrieking as a stranger pulled her on his horse? As he ravished her? He drove his horse into the current before he reached the ford. "Rachel, Rachel, I'm coming!" he muttered. "Hold on. Fight!"

Dirty blue coats, heavy horses, not the wiry breeds of the plains. Soldiers!

"There he is! That man stole the horse!" Burdette stood between two soldiers, pointed with a strange gesture, both arms raised, his wrists crossed. Bound, by God!

Will laughed and slowed his lathered horse. A misunderstanding, soon cleared up. He rode straight to the only soldier still mounted. The officer, he judged. He swung his leg over...and was roughly jerked to the ground. Hands closed on his arms, and the mounted soldier leaned down, stared with unfriendly eyes through cheeks puffy with sunburn. "Where's the rest of the horses?"

"Rest of...what are you talking about?"

"He brought the horse to me!" Burdette screamed.

"Shut up!" Will said, needing a moment to frame his explanation. The officer nodded. A noise in his skull, nearby lightning, rolling thunder that echoed and echoed.

"What horses?" he tried to say, but one side of his face did not move. He groped with his hands and felt the ground.

"I believe—" Anders's high-pitched voice "—you are sadly mistaken as to the sequence of events."

"Get out of here, greenhorn."

"But you don't understand! I am Sir Anders Trout, of
Lindenlore Castle."

"I don't care if you're God Almighty. Any man who
wears white buckskin should be tied over an anthill. Spread
out, men." The explosive shout pounded in Will's head.
"Search every gully. They've got the horses hid." Strong
arms dragged him to his feet. He wished they'd leave him
on the ground, for the whole world spun.

"Where are the horses?" The last time he had heard
those words—

"Stop!" A female voice, quite close by. Granny?
"You're mistaken. I brought the horse to camp." Rachel!

"Get this woman off me!" Will opened his eyes and
saw everything in twos. Two Rachels, two horses. By clos-
ing one eye, he distinguished a single Rachel clinging to
the officer's stirrup. Will tried to step toward her, but was
held back by weakness and bondage.

"He was all alone—the horse, that is—wandering, with
the saddle bumping his poor legs, and I took a hatful of
barley—"

The man kicked at her, but Rachel dodged nimbly, still
grasping his stirrup leather. "He came right to me."

"That sounds right, Sarge," said a voice near Will's ear.
"Tawny always behaved better for the lady."

"We found their cattle," someone yelled. "None of our
horses there."

"Of course not," Will said, but the words came out thick
and he supposed no one understood.

"Of course not," Rachel said. "Don't talk, Will, I'll
explain." That's right. Rachel would handle everything, because she had remembered to cross her fingers. "Were we
supposed to leave the horse like that? Hurting and—"

"What's going on here, Sergeant?" Will sagged with

relief. Captain Hull. Not Captain Hull, for Anders was the captain, but a man capable of taking charge. "Release these men immediately!"

"Who're you to be giving orders?" the soldier asked.

"Lieutenant Matthew Hull, U.S. Army. Artillery."

The men's hands fell away, too suddenly, because they held him up. Will closed his eyes so he did not see the ground rise to meet him. Somewhere, at a great distance, explanations and apologies. No need to listen, for Rachel knelt over him, murmuring senseless words, clasping her hands behind his neck, lifting his head into her lap.

"A cold compress," she whispered, and it touched his face, except the part covered by her kisses.

"I've put some five-fingered grass to soak for a poultice," Granny said. "You soldiers there, lift this man and carry him to a softer bed."

"No," he whispered to Rachel. "This is fine. I'll be able to walk in a little while."

"Don't talk," she said.

"I must. Things have changed," he muttered.

"They certainly have, dear. Don't talk." How did she know he had sought love for fifteen years? He had just come to know it himself. Then he remembered, she had crossed her fingers and the cloth of gold did not harm her. Everything made a crazy kind of sense.

"The horse came to me," Rachel whispered past the poultice, "because it was Mrs. Colonel Bidderman's favorite mount. An army horse who likes women." She cradled Will's head in her lap, ignoring the fact that the poultice wet her skirt.

Mr. Burdette stepped into the circle of firelight, behind him Mr. Marshall. "I have second thoughts...about captain. I suppose it's best to have an American officer as our boss. Right now, if it hadn't been for Captain Hull…'' Rachel had never noticed Mr. Marshall's stammer before. The men standing around the fire stirred and Will hooked a hand over her shoulder to sit up.

"I agree," Burdette said, rubbing his wrists. "Never know when we'll meet more dragoons on the trail, and having Matt Hull as captain, well, he knows their lingo."

Rachel laughed.

"What's funny?" Will asked.

"Men," she said.

The wind lifted ashes from the dinner fires. The tents looked like billowing sails. Will measured the sway of the tent pole as well as possible with one eye swollen shut.

"Anders is madder than a saddled bear," Godfroy said. "He expected, after we joined the Independence trail, to get two or three more parties to elect him captain, so he'd lead the biggest train on the road. I think you're right, the tent should come down. You two can sleep in the wagon."

Will had noticed before that he and Godfroy often had the same thought at the same time.

"I'm proud of you, Rachel," Godfroy said. "The men were scared to go against the soldiers. You were the only one with gumption enough to step forward."

"She saved my neck," Will said.

"The truth would have come out once Captain Hull talked to the sergeant," she said, dismissing his gratitude. "I just speeded things up by screaming." She flaked soap into the dishwater.

"Reminded me of a panther with kittens," Godfroy said. "That coffee ready, Rachel?" She dropped the soap.

"Don't bother, Rachel," Will said. "I'll get it."

"But you should be quiet."

"Don't hover."

"Thank you." She smiled, and the fragrance of sugared flapjacks washed around him. And a thin line of silk, not about his chest. Lower down.

"Me and Sampson rode out to the junction," Godfroy said. "There's a party camped just south, so Hull wants everyone ready to roll at daybreak. That way we keep the lead." Rachel paid more attention to the soap than necessary.

Will helped Godfroy fold the stiff tent. Godfroy stuck his head through the flap at the rear of the wagon.

"Plenty of room for the two of you to sleep in here, now that the extra provisions are stowed under the floor." Godfroy wrapped himself in his buffalo robe and stretched out, feet to the fire. Rachel climbed into the wagon.

"Will," she called quietly. He would suggest a stroll away from camp, although walking in the rising gale was hardly romantic. He looked into the wagon. Both bedrolls were spread in the narrow confines, and Rachel sat on the blankets, wrapped in a shawl. More comfortable than being in the wind, and what he had to say would take only a few minutes. He pulled off his boots and crawled in. She opened the shawl, causing him to stop, one hand and one knee raised. He closed his eyes against the glow of white skin. Cross-legged on his blankets, completely naked.

"Will, you're not like your brother. I won't let you."

"Rachel!"

"If the men hadn't changed their minds about who was captain, Granny meant to threaten to walk back to St. Joe. She said sometimes a woman has to sacrifice, to make men come to their senses. I won't let you be your brother!"

He drew his legs under him and crouched against the tailgate. The neighboring fire flickered and the shadows of her high breasts moved on the wagon cover.

"No. The first time you let me in your bed out of gratitude,'' he said. "Now you'll sacrifice yourself to save my soul. I've got three things to tell you, then I'll crawl under the wagon and leave you alone. First, thank you for rushing to my rescue.''

"That was nothing," she said.

"Second, so long as you're my wife, we're living together, because I want to be with you. And I want Godfroy to be my father. But nothing will happen, physically, not at my instigation, anyway." He stopped, for the agitation of lust clouded his mind and he had a hard time remembering number three. She stared at his crotch.

"I'm sorry," he said huskily. He put his hands behind him, palms down, to scoot out of the wagon.

"You said three things," Rachel said.

"Get off my blankets, Rachel."

"You're sleeping here. I've got something to tell you."

"Say it."

"Not until you're here." She patted the blankets.

He loosened the belt of his hunting shirt, threw it and the knife to the end of the wagon. He lay with his back pressed against the wagon box. Her head came down, hair falling forward like a veil, her lips parted. "I liked it, when we got married, you kissed me with my mouth open."

"Is that what you wanted to tell me?"

"No." Her small body uncoiled, rolled against him, her thighs gentle against the hardening bulge he could not control. She slid an arm beneath him, clasped her hands on the back of his neck.

"I love you." A faint admission, barely audible. Fragrance of sugar and wood smoke in her hair. "I knew today, when the soldier grabbed you. I went all hollow inside, and I knew, if you ever went away, I'd be all alone. Forever. I suppose that's how it feels, grand passion."

He curled his fingers in the placket of his hunting shirt,

resisting an embrace that would lead inevitably to physical passion on his part, pain on hers. "Don't get so close to me," he said. "My clothes are filthy."

"Undress," she whispered. She unbuttoned the flap of his trousers and shoved his hunting shirt toward his armpits.

He groaned at her touch, then sat up. Undressing in the restricted space took a great deal of wriggling, and by the time he stripped his shirt over his head, their legs were entangled, his warm, hers cold.

"A blanket?" he whispered. "You feel like ice."

She thrust a soft coverlet into his hand.

"What's this?"

"The wedding quilt."

He adjusted her head on his shoulder, and spread his hand on her back. "We have marvelous times together," he whispered, "and I love you. If you should go away…I don't want to think about it."

"You won't go looking for another woman?" she begged. "It hurt me so much, as if you'd used your knife, when you said you'd find—"

"I'll look at other women, to compare them to you, and know that you're the most beautiful woman in the world."

She moved her hips a fraction. "You do what you want."

"We'll do what we both want." The flames of the nearby fire had died and nothing remained but darkness and wind. He slid his hand down her side, to her legs, found them spread. He touched the tight bud of her sex in the tangle of hair. Star threads. Her arms tightened for a moment, she shuddered against him, and the slight movement loosed his climax before he could enter her.

"I'm sorry," she whispered.

He patted her back to tell her it made no difference. "We'll learn together."

* * *

Rachel woke to silence. The wind had died. She shifted her head on a hard pillow. Will's shoulder.

"Rachel?" he whispered.

"You're awake?"

"I've not slept. I wanted to enjoy the whole night."

"Don't think you're bound, just because this happened," she said. "I understand, a wife's a burden to a man with your ambitions."

"You're not a burden. You're what I've wanted forever."

"The time will come when you long to see what's on the other side of the horizon, and I can't go." Her whisper held a hint of regret.

"I won't go where you can't. I didn't understand before, that every time I ran away, I looked for you."

He kissed her breasts, avoiding the nipples until she moved one to his mouth. Whatever he wanted, although the pain low in her body had become almost unbearable. She arched her back, collided with his solid shaft. He lifted her leg across his hips and she held her breath as he fitted the tip of the shaft to her opened notch. The pain would change, she knew, from the throbs deep inside to a fiery stabbing as he tore into her. His hands grasped her hips, held her against him.

"Do it!" she gasped. The waiting was far worse than the minutes of agony.

"Rachel, I love you." His hands tightened.

"Do it!" Did she have to beg? Did he mean to humble her, so she would be like Louisa Tole, his crawling servant?

"I love you," he whispered. Force and energy, a great spasm, paralyzing even though she was overcome with panic and fright. She fought to bear the suffering, to stifle her scream, every part of her falling inward, embracing a rock that churned like a swollen river, echoing back in turmoil, again and again, until chaos soothed into rhythm, and the prairie sea heaved in wave after wave of rolling quakes.

"Have I hurt you?" he whispered. His fingers lifted the damp curls from her forehead. She ran her hand down his side, across his stomach, and touched their union. Every part of her wet. And him. A friendly feeling, the throbbing that eased to a gentle quiver.

"No, it's gone."

"Gone?"

"The pain that came whenever I thought of you. Whenever you touched me. It's been so bad lately, I decided nothing could be worse, even you inside me."

"Wanting," he whispered. "It hurts to want someone."

"I didn't know it was wanting. I thought I was so terribly afraid—"

"No fear. No fear when we're together. We'll cross every river that flows in our path. 'Neither was there any such spice as the Queen of Sheba gave King Solomon.' Part of the verse has come true already."

She laughed, and their connection moved in the same pattern. She pressed herself against him, loin to loin so he did not leave. "I suffered from grand passion, and didn't even know it. Can we do it again?"

"Not until this evening. The sky's turned and the hunter's star's rising. Hull will have us on the trail at daybreak."

"Anders is leaving," Godfroy said the moment Will dropped his legs over the tailgate. "He can't be head man, he'll go home. We're only ten men, and two near grown boys. I got to tell Sampson." A fog hung in the river bottom. No stars visible.

"Wait!" Godfroy turned. "Would you mind...now that Rachel and I are married...if I called you Father?"

"Seems a bit formal, between men."

"There's more between us than most men. Rachel."

"My old friends in the mountains called me Trail."

Old friends in the mountains. "Thank you."

A fire flickered in a trench, the lid of a coffeepot rattled. Horned cattle loomed in faint outline as the last watch of the night came in. Rachel's cheek pressed on his back. He turned just enough to squeeze her hand before she jumped to the ground beside him.

The fog drifted in ghostly fingers, exposing and concealing. No activity around Anders's tents. No need for them to leave early. In fact, more pleasant to let the day age, so they did not face directly into the rising sun. He led the horses from the wagon circle to graze. No riding this morning. The whole day with Rachel beside the wagon, careful not to look at any women in the Independence trains.

"Hunter." Reid emerged from a finger of fog. "Is there any man who'd take me in? I don't want to turn back. I'll work for my board."

Ten men. Reid would make eleven. "Can you drive an ox team?"

"I can learn."

"Speak to Captain Hull. He's not happy that Tildy must drive the animals when he's busy."

"Anders *should* leave me part of the provisions."

"Should, but probably won't," Will said. "Have you said anything of this to him?"

"Not until I asked. I couldn't sleep all night, daring myself…. I don't have much money, but British ships stop on the California coast and I can work my way home."

"Not to the embraces of Sir Anders's sister, I wager."

"Certainly not. Not if I abandon him. It's your fault. You inspired me, renouncing fortune and family to claim your own dream. You see, I'd been offered a position in London. My mother fainted when I told her. My brother said I'd disgrace the family, said I should come with Sir Anders.''

"Something illegal?" Will asked, curious to know what skills Reid possessed other than milking cows.

"I thought it quite respectable. Work with a publishing firm, with a partnership in the offing, based upon expectations on the death of my grandmother."

"Publishing? Books?"

"Yes. Not a large establishment, but quite well thought of. Perhaps, when I return home, the post may still be available."

"Trail won't mind if you stow your things in his wagon. For today," Will added, remembering the pleasure the bed promised tonight. "Let's find Hull."

The fog separated and the sky arched clear above them. The band of the Milky Way shone in splendor, and against that brilliant background a greater brilliance. A falling star, trailing fire and star threads.

\* \* \* \* \*

# Looking For More Romance?

Visit Romance.net

Look us up on-line at: http://www.romance.net

## Check in daily for these and other exciting features:

**Hot off the press**

View all current titles, and purchase them on-line.

What do the stars have in store for you?

**Horoscope**

**Hot deals**

Exclusive offers available only at Romance.net

Plus, don't miss our interactive quizzes, contests and bonus gifts.

PWEB

# DEBBIE MACOMBER

*invites you to the*

## HEART OF TEXAS

Join Debbie Macomber as she brings you the lives and loves of the folks in the ranching community of Promise, Texas.

If you loved Midnight Sons—don't miss Heart of Texas! A brand-new six-book series from Debbie Macomber.

Available in February 1998 at your favorite retail store.

## Heart of Texas by Debbie Macomber

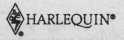 HARLEQUIN®

# COMING NEXT MONTH FROM

# HARLEQUIN HISTORICALS

---

## DON'T MISS THESE FOUR GREAT TITLES AVAILABLE NOW!

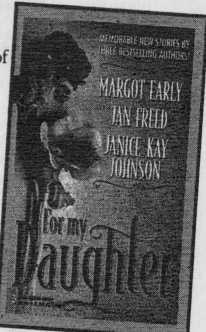
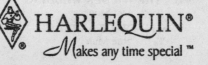